FRANKENSTEIN ON THE CUSP OF SOMETHING

Glenn Alan Cheney

PublishAmerica
Baltimore

© 2005 by Glenn Alan Cheney.

All rights reserved. No part of this book may be reproduced, stored in a retrieval system or transmitted in any form or by any means without the prior written permission of the publishers, except by a reviewer who may quote brief passages in a review to be printed in a newspaper, magazine or journal.

First printing

ISBN: 1-4137-5285-3
PUBLISHED BY PUBLISHAMERICA, LLLP
www.publishamerica.com
Baltimore

Printed in the United States of America

for Ralph

OTHER BOOKS BY GLENN ALAN CHENEY

Journey on the Estrada Real:
Encounters in the Mountains of Brazil

Journey to Chernobyl:
Encounters in a Radioactive Zone

Live in Caves

Acts of Ineffable Love

Frankenstein on the Cusp of Something

- CHAPTER ONE -
Frankenstein Doesn't Play Ball

Frankenstein sat near you in the fifth grade. You've forgotten him. If he played on your kickball team, he stood so far out in the right field weeds that you couldn't see him. No one in the history of the game ever booted one out that far. He was safe there. He could think his thoughts.

He wasn't safe in the lunch line. You stepped on his foot and didn't notice. You jabbed him with a back swing of your elbows, the punch line of a joke he didn't hear. You left him with no place to sit except with the girls. He remembers that. He remembers you.

He remembers high school worst of all. Same deal but no girls. He still played obscure positions in obligatory ball games. He never sank a basket, never made it to first base, never knew what to do when the center hiked the ball. It didn't seem to matter what he did. Usually he just stood there. Once, in gym, during a basketball scrimmage, the ball came into his hands. Somebody loomed over him, huffing and puffing, preventing any throw or movement. He looked up into the hairy maw of the kid's armpit and said, "You want it that bad? Take it." And he handed the boy the ball. Remember that? The boy looked back as he dribbled away, ran as if he had water in his shoes, tried an easy lay-up but flubbed it.

Somebody might remember the time Frankenstein threw up in the hall between classes. Somebody might remember the time in the cafeteria when he slipped in somebody else's tapioca, fell beneath his own ravioli, green beans, creamed corn, juice. Somebody might remember the empty seat in the SAT exam. Frankenstein forgot to go. At the moment the proctor said, "You may now begin," Frankenstein was lying on his back under a thicket of laurel, wondering if there was a God.

While waiting for the next SAT exam to come around, he held a few jobs. He hosed the dog doo out of the kennel cages until somebody told him what he smelled like. He dried cars at a car wash until the skin came off his hands. He was the janitor of a big Catholic church until he applied full-strength Mr. Clean to the grime of an ancient crucifix. The paint wiped right off. He actually had Christ's blood on his hands while a priest blessed him out. He just stood there feeling stupid and guilty. Stuff like that happens to Frankenstein.

Nails bend under Frankenstein's hammer. Toilet paper has never ripped straight for him. Computers crash. Silent crowds give him hiccups. Dirt seeks him out, attaches itself where he can't see it but others can. His father left him before he graduated from kindergarten.

He went to college, barely crawled out. Somehow they let him graduate without a major. Then his diploma didn't have his name on it. Somebody in Registration had thought his name a joke. They get a lot of forms filled out for Mickey Mouse, Al Einstein, Chuck Wagon, Moe Rhon. Nobody's really named Frankenstein, so they left it blank. Before he took the diploma and photo ID to Registration, he lost both. Last he saw of them, they were on his mother's Oldsmobile. Not in. On. Registration, personified by a pasty-faced gum-chewing lady with bright red hair and a New York accent, wouldn't give him a new one. It's kind of like a blank check, she said. Anybody can write their name in there. And it's kind of not like a blank check because you can't cancel it. Somebody out there had a nice new diploma. Frankenstein didn't.

Love? It's not in the cards for Frankenstein. His nose, mashed into a mailbox at an early age, sits off to the left at the top, off to the right at the bottom. One ear definitely sticks out a little too far. It looks like it could flap. His teeth buck out a bit, and there's a dark gap between the incisors. His mustache looked pretty wispy for its first two years. He grew a beard to hide the lack of meat in his chin, but somehow it got longer without getting thicker. Maybe his eyes are a quarter-inch too close together. He's worn glasses since the fourth grade, which only magnifies the weirdness of his eyes. His pupils are too dark to read. He seems to be hiding behind them. His mother described his hair as the color of a mule looking the other way. She's from West Virginia. She knows these things.

And he's short. Modeled after the common concrete block, he's squarish, open-faced and seemingly just knee-high. He's the kind of person you could practically trip over. But he's quick. He stays out of the way. He knows you won't see him. With your head up there in the rarefied air of conceit and self-concern, you don't notice much of what goes on below your haughty sight line. He's essentially invisible, and he knows it. He sees you coming and keeps to the side. You go by without noticing. Waitresses do the same. Right to his face they say, "Oh, I didn't see you."

Funny how he has the opposite effect when he hitchhikes. Drivers see him on the side of the road, standing behind his dirty white duffel bag. He doesn't hold out a thumb. He just shows them the palms of his hands. Cars pull right over, at least on good days. He tosses his bag onto the back seat, hops in front and off they go. Sometimes it's a drunk, sometimes a homosexual, sometimes a Jesus freak, a lonely person, a sleepy driver, an angel who can't help but help. Once it was a guy AWOL from the Army and just as sad as could be. Once it was some yoga maniacs on their way to a festival. Once it was nine or ten Mexicans in an old Lincoln. Once it was a guy who had a rifle across his lap. One guy had no legs. A lady with a big yellow airplane propeller on the back seat, one end sticking out the window, had no voice. She had to honk through a little hole in her throat, but that didn't stop her. She yakked and yakked and yakked, even laughed, even sort of started to cry. Frankenstein went right along, taking cues when to laugh, look surprised or give a moan of sympathy—empathy even; he found himself beginning to imitate her huffy little honk. But he never knew if she was talking about her yellow propeller, her throat problem, the price of sow bellies, the weather or what. When it came time to leave the car, he kissed her hand. Her honk became a coo. As he pulled his duffel bag from the bag seat, he ran his fingers along the propeller, the only time he'd ever touched one. For the rest of his life he would squint at any low-flying aircraft to see if the propeller was yellow, to see if it's her.

It's the Mexicans who drop him off across the street from a bowling alley. Big red letters across one wall say "Bowling." A flag over the door says "Bowling," too, its letters laden with blue icicles. This is in Arizona. The building is a refrigerator in a vast spill of lava. Frankenstein goes in. High-pitched thunder and bleating pop music fill the place. He hasn't bowled since the eighth grade, when he quickly learned that it was not his sport. It's safe to try again. He's not going to see how well he can bowl. He's going to see how long he can milk one game.

Can he bowl in sandals? A woman doesn't think so. She's just the cleaning lady sweeping up behind the counter, but she takes a look at his feet. They're filthy in their tire-rubber sandals. She hands him a pair of purple bowling shoes with a zippy little yellow lightning bolt across the instep. "You got socks?" she asks.

"Sure do." They're a thousand miles away, in Delaware, at his mother's house, neatly folded in a drawer, just in case.

"Good. You gotta wear socks."

No he doesn't. He sets up camp at Lane 21, stuffs his naked, swollen feet into the shoes. They don't like it in there. It's hot and stuffy. But he knows that if he bowls in his Guatemalan Goodyears, he'll leave tread marks on the hardwood floor. He remembers a bank teller on the outskirts of Chicago. He left tread marks on the linoleum of her bathroom. Until that point, things had been going well.

He relaxes before choosing a ball. He thinks about it before giving it a roll. When he finally develops a satisfying strategy, he prances on up to the line and lets 'er go. The ball walks a tightrope down the middle of the lane, plows straight into the center pin. Everybody topples each other over like clowns.

Frankenstein fills with a scary satisfaction. He really doesn't want to get the knack of this. He doesn't want to be a bowler. He stalls around for a long while, then tries a shot with his right hand rather than his usual left. The ball sweeps wide, veers in, attacks from the side. The pins fall with a clatter of urgency.

FRANKENSTEIN ON THE CUSP OF SOMETHING

He aims for the gutter but the ball won't go in. He sticks a wad of gum to it. No problem. It just rolls a little funny, a Caribbean two-step, tickwhump/tickwhump/tickwhump, all the way. They shouldn't all fall down on a shot like that, but they do as the ball pivots on its sticky little pink spot. He rolls it regular one time, tippy-toeing forward, sliding on his lead foot right up to the line. Even that works. A gathered crowd gasps with amazement, cheers at each strike. One ball to go and it's a perfect game.

The hush presses on him. Knowing he will fail, he refuses to do it right off. No time limit in bowling, right? Time segments. It stops and goes. It stops while Frankenstein goes to the bathroom. With his ball. He goes alone, assumes the solitary stall, a dented, black-enameled room neither clean nor dirty. His belt remains buckled, his zipper zipped. The global weight in his lap almost sparkles—*pretends* to sparkle—with golden flecks on a field of dusty black. He caresses it for the glory it has given him. It is so round and heavy, a model of the world, of heads, of atoms, the planets and distant suns, blowfish, helium balloons, cantaloupes, milk-laden breasts, globs burped up in lava lamps, bubbles, cannon ammo, the dots of I's, monkey-fist knots—so much depends on the form of bowling balls. No wonder the pins fall! How could they resist? Who are they to stand when the holy sphere rolls in? Frankenstein uses spit to clean a spot on the ball, then curls his torso forward to set his lips to the cool plastic surface. *So much depends.*

The bathroom door swings open, swings shut. Feet appear below the stall door. Tutti-frutti bowling shoes, slightly duck-towed. Their owner says, "You all right in there?"

It's a woman—a big one by the sound of her.

Frankenstein says, "No problem."

"You got a ball in there?" The shoes don't move.

Frankenstein pleads guilty.

Big pause. Then, "I'm sorry, sir. No balls in the men's room."

Frankenstein refrains from the obvious comment. He holds in his lap the model of the world, the universe and all that's equidistant from a point. An eleven-twelfth's perfect game awaits his final roll. He cools his forehead on the ball, a slow rock from left temple to right. He says nothing. It's her decision. The ball, so to speak, is in her court.

"Sir?...Sir, I'm afraid I must insist."

It's *still* in her court. She can't get rid of it unless he talks. He feels his bowels and bladder swell. They know what toilet stalls are for, so, here, atop the round-holed seat, they assume what they've been brought here to do. Like hounds in a cage at the edge of the field, they're ready to cut loose. Frankenstein would love to drop his drawers and accommodate them. He'd like to a lot, but he has a bowling ball in his lap and danger at the door. If he puts the ball down—between his feet is the only space— she might see it and snatch it away. Then he'll have to go out and confront her. On full bowels and bladder, maybe even with his pants down. He doesn't want to confront her. He wants to take a dump, a leak, and be done with it. He wants to go back to Lane 21 and finish his game.

"Really, sir," she says, not unkindly. "Either give me the ball or I call the cops."

Nice try, thinks he. What's the crime? Taking a bowling ball into a men's room? Wouldn't that make a dandy court case. Almost worth getting arrested for. He'd insist on a full jury. He'd call in the TV cameras. He'd represent himself, present charts, diagrams, photographs, the single piece of solid evidence, the gold-flecked ball, plucked from obscurity and raised to legal fame, right up there with O.J.'s gloves and Liz Borden's ax. When the woman again says, "I'm going to call the cops," Frankenstein thinks, *Good*. But when she says, "I really mean it," he knows she won't.

He takes the easy way out. He surrenders. He just rolls the ball under the door and says, "Save it for me, would you? Lane 21." He's glad he doesn't have to see her gloat.

She picks it up by the finger holes, strides out the door. Frankenstein does what he had to do. It doesn't take long.

Back at Lane 21, he finds, to utter horror, that his ball is nowhere in sight and that a bowling league team has set up camp. Four flabby people have re-set the pins, done away with Frankenstein's score sheet, rolled a few balls down his lane, busted his karma like...like....They've lit cigarettes, shed shoes and jackets, draped their socks over the back of the long fiberglass bench, dangled a large stainless steel crucifix, of all things, from the overhead projector. The bowlers' names glow on the overhead screen: Marilynn, Bob, Bill, Debbie. These people are plain vanilla to the core, but they've moved in and taken over. According to a red-on-blue nylon jacket, they are Cindy's Country Skillet Sharks. They have seized his territory. If bowling alleys had historians and if these invading hordes had left any evidence of him, Frankenstein would be history.

What's he going to do—take on four flabby people? Not only do they fancy themselves sharks, but they have a whole bowling league behind them. Frankenstein's alone, a wimp out of Delaware. The hierarchy of authority here begins with the woman in the tutti-frutti bowling shoes. Above her, he supposes, are the police. Above the police are their grandfathers, the Supreme Court. Above them is God, if any. Given the incident in the bathroom, the embarrassment of police action, and the big steel cross, Frankenstein has no hope. He has lost his lane, his ball and his last shot at a perfect game. Grounds for murder? He figures it depends whether the judge bowls. He treats himself to the image of a black-clad man billowing up to the lane line like a thundercloud, delivering his shiny black ball like a finely honed legal brief.

So Frankenstein can start a ruckus or just pay up and move on. Paying won't be easy. The lady at the counter is his friend in the tutti-frutti shoes. Now he knows more than her feet and ankles. She has the shoulders and broad back of a heavy-duty bowler. Her hips and thighs show signs of diet grazed at the bowling alley snack bar, fat rendered suet by lackadaisical exercise. Her face shows a certain ingrained sadness, perhaps a touch of shame for reasons he cannot guess. He feels a little sorry for her. Her face, he is sure, has never, at least since childhood, been gazed on as an object of beauty, an object of desire. If a man ever told her she was beautiful, he lied. For reasons that cannot be called reason, men avoid the pointed nose, the concave face, the down-turned lip line, the fatted underchin, the overbite of a suppressed IQ.

Frankenstein walks away from his lane, approaches the flier-and-warning-strewn glass counter. *Socks required. No practice frames. Balls waxed: $1.00. Bowl a perfect game? Get one free!* He leans into the counter, grips its cold chrome edge, looks up at the lady and says, "Nice eyes."

Taken aback, she shows surprise, then a second thought, the possibility that she might indeed have nice eyes. Frankenstein says, "I like brown," but that pushes it too far. She has indeed been told she's beautiful, it seems. Someone said that, ejaculated, and left. Now she looks at Frankenstein as if it had been him.

"Lane 21?" she says in cold business terms. He knows she really means to say, "You the guy with the ball in the bathroom?" From behind the counter she lifts his sandals and score sheet. "One game," she says. "One shoes. Plus tax. Five-fifty-eight." She scans the lanes behind him, her clay-brown eyes unavailable for argument.

"I didn't get to finish," Frankenstein says. "The Sharks took my lane. I would've bowled a perfect game and you'd owe me a free one. Know what I mean?"

She glances at the score sheet, checks a machine that counts the frames of all the lanes. "Says twenty-three frames here. What do I look, stupid?"

Eighty-two percent pissed is what she looks. He's sure she's been pursuing the perfect game since she was waist-high to a bowling ball. He walks in out of nowhere and does it—boom, boom, boom—almost. No wonder she wanted his ball so bad. She probably thinks there's something about it. He searches her heavy concave face for signs of stupidity. It's in there somewhere, he can tell. He wonders how it is possible to see ignorance in the topography of a face. He almost feels like asking, but he knows he'd be barking up the wrong tree. He just wants his sandals back. "Damned near a perfect game," he says. "*Look.*"

She does, giving the score sheet but a flicker of attention. "Yeah, right," she says. "You come in off the street, take twelve practice shots, which you're not supposed to do under penalty of law, then bowl eleven strikes, then take your ball into the bathroom. A *house* ball. And house shoes. Sure. I'll let you get away with five-fifty-eight if you cough it up now and," she drops to a whisper, "never show your miserable ass in this bowling alley again."

Maybe she *is* ugly. To the core. Ugliness on the hoof. Ugliness defined, the very quintessence of the stuff. Right before his eyes and miserable ass. In a way, it's an honor. Why hurry through the experience? Better to linger in her shadow, savor the moment, milk it for all it's worth. He searches for her eyes, but they dodge him. They *are* beautiful, as all eyes are, and they accent her less palatable parts. They float like little brown lifeboats in sea of bloodshot moonlight. He wants to save those lifeboats. He knows what it's like behind them. "I'm sorry about the ball," he says. "I didn't want anybody to take it."

"Still gotta pay five-fifty-eight." She keeps her eyes high in their sockets, pretending to check scores on the bank of screens above the lanes.

What's he supposed to do? Stand there and keep refusing to pay? Abandon his sandals, walk away, out the door in bowling shoes, forcing her to do something painful? Cough up the five-fifty-eight and call it a day? Tough choices all of them, each pitting his ego against hers. He wishes he knew the magic formula that would enlighten her eyes and let her love him just because for a moment he had loved a bowling ball that for eleven frames had done exactly what bowling balls are supposed to do. She runs a bowling alley! She wears bowling shoes to work! She probably knows the names of the ten best bowlers in America and their averages. Can she feel nothing above disdain for the house ball that made good?

She says, "Five-fifty-eight or I call the cops."

Frankenstein forks it over. Six bucks, keep the change. He pulls off his bowling shoes, tied, and holds them to her low and not quite far enough. Just as her fingers touch them, he retracts them an invisible bit, pulling her an invisible bit closer. He leans in and slides her a whisper audible only because it's on a frequency not reached by the rolling thunder and gentle explosions of bowling games. He says, "Want to know the secret?"

He senses her breath stop short. Their eyes meet. They are just as brown as can be, shot with black radii and glazed with melted glacier ice. The shoes between them conduct a certain juice, a voltage sufficient to make his face buzz hot. "Just roll the ball," he says in a sincere and caressing tone. "Just let it go."

She jerks back as if he's just nipped her with a hickey. His sandals fly from her hand as if bursting with roaches. "Get the fuck out of here," she says, eyes burning. "Just get the fuck out."

With great relief and no regrets, young Frankenstein steps out of the stale cold air and into the warm humus of a summer's afternoon. The glass door closes on the explosions of devastated pins and the relentless bleating of pop music earwash. Frankenstein will never bowl again, of that he is sure, not if he has to do it in a bowling alley. He wonders how far he'd get if he invented cross-country bowling. Would people bowl in the woods if their balls drifted across pine needles and silently toppled logs into a bed of moss? Would they know they were having fun if they weren't pounded with pop tunes and parting with cash? Would the lady with the brown eyes and tutti-frutti shoes find happiness in a place that didn't need its rules posted? So many questions for just one bowling alley, but Frankenstein must move on.

- CHAPTER TWO -
Frankenstein's Trip

In West Virginia, Frankenstein rode four feet from death. To save on gas, the driver of a rusty, yellow car of no discernible make slipstreamed an eighteen-wheeler almost all night long. He tucked his little car into the relative vacuum behind the truck and let it pull him through Appalachia. They rode so close to the bumper that Frankenstein could see individual flecks of grit where the one working headlight shined hard and close. The vast, towering back of the truck filled the little windshield. It seemed to move in slow motion, a surreal, neon monolith cut off from the night that sped by around it. Someone had fingered "Wash Me" in the grit. More grit had almost filled in the letters. Frankenstein just stared at the short, time-worn message. He wished he could lower the windshield, lean out and write, "Frankenstein was here." The truck was certainly close enough, and Frankenstein certainly had the time. But he feared he wouldn't need to write that message. If the truck driver just touched the brakes, Frankenstein's face would have left a graphic impression on its back door, his face and that of the tightwad at the wheel.

All night long he kept nodding off, even in sleep assuming he'd meet his maker with a dirty face and nothing but nubs where his teeth used to be. Each time his head tilted forward, he snapped awake and for a terrifying second forgot that he and the truck were headed in the same direction. This continued until the shaky glow of false dawn, when the car ran out of gas. Frankenstein stayed in the passenger seat for a polite interval, then walked away.

In Georgia, on a straight state highway through fields of soy, a black Firebird thundered by. Flames graced its hood and front fenders. As it whumped by, an eight-foot orange rat snake leaped up out of the pavement, its spine crushed. In its horrific throes, it flitted as lightly as a butterfly and came right at Frankenstein. Aghast, he abandoned his duffel bag and scrambled away like an upside-down crab. The snake's agonized contortions wrenched it into a flapping, knee-high, upper-case *W*, a back-biting *C*, an impossible *Q*, an inverted *z*, a frantic *S*, a withering *j*, a spitting *i* in Palmer script, and finally an apostrophe draped across Frankenstein's bag. If it spelled something, Frankenstein didn't catch it. He was backing up fast, sucking in air through a constricted throat, screaming inwardly as if it were his own spine, his own ineffable anguish. The mashed nerves didn't let the snake die. Its tail twitched and its rust-colored head, as blunt as a bullet, convulsed to the side as if it might lick its wound with its little red forked tongue. The white ribbed roof of its mouth was as horrid as the underbelly of a cockroach. When it finally stopped twitching, pale goo oozed from its mouth. Frankenstein threw up.

For a long, long time he sat twenty feet away, spitting and wiping salt water from his eyes. His duffel bag had snake goo on it. If the bag hadn't contained everything he owned, he would have abandoned it. He could have lived without his dirty underwear, but he had a letter to his sister in there, over twenty pages on paper place mats from diners, segments of paper trash from the side of the road, napkins, even a regular postcard featuring the biggest truck stop in all of Oklahoma. He kept meaning to buy a notebook and transcribe it all to a coherent whole, but notebooks never crossed his path. Now it all lay under a dead snake from the Peach Tree State. It took almost an hour to become a reasonably normal situation. Then he crept forward, yanked his bag from under the snake, and wiped the worst of the goo off on a tuft of grass.

In Missouri, Frankenstein kept thinking about home. He imagined his bed with clean sheets smelling of a thunderstorm. He conjured up an impossible trove of chocolate chip cookies. A mockingbird tootles its repertoire as he snoozes in a hammock in the dense shade of a sugar maple in his backyard. His mother brings him great books and calls him *dear* and has nothing to complain about. At night he watches hilarious TV shows, and a girlfriend he doesn't quite recognize comes over to stick her tongue in his ear and whisper things in a Swedish accent. Mid-state he crossed the highway and started hitching back the way he'd come.

But before long, he thought of the damp gray sheets of his unmade bed and his mother's high-pitched opinion of his unmade bed, the dearth of edibles in the kitchen, the brutal noise of the neighbors' lawn mowers, his mother reminding him of certain facts, a girl with cold fingers and a tendency to whine. He crossed the highway again and wondered what it must be like in Utah.

The Swedish girl stayed with him for a long time. In Michigan, early winter, a fat guy asked about her. Was she cute? Did she have long legs? What did she wear in the summer? Was she blonde *everywhere*? What, exactly, was she like in bed? Frankenstein made up all kinds of stuff. He made up stuff about her sister, too. And her girl cousins who came to visit from the old country. He took the man on America's most erotic canoe ride, across a lake, down a river and over a waterfall. Everyone was killed but him. The man mashed down on the brakes, sending the car swerving and screeching across the road. "Get the fuck outta here," the man said, angry in his disappointment.

Frankenstein got the fuck out. He stood there as the car sped away, his duffel bag in the back seat. This was on the Upper Peninsula. They hadn't passed a town in hours. He didn't remember seeing another vehicle all day. He started walking in the same direction he'd been going in the car. He thought about the Swedish girl all the way. He wished he had a Swedish girl to travel with, a real one. If they got stuck walking across the

Upper Peninsula, every couple of miles they could go into the woods and make love on a bed of pine needles. It wouldn't be so bad. But he didn't have a Swedish girl. All he had were sore feet and sense of worsening chill. Still, he couldn't complain. After walking for most of the day, he found his duffel bag on the side of the road. Things tended to balance out like that. Not that he'd trade a Swedish girl for a duffel bag with a snake goo stain, but it certainly could have worked out worse. Frankenstein doesn't complain.

In Texas, Frankenstein found a perfect place to sleep—a sloppy pile of hay under a broad, lone tree at the corner of a pasture. It wasn't dark yet, but he wasn't going to pass up sleeping quarters that good. He thought it would be a nice place to do his plastic bag trick.

He does this sometimes, lies down in a comfortable private place and puts his head in a plastic bag. Alone in there, he thinks about home a long time ago. On the wings of a deepening buzz, he can take himself back to the sunny age of five, a time when once his father knocked over a glass of milk at the dinner table. Like fanged slime, the milk lurched from its cave, stretching at his mother, slithering into her lap faster than she could back away. She screamed and leaped up, sputtering fire and crackling with little black lightning bolts. Daddy, silent, fuming, rose from the table, stomped quietly to the back door, slammed it so hard the house boomed.

His mother's anger, as wild as wasps, attacked not only Daddy but little Frankenstein, his big sister, and all the other vile, useless subspecies of the world. Growling bad words from the top of her throat, she lashed at the milk with a dish towel, wrung its neck at the sink, came back for more, rubbed the table beyond all visible milk, rinsed the towel again, wrung it, rinsed it, wrung it, folded it into a tight little wad, dropped it into the trash can under the sink, then removed the white trash bag, twisted *its* neck, tied it shut, carried it outside like a dead thing, dropped it into a bigger trash bag and tied *it* shut. Then she went upstairs and took a long, long bath.

Daddy didn't come back, not even after dark. Frankenstein snuggled with his sister that night, both of them listening to the dirge of crickets, waiting for the back door to open again and trying not to wrinkle the bedspread. Somehow, next morning, he knew to go look in the shed.

That's what he thinks about most when he does his plastic bag trick. It's an old habit now, but he still thinks about how it must have felt to lie there in a dusky shed, stifling among tools and old paint cans. He thinks about the last sound his father heard, the same rhythmic crinkling of thin plastic, so soothing at first, so slow, then faster as he gasped at the humid warmth of his own exhalation. As he breathes more deeply, the moist plastic compresses against his cheeks and forehead, then expands away. He does this until he gets dizzy and desperate for breath. Then he removes the bag, sucks in delicious air and pants himself to sleep.

When he did this on the bed of hay in Texas, he emerged from the bag to find a black and white cow standing there looking at him, mulling its cud and breathing through its huge wet nose in the heavy way of someone slightly short of oxygen.

Up in Canada, he got hit with a bag of garbage—not some little litter sack but a thirty-gallon Glad formerly owned by someone who smoked Craven A's, had a baby, and ate lots of fried chicken. The bag had launched from the back of a pick-up truck and scored a bull's-eye. He saw it coming for about two seconds. It hovered beside the little truck, an impossible asteroid with Frankenstein written all over it. It exploded when it hit him, sent him reeling westward and then down to the sandy asphalt. This was in sunflower country, middle of the summer. Frankenstein had just been thinking what a wonderful place it was, an infinite sea with waves of sunny faces. If he had known how to paint, he would have set up an easel right there. But Frankenstein couldn't paint the broad side of a barn. Suddenly, that didn't matter. He was covered with household trash. Later, upon reflection, he thought he might have learned something from the experience.

Also up in Canada, coming into Vancouver, he got picked up by a drunk percussionist in a giant Oldsmobile. What a jolly fellow! How he loved his rye. Drank it from a leather-covered flask. He was driving all the way from Moose Jaw just to play the cymbals in a Rossini overture. It didn't pay much, he said, but it was easy and nothing in the universe was more satisfying. He described it in poetic detail, the swelling excitement, the build-up of tension, the climactic *q'wizscj* of the cymbals. Tchaikovsky's *Romeo and Juliet*, for example. Had Frankenstein ever heard it? Not that he could recall, not the cymbals, anyway.

"Not the cymbals," the man gasped with utter incredulity. "*Not the cymbals.*" He gripped his flask between his legs and fished around in the glove compartment until he found the right cassette. "*Listen,*" he said. With broad drunken sways of his arm, he led an invisible orchestra toward orgasm. As the big moment approached, his eyes teared over and his jaw thrust toward the horizon. As the cymbals clashed in what even Frankenstein recognized as a sword fight, the man punched the air.

"*Those* cymbals," he said when it was all over. "See what I mean?"

Frankenstein saw it. He knew Rossini and could imagine cymbals in this man's hands as they burst with all the glory of the Italian renaissance. He asked if the man could sneak him into the concert hall, back stage, to watch it close-up. The man said he could do better than that. He'd let Frankenstein play them. Right there in the concert. *Q'wizscj.*

Frankenstein knew better than to say, "Yeah, right." He'd been around. He'd seen plenty of stuff weirder than himself playing cymbals in an orchestra. But he also had a certain sixth sense for situations where he was likely to screw up. This was one of them. Out of respect for the music, he warned the man. With a wet, flabby-lipped embouchure, the man discounted the danger. He'd be right there. Frankenstein would feel the rhythm. When the man pointed at him, Frankenstein was to hit the cymbals three times in a row. They listened to the overture on a cassette. The man marked the rhythm with bouncy fingers, indicated the big moment coming up. Frankenstein could feel it. Yes, *q'wizscj, q'wizscj, q'wizscj.* It would be easy.

They walked into the concert hall as if they owned the place. The man was pretty well soused, but he found the rack of white shirts and black pants and had Frankenstein suit up. They practiced a couple of times. The man warned him not to hit the cymbals dead-on because they'd stick together, locked in suction. Frankenstein worked up a big sweat as he loitered just off-stage, two steps away from the percussion section. The cymbals stood on a special rack. The drunk percussionist did just fine with a series of gongs, raps and clicks. He was almost dancing to the rhythm. Frankenstein could hear the cymbals part coming up. The man nodded for him to come forward. The conductor did not notice as Frankenstein took up the cymbals, but the entire audience had their eyes on him, the only guy in the orchestra with a beard half a yard long.

The big moment arrived. The man punched the air at the moment the conductor whipped the percussion section with his baton. Frankenstein slammed the cymbals with all his might. *Q'wizscj*. They didn't stick together. Rather, they inverted. The man didn't notice. He punched the air. Frankenstein had no time to think. He slammed them again. *Klank*. He then had everyone's complete attention. The orchestra played on but with a clear shift in intensity. It wasn't the Italian renaissance anymore. It was deepest, darkest Africa. The conductor stood there like a scarecrow, his mouth open, his baton frozen. It took two seconds for the next downbeat to come around. The conductor whipped his baton weakly, experimentally, as if only half hoping to repeat an experience. *Klank*.

And with that, job done, Frankenstein placed the cymbals on their special rack. He turned and walked off stage. As the orchestra played on, he hung up his white shirt and black pants, pulled on his bibbed overalls, and walked right out of the place. He would always wonder what became of the drunk percussionist. He probably never played in a concert again. He probably crept back to Moose Jaw, where until this day he sits sipping rye and not listening to Rossini.

Coming down the coast of California through a corridor of redwoods, Frankenstein got into the car of a woman who cried and cried and cried. It took him a few minutes to realize this. Though her eyes were brimming when he got in, she was smiling. Frankenstein took it for a warm and loving look. He hoped it wasn't that because she looked about fifty-eight years old. He had a way of attracting post-menopausal women. When he was a little boy, they used to come over to his family's table at restaurants. One lady buttered his corn-on-the-cob for him, right there in public.

Another smeared spit on his cowlick. They'd been chasing him ever since.

So when this one smiled at him with those bleary eyes, he kept his own eyes pointed elsewhere. She didn't say anything for a long time. When she sniffled and mopped up under her left eye, he noticed. He suspected a trap but asked her if she was all right. She gave him the damnedest nod. It tried to say yes but at the same time shook no. Her golden earrings, fancy things that looked like wind chimes, clinked as they bobbled around. She sniffled again, hard, and dabbed at her eyes with the cuff of her blouse. Frankenstein offered to drive. She shook her head, choked a bit, kept both hands on the wheel. Increasingly upset, Frankenstein begged her to say something. He tried guessing if the problem was love, sickness, death, age, money. She just shook her head. She moaned through her gritted teeth and sniffled as hard as a bath tub draining the last of its water. She looked like she might bite her lower lip off. Spasms heaved her belly and chest. How could she drive? Frankenstein took a worried glance out the windshield. A logging truck stacked with redwoods came at them but rumbled by with only a warning. When he suggested stopping, for coffee or something, she just huffed uncontrollably through her nose.

So then Frankenstein started to cry. He knew exactly what the woman was crying about, but he couldn't put a word to it any better than she. They were crying simply because it was sad—the same "it" as the "it" that rains, the "it" that's hard to say, the "it" that doesn't matter, the little pronoun that means everything except itself. Frankenstein and the woman just cried and cried and cried.

In eastern Tennessee, Frankenstein dallied over a local paper in a little downtown diner. He read about the most horrific thing he had ever heard of. Somebody was in a one-car accident, got all busted up but not killed. He was stuck in his car, hanging out the open door, held in by his seat belt. Along came another motorist. This was up in the mountains somewhere, on a back road. The other motorist came over and just squatted beside the dying man for a while, watching, not saying anything. After a little while, without a word, he took out a pocket knife and slowly slid it into the driver's eye. Then he squatted there for a while and watched. Then he punctured the other eye. Then he patted the driver on the cheek and left. The image of the bad Samaritan haunted Frankenstein for weeks. He could picture the man's face, not cold exactly but serious and a little sad and a little excited, kind of like the face of an impotent man watching pornography. He always wondered if the man picked up hitchhikers. He supposed so, and he knew the face to look for. He was sure of it.

Frankenstein slept the breadth of Indiana. In the back seat of a Chevy station wagon, his head in the harsh embrace of his canvas luggage, he swam, stumbled and struggled through three hundred miles of turbulent dream. He lost his voice in a riot of children. He fell into a bottomless hole. Something hot got stuck in his left nostril. He failed at more responsibilities than he could keep track of, something to do with his old job at the dog kennel, something else demanding intense thought at a computer screen from which damp, rancid breath puffed like smoke from a locomotive. A truck ran over him. A nasty-looking woman picked him out in a police line-up and accused him of not caring. He slid down a telephone pole. An asphalter laid pavement over his sandaled feet, pinning him to the sunny side of a dune. Bugs crawled on him. A medium-sized rat with a shiny black nose squeaked at him, but in a nice way that made a certain sense. A cop gave him a ticket for standing there. Somebody put him on hold so long that his skin grafted to the phone. Somebody else beat him up for the pleasure of it. He got gangrene. He woke up in the Land of Lincoln when a big burly guy with a beard shook his shoulder and asked him if he wanted to get out or go to Chicago. He still doesn't know what a Hoosier is.

At a truck stop in Iowa (he thinks it was), he drank eighteen cups of coffee. A sky-blue waitress named Tina kept track. Frankenstein barely kept control of his mind. He had a booth to himself during a god-awful sleet-rain-hail-snow storm. Not entirely sure tornadoes couldn't happen in the winter, he kept asking for more coffee and place mats. On the back of the place mats he wrote letters to his sister. As the caffeine and sleeplessness snaked into his brain, his writing electrified into frantic, illegible scribbles. He kept wishing he could cry or something. He kept saying he was sorry: sorry he had smoked pot before being an usher at her wedding, sorry for the time he lit the leaves on fire under her tree fort, sorry he was such an inadequate uncle, sorry he had told her, fifteen years earlier, that Santa Claus had stabbed the Tooth Fairy, suicidally sorry he had shoveled his bit of dirt onto his father's coffin before he was supposed to, sorry he had left home without saying good-bye to his mother. He told her which parts of the waitress he desired most, then told her he was sorry he had told his sister such a thing. He told her he wished he could crawl into a dark little hole and just stay there.

He listed eight reasons to die (because why not, because it made a certain sense, because he wanted to see what would happen, because he was so sorry for what had happened so far, because he'd forgotten if he was on the westbound or eastbound side of the interstate and didn't see how it mattered but knew that it did, because absolutely everything went wrong for him, because he didn't know how to have fun and didn't think he'd ever figure it out) and two to live (because he wanted to see what would happen and because he was sure that dying would end up being a mistake). He told her about the lady who kept crying, the snake who got run over, a prissy middle-aged man who drove with a Raggedy Ann in his lap, a guy who had been eating a Bible for the last three weeks and proved it by chewing on a page of Leviticus for half an hour but then choked on it so bad that Frankenstein had to slam him on the back until he coughed up a gummy wad which he looked at with disgust but said he'd save for later. When a drip of coffee plopped onto a blank space in his letter, Frankenstein doodled it into a face that looked shocked and windblown. He drew a bubble over it and wrote, "I'm sorry! I'm sorry!" and let the rest of the letter flow around it.

- Chapter Three -
Mud

A lady with half a brain dumps Frankenstein at the center of a rat's nest of interstates and ramps off ramps. A viscose rain, atomized by traffic, wraps around him like wet cobwebs. Overpasses soar above him. Underpasses pass below. These death ribbons have no walkways. Safety, a distant clearing of soggy twilight, hunkers beyond a forest of concrete columns that support an upper-story interstate. He stands at a bifurcation. Neither road is less traveled than the other. One curls around toward where he just came from. The other peels off toward infinity. Gross death roars all around. He's standing right in front of a giant yellow barrel that's supposed to absorb the vehicles of the sleepy, the stupid, the stoned, the indecisive. An amber light marks his location with a languorous flash. He cowers like a mouse among diesel cats, a fly among a mad flock of swatters, a tiny matador beset by Brobdingnagian bulls. He considers the easy way out: dashing to the guardrail, vaulting over the edge, tumbling into a murkish underworld of homeless Dumpsters, crumpled fencing, petrified car parts, fast-food excrement, flames of graffiti, chilled brimstone and wet litter.

But why risk a sure thing? Better to just start walking, see if he gets hit.

With a little luck he'll get a ride in a cushy ambulance, a few days in a nice clean warm dry hospital bed. Nurses will attend to his every need. He won't even get up to pee. He'll just watch TV all day. TV's a little better than hanging out at the big yellow barrel, waiting for a three-ton spear. It tips the balance. He goes for it. Sliding along a left-side guardrail, duffel on his shoulder, leaning away from the swish of traffic, he slouches toward somewhere else. By the time he gets there, his teeth are chattering with cold despondency. This other place is at the frontier of civilization. It's a body shop half buried in the carcasses of automobiles. The window beside the office door is protected by steel mesh and patched with cardboard and duct tape. The only light comes from behind an oily garage window, a dull glow and the sparky throb of a welding torch. The pavement between the curb and the door is slippery with rain and old oil. Frankenstein lifts his cold, naked toes away from the edge of his Goodyear sandals. The balls of his feet squeak against the wet rubber.

He touches the doorknob. In a heartbeat, a ghastly rampage of used lubricants creeps across his fingers, embeds itself beneath his nails, thrusts under his cuff, shoots up his arm, coats his armpits, swirls around his neck and dribbles across his torso to congeal at his crotch. A stalactite forms at the back of his scrotum. He thinks he feels the same stuff clogging the gaps between his toes, too. It is filth that will not leave him soon. It bonds with his coat of perspiration, a three-day build-up he had been hoping to scrape off in the comfort of a hot shower. Now impermeable to water, it has a half-life of at least a week.

He enters. The welding torch crackles just out of sight in the garage. Frankenstein says, "Hello?"

He peers in. A low dim light crouches behind something huge. With a little explosion of lightning, the torch crackles again. For a flicker of an instant, he sees an unearthly giant, a robotic thing, a mechanical cactoid as broad as a tree, a Godzilla of crankshafts, mufflers, axles, tie-rods, radiators, hubcaps, gears and junk he goes on to imagine in the dark. Less sure of himself, he says, "Hello?"

A man with a voice like a welding torch says, "Ain't that door locked?" He's behind the thing he's welding. Frankenstein can't see him.

"It was open," he says. He's never felt this cold, at least not cold this way. "I just wanted to use the phone. If you've got one."

"Be my fucking guest."

Before Frankenstein can decide if that's a yes or a no, the torch crackles and the lightning flickers. Blue orbs swim between him and the thing in the garage. He turns away. The orbs float around to a cast iron telephone, a junkyard dog of a pay unit on the wall. By the touch he can tell it's filthier than the doorknob, a phone that has never known a loving touch, that has tasted spittle tainted with the residue of Bazooka gum, Eldorado cigars, cold Chinese food, coffee sludge, yesterday's plaque, a phone that has transmitted every vulgarity known to men, a phone at one with the world around it.

He's heard better dial tones, too, but when he cranks the dial around for zero and the number of his sister outside of Bethesda, he gets the robot that talks him through the collect call routine. When it asks him to state his name, he hopes it's her, not her husband, who listens on the other end. If it's him—a computer peripheral sales rep with an almost erotic love of professional ball players—he'll say, "Yeah, what is it?" Frankenstein will tell him what it is, and he'll say that she's not home. Frankenstein's brother-in-law doesn't like collect phone calls, and he likes Frankenstein even less. They have opposing philosophies, and there's nothing either of them can do about it.

But it's her. She says, "Fred!"

It's not his name. It's an old joke. Nobody calls him that but her. In a dirty-old-man tone of voice, quivering through his filth, stretching his vowels, he croons, "Soooosie Creamcheese."

"Where *are* you?" she asks.

He looks around. He doesn't quite know how to answer. He'd never say to her something as simple as "greater Seattle." If he did, she'd say, "Yes, but where *are* you?" She's quite a sister for a guy like Frankenstein. He says, "I'm in a dark hole."

"Wow!" she says. "How *is* it down there?"

With those few words she resurrects him. Now he's glad he's in a dark hole. He remembers that this is where he wants to be. He says, "It's real clammy."

"Dandy?"

"*Clammy!*" he shouts. The little holes in the mouthpiece of the phone are clotted with somebody else's coagulated breath.

"*I hate clammy!*" She hollers it as if to someone at the bottom of a well. Her voice clatters out the earphone in metallic shards.

Frankenstein doesn't want to shout. He doesn't want the man in the other room to hear. Not that it matters. He just wouldn't want the guy to come stomping out with his welding torch and growling, "What're you calling clammy?"

He pictures his sister all in denim, shirt untucked, sleeves rolled halfway up her forearms, her hair in a ponytail tied with a rubber band looped around something she found at the beach. Bare feet. Traces of dried bread dough in the grooves of her knuckles, a smudge of oil paint on her cheek, a Band-aid around her little toe, Little Tom anchoring one foot to the floor. This is how she survives Big Tom. She keeps busy. She pretends he doesn't exist or maybe that he's someone else. She never said this. Frankenstein just knows. She's in a bit of a dark hole herself, but she makes the best of it. Frankenstein admires her spirit. She's always gung-ho. He can picture her in this grubby little auto body shop. Within ten minutes she'd have daisies growing out of the ashtray. She'd paint a sunny Van Gogh-esque hayfield on the wall. She'd have ferns in the corner and vines across the window. She'd cook muffins on the coffee maker. She'd paint the steel desk yellow and put her feet up on it while she taught herself to play the accordion. Everyone around her would laugh a lot and keep their language clean. Under similar circumstances, Frankenstein might likely write a poem about the discomfiture of rigor mortis.

"I hate clammy, too," he says to his sister, "but sometimes it's all you've got."

"Sounds like you could use a nice hot bath."

Somehow she always knows these things. He wishes she'd guess why he called. She's pretty close already. He doesn't want to come right out and ask. In due time he'll drop a hint and, if necessary, segue into a request. He says, "What's your mother up to this week?"

"You won't believe it," she gushes with half a laugh. "She has tilted her lance at the town dump. She says the place is a mess and she wants it cleaned up."

FRANKENSTEIN ON THE CUSP OF SOMETHING

Frankenstein wrinkles his forehead. *Clean up the dump.* It sounds like the kind of oxymoronic impossibility she'd ask *him* to do. But he has trouble imagining his mother anywhere near the town dump. He didn't think she even knew such a place existed. He can, however, imagine her raging through town hall, berating, blaming, accusing, threatening, stabbing the long red nail of her forefinger into state statutes, federal mandates, the mayor's gut, the sanitation department's gut and the guts of all others who look like they could use a little improvement.

"She got an editorial in the paper," his sister says. "She wants everybody to put their trash in white bags, and she wants all the bags laid out in even rows in an even layer so they can be sprayed with deodorant and disinfectant by a crop duster before they're buried."

"A crop duster!" It sounds like something he'd think up. He can see the lady with the yellow propeller swooping over the dump in her biplane, smiling down over the edge of her cockpit and cooing through the hole in her throat. "I wonder if she'll ever be happy," he says, meaning his mother.

"Not till she's got every speck of dirt in the world sealed up in white trash bags."

"That wouldn't leave much of a planet, would it? Where would she stand?" He pictures himself curled up and weightless in one of ten billion white trash bags orbiting the sun in a tidy row. His father's about ten bags ahead of him.

His sister giggles. She always does. "Antarctica!" she says in a tone of gleeful hope. "All alone in the clean-driven snow, queen of all she sees and happy at last."

"If she were there, I'd be happy, too." He lets two heartbeats pass, then says, as casually as he can, "Has she mentioned me?"

Two more heartbeats pass as his sister shifts gears. "Sometimes," she says.

He tilts his forehead to the concrete wall and says, "Like what?"

"Like…I wonder where he is."

He says nothing. He just waits. She adds, "Like…when's he going to come home or get a job or something?"

Yeah, he knows that. He says, "Tell her it's not time yet."

"I'm not going to tell her anything. You tell her. Call her."

"I will." But he knows he won't. It isn't time yet. Besides, he hates talking on the phone. He remembers that now. So he doesn't wait for her to ask. He says, "I'm in greater Seattle."

"Ah, Seattle," she sighs. "Land of…what?"

"Milk and honey. Nothing here but milk and honey."

"Hey…you know who lives in Seattle?"

He sure does. He says, "Who?"

"Angelica Pascapelli! Remember her?"

Frankenstein says, "Hmmmm. Rings a distant bell."

"My next door neighbor in the dorm, at State. Remember? Senior year?"

"Ohhhhh, yeah. *Angelica*. She used to wear dresses, right? Little matching outfits? Even to class?"

"That's her. Last I heard, she was living in Seattle. She became a flight attendant."

"I'll be damned."

Truth is, he's been thinking about Angelica since southern Idaho, and to that thought he has added a nice warm bath. Now he remembers her last name. Things are fitting together. And then his beloved sister says, "You should call her!"

Beloved and omniscient. She knows why he called. He can tell. But he plays right along. He says, "Have you got her number?"

She says she thinks she can find it. Her phone clunks down. From Seattle he can hear her feet thump lightly across the room. They are indeed bare. A dog barks. He didn't know she had a dog. It's a mutt. He'd bet money on it. Unless it's Big Tom's dog. If Big Tom went nuts and bought a dog, it would be the kind that's worth money. By the sound of the bark, Frankenstein guesses its something between a beagle and a poodle, with a high IQ and very twitchy tail. A good dog for a kid like Little Tom. A pain in the ass for Big Tom. When Frankenstein's sister pads back to the phone and blows her bangs up with a *phew*, he says, "Did you get a new cat or something?"

She says, "Oh, that's Uncle Sam. You'd like her. Put her out and she wants to come in. Let her in and she wants to go out. You two would get along well. And boy could she use a bath."

"I know how *that* feels. You don't suppose Angelica's got a bathtub?"

"If I know Angelica, she's got two. You ready to write this down?"

Of course he's not ready. Frankenstein hasn't been ready for anything since birth. He wasn't even ready for that. He was still working on a double back gainer with a twist. He assumed that's what life was all about. But then he saw the light at the end of the tunnel. He got curious. It was his first big mistake. He went for a peek, and *boom*—he's a person. He hasn't done a gainer since, let alone a back gainer. Twists? Forget it. He's lucky if he can keep both feet on the ground.

"Wait," he says to his sister. He's got a dusty old Bic in his duffel somewhere, but it could take days to find. He's not about to ask the welder for a writing instrument. The little concrete block office doesn't look like a place to find such a thing. The gunmetal desk no doubt seized up decades ago. There's nothing on top of it except an ashtray dating back to the Mesozoic era. The trash can looks unfit for trash. Frankenstein's going to have to use his memory. He winces at the thought. He has no capacity for arbitrary data. Seven unrelated digits don't stand a chance in his brain. Just in case Angelica has one of those magical numbers like 345-6789, he goes ahead and asks. In a voice bogged with incipient depression, he squeaks, "What is it?"

"Area code two...."

"*Fuck* the area code."

"Okay, *okay*. 843-9271. Got it? 8-4-3-9-2-7-1."

He wouldn't talk like that to anybody but his sister. She understands. She knows he's standing there in semi-dark with the top of his forehead against a wall of concrete blocks painted with enamel and tobacco tar. She's just handed him the world's toughest phone number. It makes no sense whatsoever. She knows what he means when he says, with quivery desperation, "Does that spell anything?"

She hums for a while and mumbles combinations of letters. Then she says, "Well, there's no letters on the one, so forget it."

"How could they be so *stupid?*"

They being the phone company that didn't put letters on the one. But he knows who the stupid one is. If Angelica Pascapelli didn't have big brown eyes and a bathtub, he'd give up right there. She has a one in her phone number. He might as well go back up to the big yellow barrel at the fork in the road and wait for the first Buick with bad tie-rods. "Never mind," he says. "Give it to me one more time. Then I'm going to hang up and dial it quick. Okay?"

"I gotcha. Here it comes. I'm going to sing it. Ready? Eight-four-three-nine-two-seven-one." She makes it sound like "Twinkle, Twinkle, Little Star." "Got it?"

He sings it. She says, "*Yes.*" He sings it again. He feels a little pilot light of happiness blip into the darkness of his chest. He sings it again. His merriment means thanks and good-bye. He slams the receiver into the hook.

Eight-four-three-nine-two-seven-one.

He paws at his pocket for a coin.

Eight-four-three-nine-two-seven-one.

There's something in there!

Eight-four-three-nine-two-seven-one. How I wonder what you are.

He scoops them out, squints down close.

Eight-four-three-nine-two-seven-one.

It's a puddle of pennies. Not a bit of silver among them. He flings them across the room and slams his forehead to the wall. He's been lugging those damned things around for days.

Now he can't sing the number. He couldn't sing "Twinkle, Twinkle Little Star" if his life depended on it. Which it practically does. His belly undulates with the start of a good cry. All he wanted was a bath....

But God's good graces touch the telephone, and it belches Frankenstein's quarter. With a sense of biblical significance, he extracts it from the little slot. He kisses it as if it were Angelica Pascapelli herself.

Eight-four-three-nine-two-seven-one. Like a diamond in the sky.

Whispering the numbers, he spins the black steel dial. The eight takes too long to mosey back around. It messes up the rhythm of the song, but he keeps cranking. He gets it right, he's sure of it. The ring sounds distant but cautiously optimistic. It rings again. It rings again. She's on a jet to Tokyo, he's sure of it. She's serving TV dinners in the stratosphere. Her answering machine is going to eat his last quarter, and he won't even have a message to leave. It rings again, and she answers. It's Angelica, yes, and yes, she remembers him.

Things move along well after that. She figures out more or less where he is. He walks to a certain intersection, waits on the corner for no more than a minute before a white Cadillac pulls up. It's far from new but remarkably clean and polished. The electric window glides down. A chubby-faced woman he would hardly recognize says, "Frankenstein?"

He's surprised most by her eyebrows. They're as thin and precisely defined as arcs drawn by a fine-point pen. She was working on them when he called, he can tell. She has a towel wrapped around the top of her head, a floppy mound stuffed loosely with hair. Sitting in the passenger seat, his cold fingers gripping each other in his lap, he wonders if she still has great gobs of black curls. She looks different than she used to, back when she lived next door to his sister in the dorm. Her former voluptuousness has rounded out to jolly curves. When he last saw her, he was a senior, she a freshman. Now she looks like a grown up and he feels like a kid.

The Cadillac moves through the washy-gray streets of Seattle like a fluffy cloud. She has the heater on full blast, but it seems to produce only steam. It fogs the windshield. The wipers squeak as they rub away the misty rain. The bare areas remind him of the angels he and his sister used to make in the snow by waving their arms and legs. Then he notices the key ring dangling at the ignition. It's an angel, pure white and as big as a saucer. Angels, he guesses, are her personal motif.

She smells of soap. He's sure he smells of stale sweat. She cranks the defroster to full blast, but when her fingers touch the window controls, it's his window that opens a crack. She says, "Do you mind?"

He's almost sure it's an oblique reference to the odor he's brought in from Idaho. All he can say is, "A little fresh air should help." It's an oblique confession of stench, an implied apology.

He likes Angelica's face. It reminds him of a pumpkin, but cute. The crowns of her cheeks are a little pink, not with heat or blush but well-fed health. She'll be fat someday, he thinks. At her current stage of development, she's at voluptuous-plus but teetering on pudgy. She won't be fat, he decides, just buxom.

She asks about his sister. He tells her what little he knows. Angelica says she's quite a character. Frankenstein whistles softly. "I don't know what she's doing in Bethesda," he says. "I think she lives in an apartment."

"What's wrong with that? *I* live in an apartment."

"Oh, I didn't mean it that way. I meant, like, she ought to be on a farm or something. Out in the country."

"Yes," Angelica says drearily. "With *chickens* or something."

He doesn't like the way she said that. Just by the sound of it, he knows that Angelica has never come, nor will she ever come, within a hundred yards of barnyard fowl. He's not too surprised to hear her ask, "Do you know anything about computers?"

Frankenstein tilts his head. "Computers," he says thoughtfully. "I know a little, but not much."

She says nothing in return. He's glad. He hates computer conversations. Back when he used to use one, he always felt a moment of quiet joy when he turned it off. He really enjoyed seeing the screen die, hearing the hard drive croak and the little fan sigh its last. He wished all his problems could be turned off with a little button.

Eager to change the subject, he says, "Do you still play harp?"

She turns her head to look at him. She looks longer than a Cadillac driver should. Then she turns back and says, "Yes…I do. Not as much as I should. But every once in a while."

"It's a beautiful thing, a harp."

"Sometimes I miss it. I'll be halfway into an all-night flight and all the passengers will be sleeping and I'll imagine sitting back near the galley, playing harp for everybody."

"That's beautiful," Frankenstein says, almost whispering. For the first time he ties together her name and her chosen instrument. He's now fully in love with Angelica Pascapelli—except those eyebrows still scare him. Why does she pluck them to such perfection when she could be playing her harp? Maybe it's in her contract. Would an airline claim that bushy eyebrows are a safety hazard? Frankenstein doesn't doubt it. Sex appeal would have nothing to do with it, of course. Eyebrow growth would have to be tightly controlled to prevent occlusion of the eyes during an emergency. Worse, unrestrained thickets of brow hair could burst into flames at the very moment when flight attendants have to remain calm and clear-headed.

Frankenstein doesn't share these thoughts. They go without saying. It's possible she likes to pluck her eyebrows. Some girls do.

And some guys have fantasies about having their back scratched by a harpist. Frankenstein's one of them. He thinks about it, then fully imagines it, all but feels it as his back breaks out in rampant itch. The itches march across him like a ragamuffin army through a salt marsh.

Angelica's apartment building looks like a motel, a two-story horseshoe with a swimming pool in its lap. She leads him up a short, wide flight of outdoor stairs, down a concrete walkway overlooking the pool, around a corner to 14-B. Neither of them speaks along the way. He lugs his duffel bag. She fiddles with her keys, finds the right one and isolates it with a jingly flourish. She opens the door and says, "Well, this is it."

It's an apartment with deep cream-colored wall-to-wall carpeting, matching couch, love seat and chair, a coffee table with two neat stacks of magazines set at a jaunty angle. The back of the couch marks the border of the dining area, and a counter marks off the kitchen. The other rooms are down a short, dim hall.

Angelica removes her jacket. She's wearing a loose denim shirt unbuttoned to a hint of cleavage. Frankenstein notices this right off. It's a good sign. He lowers his duffel bag to the floor. Just to say something, he goes, "Whew."

Angelica looks back from the coat closet. "No, no," she says, signaling for him to pick it up. "Not there." The wag of her finger makes him feel like a bad boy.

He raises his grungy duffel bag from the cream-colored carpet and follows her down the dim hallway. She's not bad looking from the back. Her hips sway below her waist like a pendulum. She opens the other door at the end of the hall and stands back. There they are: the computer and the harp. Angelica says, "This is where I store junk."

She means his duffel bag. Granted, white though it might once have been, it doesn't exactly match her decor. Still, she could have phrased it better. But it's her apartment, not his, and she seems to have included her computer and harp in the category of junk. So his duffel's in with respectable company. He can't complain.

The computer looks like something dragged out of the sea. She hasn't been using it lately. A tangled glob of wires splays atop a tight crowd of stacked peripherals. Nothing's hooked up. It's waiting for somebody to come along to do it. Frankenstein inhales.

The harp looks even less used. It stands deeper in the room, beyond the computer, behind some file boxes, back among some milk crates and stuff in shopping bags. A dry-cleaned flight attendant's uniform in a plastic bag hangs from the pinnacle of the harp. It looks a little like a skeleton dancing with a ghost. He briefly considers asking her if he can take the plastic bag when he goes. Hoping to prevent mention of the computer, he says, "I thought harps had to stay in some kind of humidor or something." That is absolutely everything he knows about harps.

"*Good* harps, yes."

"What did it do," Frankenstein chuckles, "bite somebody?"

She smiles with only half her mouth. "I got it at a pawn shop. Cheap. Sounds like shit."

For an instant, Frankenstein wishes she wouldn't talk like that in front of it. "It doesn't *want* to sound like that," he says.

"Yes it does."

There's no discussing it. If Angelica says the harp wants to sound like shit, that's the way it wants to sound. It's her harp and her apartment. She says, "I suppose you want to take a shower."

"As a matter of fact...."

She points to the bathroom. "Right in there. I suppose you've got laundry."

Laundry would be putting it nicely. Filthy rags is more like it. Biohazardous waste. But not junk. It's all he's got. He says, "Well, yes, if I could borrow the use of a washing machine."

"You wash you, I'll wash the clothes." With a single finger to his shoulder, she pokes him into the bathroom and closes the door behind him.

Nice can, thinks Frankenstein, maybe a little *too* nice. Everything's pink—pink sink and toilet, pink bath mat, seat cover and towels, pinkish wallpaper, pink tiles in the shower stall, pink angel around the light switch, pink silk flowers beside a bowl of pinkish potpourri replete with colossally pink odorizer. Pink, pink, pink, pink, pink. This crapper needs something like Frankenstein, something firmly unpink. His image in the mirror is so gross it's almost good, something salty after an overdose of sweet. He strips. He turns on the shower. The water looks so clean and steamy. Then there's a knock at the door. The door knob turns. Frankenstein thinks, *This is it.*

But it isn't it. It's only her voice and her hand with its bright red fingernails. She says, "Dirty clothes?" Her fingers snap. Frankenstein rolls them up, hands them over. The hand withdraws. The door closes. *Oh, well.*

It's a good shower. Even though the water temperature jumps around a bit as the washing machine commandeers the flow, Frankenstein appreciates the luxury as much as the wealthiest emperor might appreciate a trove of gold. He could live in a cave and eat charred rats off the end of a stick as long as he could take a hot shower at the end of the day. Modern technology hasn't developed much else of real import. Hot showers and the polio vaccine, that's about it.

While he's in there letting the wet warmth caress his skull, there's another knock at the door. It opens. He wipes a peephole in the fog on the ripply shower door. She enters. He barely makes out the creamy blur of her flesh as it twirls in. The door closes. He is immediately aroused. He wishes it didn't come on so fast so he could at least pretend not to have been thinking about it. The way things stand now, there's no pretending. It's as plain as the nose on this face. He lathers like crazy and sucks in his gut.

But she just stands there by the door, a smeary phantasm the color of moonlight. Frankenstein peeks again. She doesn't move. Something's wrong. He waits a while. Then he slides the shower door open a bit. It isn't her. It's a robe, hung by the scruff of its neck on a hook on the door.

Oh, well. What did he expect? She wouldn't be interested in someone like him. Maybe if he'd showed up with a couple pounds of roses and a bottle of good wine he might have inspired her. But all he'd brought was a sack of rancid clothing.

With a clunk of the plumbing, his shower goes cold. Frankenstein hops out, dries off, folds the towel as neatly as he can, hangs it back up nice and perfect-like. He puts on the robe, cinches the belt, looks down at his knobby white knees. He doesn't recall wearing a robe before. He feels silly—vaguely Roman, slightly gay, very naked underneath. If she didn't mean for him to put it on, he's in big trouble. But what else can he do? She has his clothes.

He steps into an aroma of frying onions and garlic. Angelica's in the kitchen, stirring up some food. She's smooth and slow with her motions, swirling the stuff she's cooking, rapping the wooden spoon on the cast iron pan, peeking into the steam under the lid of big pot, jerking open the refrigerator, snatching something out, spinning off a lid, tilting something into the pan, peering into the jar, dumping the rest in. If he were on TV, he'd come right up behind her, slip his arms around her waist and kiss her neck. She'd lean back and say, "Mmmmm." But something tells him to keep his distance. Feeling quite the soap opera stud, he says, "Smells good!"

"Pasta. I hope you like it." She doesn't sound optimistic.

"I love it. I really hadn't meant to impose...."

"No problem." She rinses her hands at the sink, wipes them on a dish towel. "Your laundry will be dry soon. It sure needed washing."

Frankenstein says, "I've been out there a long time." He likes the way it sounds, as if he's been up in the hills, fighting with the Resistance.

"And what are you doing?"

Standing there in a robe is what he's doing. That is absolutely all he can think to say, but he holds his tongue. She isn't looking for a wisecrack, and he doesn't want to author one. He considers saying that he's been fighting with the Resistance, then seeing if he can make it sound like he means something, something heavy. Resisting capitalism. Resisting American materialism. Resisting the System. But he isn't resisting anything. In fact, he's pretty much following the path of least resistance. *Wandering around* would sum it up well enough, but he says, "Just traveling."

"Traveling where?"

If she needs to ask, she'll never understand the answer. Trying not to sound too-too mysterious or stupid, he says, "To wherever I end up." He hangs humility across his face and shows her the palms of his hands.

FRANKENSTEIN ON THE CUSP OF SOMETHING

"That's where we're *all* going," she says. "Do you think you could take a look at my computer?"

That's all she's been thinking about since he called from the body shop. That's why she did his laundry and is making pasta. She thinks he can fix a computer.

With weak hesitance, he says, "I don't know...."

"Guys know. It's a tool. Come on."

She takes him by the hand. He likes that. This is the first female to touch him in weeks. She drags him down the hall, *past* the bedroom, into the junk room. There's the computer, looking as morose as a teen at the opera. The ghost and skeleton dance behind it. Frankenstein swells with the best idea in the world. In the most seductive tone he can muster, he sings, "I'll fix the computer if you'll play the harp."

He's lying, of course. He can't fix a computer. But he can sure look like he's trying. And who knows...maybe he'll get it all connected and it'll start right up. Sometimes they do that. Like kids with sniffles, they get better. Whether he succeeds or not, he'll get to hear some harp. Live and close-up. It'll be like sitting in heaven while working on the tool from hell.

It takes Angelica a long time to finally say, "I really don't play very well. And this harp..." She shakes her head with something like disgust.

"How bad can a harp sound? You don't have to actually play. Just practice. I promise not to laugh."

She looks at the harp as if not trusting it. Frankenstein resorts to a whine. "Please," he says. "Please?"

Angelica backs up three inches and says, "I can't play harp."

"And I can't fix a computer." He's not lying. She is. He says, "Let's do it anyway." By "it" he means go to the clean sheets of her bed and make love, but he doesn't expect her to guess this, let alone do it. He'll be satisfied to hear her play the harp.

Finally she says, "I'll *tune* it." Like that's all he's going to get. No more.

"Good," he says. "A harp should be tuned now and then. You tune the harp. I'll tune the computer. This is going to be *fun*." He steps around the computer, slips a foot between two boxes of books, plucks the dry-cleaned uniform from the harp and hands to it Angelica. Without a word, she whisks it away to a closet. Frankenstein feels gargantuan as he leans here and there to pick up boxes and stack them away from the harp. Moving fast, he collects the stuff from a fold-up table, piles it on top of other stuff. He stacks the computer stuff into a precarious, teetering tower and lifts it all to the table. Now the harp stands in a little clearing. It already looks happier, even stately, a castle in a moat. By the time Angelica returns, he's set a milk crate upside-down beside the harp. With a flourish of his hands he says, "And now, Angelica Pascapelli on the harp."

Angelica Pascapelli says, "Wrong side." Gently, precisely, she kicks the milk crate around to where it should be. "Got that computer hooked up yet?"

The last person to mess with this computer must have really hated it. It took someone a lot of time to form such a convoluted ball of wires. They aren't just bunched together. They're tied in an ugly, senseless macramé of wires knotted around wires and plugs unnaturally inserted into odd sockets. Angelica is opening a little steel toolbox when Frankenstein asks, "Did you do this?"

"That was my *ex*-husband."

He likes the way the emphasis fell on *ex*, but still, he's a bit shocked, maybe even just a teeny-weeny bit jealous. Some jerk who hates computers and can't appreciate a harpist has already been there and gone. On top of that, Angelica has already done the marriage thing. Frankenstein hasn't even learned to balance a checkbook. Again he feels way out of his league. She's a grown-up; he's a kid. He says, "Didn't like computers much, did he?"

"He didn't like *me* very much. He *loved* computers. It's all he did all day. He used to send me e-mail."

"He didn't live here?"

"Oh, he lived here. Right here in this room. He hardly ever came out except to go to work. He sent me e-mail so I'd have to use the computer."

"Not love notes, I take it?"

"Ha! That man couldn't write a love note any more than he could…could, I don't know, play the harp or something. He could *download* a love note off the Internet, assuming of course he ever thought of it, which he wouldn't."

FRANKENSTEIN ON THE CUSP OF SOMETHING

Angelica places a winding key at shortest string of the harp and gives it a pluck. It sounds good to Frankenstein. He could listen to that note again and again. As long as she didn't pluck any other notes, that first one sounded fine. Without meaning to be funny, he says, "*That* sounded good."

Angelica's pinkie and thumb reach across an octave to pluck two strings. They aren't quite right. Now he can tell. He's standing with his back to the table, half sitting on it, grappling with the ball of wires. This is modern life, right here in this room and in his hands. He's in a white robe and quite naked underneath. A chubby little cherub—named for angels, no less—plays harp for him. Wires, however, demand his full attention. He wishes he could hurl them out a window and get on with life.

They are not easy to untie. Since they have big plugs and sockets on their ends, they don't slip through knots easily. The knots have to be loosened at various points along a given wire until finally an end can fit through. They're all the same color, so Frankenstein's fingertips have to feel their way along each wire like plumbers working in the dark. The minute precision of it makes his hands shake. He breathes hard and feels a little faint. He clings to the off-key harp notes as if they floated and he might not. "What did he *do* this for?" he asks.

Angelica plucks a string repeatedly as she tweaks the key that tightens it. The notes rise by the faintest nuances. She squints at thin air as if she can see the sounds. Only after she gets the string just right does she speak. "He took the computer, to which I said good, take it, go. But then I got made secretary of the Friends of the Goddamn Library so I have to type up minutes and get e-mail and maintain the web page and stuff. So when our court date came up, I said I wanted the computer. The judge said I could have it, so Frank brought it back. Like this. See, the judge didn't say I could have it *not* tied in a knot, so that's what he did. He was that kind of guy."

Frankenstein doesn't say anything. He's got his fingers worked deeply into the ball of wires. He's trying to picture what it looks like in there, what kind of sub-knot he's working on. Somewhere in there is a knot which, untied, will release all the rest. The ball will come apart into beautiful individual strands. Then he will be able to breathe normally.

Plim-plim-plim, ploom-ploom-ploom, boing-boing-boing—little by little, Angelica brings together the tones of her harp. It doesn't sound like shit. It sounds like droplets of condensed heaven coming down. She starts playing chords, then riffs of chords. Frankenstein gives his loose knot of wires a spastic shake. He's falling behind. She's practically tuned a harp and is moving fast toward Bach. All he's got to show is a three-foot monitor cable with a ball of dead snakes at one end.

Little by little she turns her tuning chords into long strokes of music. When she gets it wrong, she goes *tcht* and reaches for it again. Not that it sounds wrong to Frankenstein. If he could play the harp as wrong as that, he'd buy one and carry it wherever he went. He'd play it here and there, wherever he got the urge. He'd be a musical Johnny Appleseed. They'd call him Frankenharp. Future generations of kindergartners would sing songs about him. They'd draw crayon illustrations of him strumming a lyre in front of fast-food joints, in bus depots, near funerals, here and there on the interstates, calming the world one spot at a time. He'd become a myth, a legend, a folk hero. Kids wouldn't believe in him. They'd assume he was just more grown-up propaganda. They'd hear about him and think, "So what?"

But he can't play harp and could never learn. His fingers could not do what Angelica's fingers are doing, and she's just getting warmed up. He watches them while fingering the ball of wires. She isn't just stroking her harp. She's embracing and caressing it. Her fingers crook and stretch to find the right strings, set upon them as lightly as birds, grip them with just the smallest bit of finger-flesh, and pull them just so. Each gentle burst of sound becomes a glorious moment in the universe.

It's a glorious moment in the universe when Frankenstein's wires suddenly loosen and separate. In the time it takes to breathe once, he lifts them apart. They look good lying on the table, limp and roughly parallel. Harp strings they aren't, but he's just a little proud. She gave him chaos; he gives her order. Not that she notices. She's playing harp. Computer wires are as far from her mind as Mars. Frankenstein says not a word. He just sets about the business of figuring out which wire goes where. He kneels at the table, turns the computer around, tries to match up the wires with their outlets and peripherals. With the harp to his back and his nose to the ass-end of an electronic device, he feels like he's reading pornography under a pew in church.

The more she plays, the more futile his efforts feel. So *what* if he gets it all plugged in and working? Angelica Pascapelli should not be futzing with a web page. She should not be receiving e-mail. She and all other harpists should be banned from the Internet. Incoming correspondence should be censured of all but letters on parchment in the cursive handwriting of a fountain pen. Their radios should not receive the trash of hoi poloi. They should not be called upon to befriend the goddamn library or to rescue wet mutts from the rain, let alone do their laundry. They should live in cultural humidors and just let their eyebrows be.

Her music is too beautiful now. Her practice chords have evolved into "Greensleeves." Frankenstein hasn't the faintest idea what greensleeves are, but their music tends to make him cry. He pictures lambs frolicking in a meadow of buttercups and rye. They frolic so well that they soon lose their way, and everyone wonders what happened to them. He vaguely recalls a hymn to the same tune. It's not about lambs but Jesus. *What child is this, hmmm, hmmm, hmmm, something, something, something.* Frolicking in a meadow of buttercups and rye, for all he knows. The image, the music, it's all too beautiful. A wetness swamps his eyes. He can't focus on the little dark sockets in the computer, can't even bring himself to stick in a wire. Something tells him that if he does, he'll short out the harp. Its strings will spit sparks and flames. Sweet Angelica will fall away, her fingers charred and smoking from the knuckles out. The invisible vastness of the Internet will not laugh. For all its omniscience, it won't even notice.

Frankenstein's not going to be the one to do it. He won't plug it in. In fact, neither will anyone else. He gets a great idea. His plan unfolds as if by divine inspiration. He never would have thought of this himself. The modem cable has a little transformer on the end, to reduce the power of the incoming electricity. He takes the modem power cord and loops it through the hinge of the leg of the table. Holding the table up with his shoulder, watching Angelica to see if she notices, he folds in the leg just far enough to snap the wire right near the little transformer. With his fingernail he slices between the two wires of the cord, then uses his teeth to pull off an inch of insulation from each. He plugs in the computer and turns it on. He plugs the modem into the back, then sticks the naked wires into the outlet in the wall. A hundred and twenty volts shoot into a unit built for six. He gets a little puff of smoke from the modem and suspects the same has happened within the computer. It's going to be a long time before Angelica Pascapelli goes online.

Angelica sniffs. The last of her harp notes fade. She says, "What's that?"

"Something's wrong here," Frankenstein taps the computer, clicks the mouse, looks as worried as he can. It isn't hard. He's got a lopped-off transformer on the floor and a lopped-off wire stuck in an outlet. Even the most dedicated harpist would recognize a problem.

"*Damn Frank*. I bet he screwed it up on purpose. I bet he gave it a virus."

"That's what I think it is," Frankenstein says knowingly. "You've got a virus in there. A *bad* one."

"Can you fix it?"

She's come closer now. She's right behind him, slightly to the side, with one hand on his robed shoulder. He's still on his knees. He clicks the end of his tongue and shakes his head as if he has a sore neck. "For a virus like this," he says, "you need a real expert. A *specialist*."

"I should throw the damned thing out the window and just play harp for the rest of my life."

"*Yes*."

"Unfortunately, Mr. Frankenstein, life's not like that." Having spoken her final word, she turns and marches back to the kitchen. Frankenstein hurries after her. She's moving very fast, her spine straight, her head back, her little hands in little fists. He almost runs to keep up. His robe flaps. Fresh air wafts in from below.

"Life *should* be like that," he says, wanting to grab her by the shoulders and impress her with some sense of the goodness of what he's talking about. "It *could* be like that."

"It could if you're willing to live out of a duffel bag and beg to have your laundry done. Then you can throw anything you want out the window."

He's about to say that he never begged, but that's not the point. The point is the part about throwing stuff out the window. She's not talking about computers. She's waxed philosophical. Normally he'd like that. But she's talking about him, something he's thrown out his personal window. He's not sure he wants to know what. Whatever it was, the lack of it left him standing filthy in the rain at a fork in the interstate with a bag full of clothes too rancid to wear. That's what she means. So the question isn't about what, if anything, he threw out his personal window but whether it was worth it. It *would* have been worth it *if* it had left him playing the harp. But it didn't. It just left him clammy.

How's he going to explain all that? He can't. All he can do is sit and eat fettuccine served with tomato sauce and guilt. He's sorry he let her wash his clothes, but he doesn't say so. He's not sorry he destroyed her computer. He doesn't say that, either. But he remembers he left the little transformer and the sliced wire on the floor in the junk room. He excuses himself for a moment, goes to the room, picks up the evidence, weighs it in his palm. If she finds this stuff, he's dead. All he can think to do with it is throw it out the window. What could be more appropriate? Only trouble is, the window squeaks when he opens it. He lets the peripheral amputations fall into an evergreen bush. The window squeaks as he closes it.

When he returns to the table, Angelica says, "What was that?" Her voice is cold, her jaw clenched. A tad of tomato sauce sticks to her tight lips.

Frankenstein packs fettuccine into his mouth before he says, "Nothing." He knows the lie won't work, but he has to say something.

Angelica resumes chewing. She gets up, clears her throat, walks to her bedroom and closes the door. Soon he can hear her in there talking on the phone. Figuring he has nothing to lose, he hangs around the door, listening. He can't make out much, but he does hear her say, "What I am I supposed to *do* with him?" He hears her hang up and then dial again. Then her voice murmurs in hushed conspiracy.

Afraid she'll suddenly open the door, he goes into the junk room and turns on the computer. It seems to be working, all but the modem. He goes to the harp, sits on the milk crate and very, very cautiously gives one string a little tug. A clear and perfect note hums forth. He tries another string. Again, the note is perfect and beautiful. Hoping to get an octave, he counts out eight strings, positions his fingers on them as Angelica had, and gives them a little tug. It's a sour combination. This is life, he thinks, right here in a harp.

Angelica opens her door, comes into the junk room. She looks quite relieved. Frankenstein says, "It works. I think I fixed it. See?"

She doesn't look at the computer. She just looks at him. She's smiling, but he'd guess it's against her will. She says, "I have some good news for you, Frankenstein. How'd you like to take a nice little trip on an airplane?"

- Chapter Four -
Frankenstein Flies

Phoenix, it seems, is as far as she can fling him. With a wink to a buddy at Gate 14, she escorts him and his clean white duffel bag right into the tunnel that attaches to a 727.

"Seat 27B," she says. Her smile is harsh and professional. "Have a nice flight." Then she turns and walks away.

Frankenstein can't even fly right. As soon as he's tucked in between a couple of over-fed sales-rep types, he wants out. He wants to travel by bike. He'd gladly sacrifice speed for elbow room. Now he knows, but it's too late. A woman with a face painted absurd shades of red, black and blue cranks over the big lever on the door: *ka-lunk*—locked-in freshness. The reps snap open their newspapers. Their elbows stake claim to the miniature armrests. Frankenstein pulls in his wings. The men have not noticed him. Now he's sorry he bathed at Angelica's. He wishes he stank. He wills bowel gas, but nothing comes. He's a fart manqué wrapped in Self-Esteem™ After-shave.

He does not believe, has never believed, that this bulking tonnage of plane can actually raise itself from the earth. Nor can he believe it will fail. He remembers, from a science class years ago, a schematic of a wing with fat white arrows flowing over and under it—the miracle of the airfoil. He thought, "Yeah, right," then; he thinks "Yeah, right," now. It cannot fly. At the same time, it cannot fail to fly, not with Frankenstein aboard.

    The reps don't think such things. One focuses on an in-depth analysis of a crucial golfing event. The other peruses stock prices. Frankenstein does not wish to disturb them with his concerns. If they thought about the impossibility of flight—they and enough other passengers and, god forbid, the pilot—the plane would just weigh more and more as it sped down the runway. The prayers of the minority would not lift it. The plane would trip at the end of the runway like a marauding brontosaurus, would skid face-first into greenery. Philosophers of aviation would arrive to investigate. They'd swat through the clouds of attorneys, have a look at the corpse with its crumpled, frowning cockpit, its crinkled wings, its broken spine, and they would draw the conclusion which they'd suspected all along: a hundred thousand tons cannot fly.

    The plane lumbers around runways, turns left, turns right, gets into line like a sullen kid waiting for cafeteria food. Frankenstein checks for exits. He imagines them clotting up like a toilet drain as ten dozen people forget their manners completely. The plane moves ahead fifty feet and stops again. He yanks out the contents of the little pocket in the seat ahead of him—a catalog of slick gizmos, an in-flight magazine, a barf bag, the emergency instruction card. He can't afford the gizmos. The magazine doesn't offer much hope for anyone not on an expense account. The bag's plastic but too small for his head. The emergency instruction card, however, depicts real-life drama. In simple, primary colors, it tells the tale of a plane wreck. A wingless jet dives at a forty-five degree angle into a rippling sea. Oxygen masks drop down. A lady with a baby knows just what to do. Everybody knows. No one screams. No one fouls their pants. Everyone's seat belt is on. A man puts out his cigarette before the whole plane blows up. A woman vomits between her knees. The flight attendants are nowhere in sight. Suddenly the plane is floating in a calm sea. Everyone stands back from the emergency exit while a lone man activates the slide. Everybody slides down. Whee! It turns out they have not landed in the sea. They are on land. Everyone runs for it. A man and a woman hold hands as they hasten away.

FRANKENSTEIN ON THE CUSP OF SOMETHING

The back of the card bears the small print. If you're sitting near the exit, you must be able to speak English, lift "something like an emergency exit door," follow instructions, read, rotate, open, stand back, assess, use caution, jump feet first, push and, if it comes to this, shove. Frankenstein locates his exit. It's just across the aisle, up one row. It is under the command of an absolute sleazeball, a man who pees with the seat down, a resolute imbecile whose English is at best a dialect of Neanderthal. Can he follow instructions? No. Will he turn the door crank up and over the way the arrow indicates? Not likely. Can he activate an inflatable slide? No way in hell. Will he think the picture with the cigarette means you should pull a butt *out* of the tiny ashtray and light it? Sure might.

Frankenstein's concerned. He feels morally obliged to ask the flight attendant to see if the man speaks English. Does he know what he's supposed to do? Isn't there some kind of IQ test for these people? Has he read the small print on the back of the card? Most certainly not. He's looking at the gizmo catalog. By the slick, cracked pout of his lower lip, Frankenstein knows for sure that the man's leering at the photo of the blonde with the red lipstick in the floating beach chair with the built-in waterproof stereo CD player and four cup holders. Frankenstein himself looks at her for a long, long time, thinking, thinking, thinking. Emergency egress is far from his mind.

But hey, what's death? Just a recycling of molecules. It has to happen. Frankenstein leans forward to look out the window. Beyond the sales rep, grass and runway flicker by. The engines give it all they've got. The plane bounces like an overweight albatross getting a running start. Prayer fills the plane. The sleazeball turns his head to the window. The sales reps inhale just enough to get the wheels off the runway. Almost immediately, the plane banks to the starboard, preliminary to the famous cartwheel of death. Frankenstein squeezes his eyes so hard he sees globs of light, and he tells himself there *is* a God, there *is* a God. The plane, convinced of same, tucks up its landing gear, levels off, flaps hard for the horizon. The seat belt light goes out. Everything's going to be all right.

"Snack, sir?"

It's the winged serving wench with the cyanotic eyelids and burgundy lips. She extends a slender package to Frankenstein's aisle-side neighbor.

She holds it as if to imply that it's only a joke, that she really doesn't expect anyone to accept the obligatory offer. One side of the man's face curls up with suspicion and curiosity. He accepts her generosity, smiles at it and sticks it in his shirt pocket.

"Snack, sir?"

He wonders what she means by *sir*. For that matter, it isn't much of a snack, either. It's a delicious, nutritious lo-fat multi-fruit-flavored health bar the size of a turd in a package every bit as slick, the kind of facsimile foodstuff that gives *snack* a bad name. *Shit, snot, crap, snack.* The swirly chocolate script of the word "flavored" blends into its background, a tapeworm on a bed of spaghetti, dog doo on gutter-scum, a camouflaged satisfaction of federal law. Why do they hide it so? Are they afraid their mothers will find out and yell at them? Frankenstein's sure that somewhere on this package a warning in microscopic Swahili says, "Not for Internal Use." He checks the ingredients. He's never heard of any of them besides that old workhorse, high fructose corn syrup, and its underachieving cousin, just plain corn syrup. The rest look like words he'd make up in a Scrabble game. Who dreamed up such a formula? Why don't they just make strawberry-rhubarb pie, sweetened with honey? Who are *they*, anyway? Motherless manufacturers in New Jersey, that's who. Their factory extracts polysnackivate from industrial sludge and condenses it into a thick orange paste suitable for stuffing into a health bar, and boy does it stink.

The in-flight magazine stinks, too—Discover Orlando! Relive Gettysburg! Eat History in St. Louis! Aloha from the Land of Frangipani! The slick, high-fructose pages offer absolutely nothing of interest until he flips to the story of a North Dakota hamster farmer with a blimp. The guy has seventeen acres of open-air hamster pastures just outside the town of Lark. He's had as many as two million, eight-hundred and fifty thousand hamsters. His philosophy: just give them fresh air, open sky, earth beneath their feet, good food and plenty of elbow room. Cages are a lot of work, expensive, and they lead to disease and unhappy hamsters. He lets them graze and breed in the way of the deer and the antelope. Only one problem: buzzards.

"Nothing a buzzard loves more for lunch than a nice, tender, ranch-raised hamster," the man says. His name is Walter, after his father.

God bless America. You don't find Walter-types in France or Japan. Walter hovers over his ranch in a helium-filled blimp, listening to the radio and blowing buzzards out of the sky with a 12-gauge shotgun. If you've ever bought a hamster from a pet store, odds are eight to one it was raised under Walter's wing and has seen the frazzled remains of carnivores dropping from the sky.

Once Walter's tether came loose in a thunderstorm. He drifted off at an estimated thirty miles per hour. He released helium as fast as he could, but updrafts got hold of him, kept him going.

"All their little heads tilted back as they watched me fly away," he said in the article. "I can't *imagine* what must of been going through their minds."

Walter's half-deflated blimp floated over the Missouri and halfway into Emmons County before it dropped into a wheat field. He had to tow it home with his brother-in-law's tractor. At every power line he had to heave a rope over the line and re-tie the blimp before proceeding. Their progress titillated the local press for a week. He could see the buzzards circling his ranch. He had his wife, Margaret, out there with the shotgun, but, as he said, "She couldn't hit the broad side of Bismarck with a stick."

Frankenstein's flabbergasted. A story like this belongs in a tabloid with pictures of aliens and vinegar cures. But it's real. Walter's a real guy. Lark's a real place. The story must have made it into an airplane magazine because it's about flying and cute things. Photos show him in his blimp, an aerial shot of his ranch, and a close-up of a hamster chewing on a strand of wheat. The story makes no reference to Margaret besides the wisecrack about her marksmanship. Frankenstein wonders what she looks like. He pictures her in polyester slacks, button-up blouse, Keds, a seed cap on her golden hair-do, maybe sunglasses when she's buzzard-hunting. He wants to meet her. He wants to eat her biscuits. He wants to slobber over her green beans while Walter expounds on the history of hamsters, how to tell if they have worms, their advantages over white mice—if the medical profession only knew! He's sent letters to Washington, but no one ever answers. He writes to state legislators, asking for hamsters to be declared the state rodent. They don't write back either. None of that's in the article, but Frankenstein knows the type. He knows their wives, too. They look down at their knitting while the TV's on. They don't talk much. It might take her three weeks of thinking about it before she finally gives her yarn a long pull and says, in nasal North Dakota twang, "I don't see why you don't give those hamsters of yours some *shade*."

Frankenstein's never fired a shotgun, but how hard can it be? High school dropouts have done it. He wouldn't mind floating over the North Dakota prairie and taking potshots at buzzards. Not that buzzards deserve to die any more than the next guy. But if you're in the business of murdering friendly rodents, he figures, you have to face certain facts. One of those facts just might come floating along in a blimp. If you want to get old and fat, stick to your high fructose snacks. If you want to live off tender, ranch-raised hamsters, you really can't complain about getting blown out of the sky.

So, thirty-five thousand feet above the earth, zipping along in the wrong direction at damn-near the speed of sound, Frankenstein hatches a plan. He bets Walter needs a vacation. He bets Margaret does, too. He bets they'd be mighty glad if a guy showed up and offered to shoot buzzards for free. Wouldn't that look great on his resume? Room and board are all he'll ask for. He lets himself sink into fantasy. Someday he'll own his own blimp. He'll migrate across the grain belt, performing aerial services for farmers. He'll shoot crows from corn fields, sprinkle fertilizer over oats, seek out lost sheep, advertise chewing tobacco. He'll build up a fleet of dirigibles. It wouldn't take many to be the world's largest. He could become a force to be reckoned with. Who could stop a fleet of blimps? Who could tell them where to go? He supposes they could be shot down, but if enough of them carried, say, a hydrogen bomb, well….he doesn't want to think about it. He wants to think about a thousand dirigibles drifting in the jet stream, their motors shut down, their passengers drinking fine wine, making love, catching up on their reading, hearing lectures on astronomy, listening to a string quartet, eating strawberry-rhubarb pie, looking out the window at Africa and erasing from their minds all memories of new delicious strawberry (flavored) health bars. He supposes no one has yet thought of a law against this.

FRANKENSTEIN ON THE CUSP OF SOMETHING

Couldn't a thousand dirigibles constitute a country? If not, well, how about ten thousand? Where does it say you need an solid piece of the planet to declare your independence? *Air's* part of the planet, isn't it? Couldn't a people lay claim to a bit of it?

It feels like the kind of plan that could lead to trouble, but as long as he keeps it in a closed container, nothing should go wrong. He leans back into the saccharine mist of after-shave. He dreams of blimps floating so high that down looks like up, the earth a shade of blue that looks like sky. Up there, direction makes no difference. Even now, as he shoots through the air toward Arizona, in the space of his mind he knows where he's going. He's going to North Dakota.

- Chapter Five -
Frankenstein Loves Asphalt

Earth looks bad at an interstate exit in northern Arizona. Road crews have waged war on the place, tearing away a mountain of rock, blocking part of the interstate, shunting traffic into a temporary sluiceway of death, raising up monolithic pylons in a massive federal project to re-tie a cloverleaf.

Arriving in an old yellow station wagon piloted by a drunk carpenter, Frankenstein grips the door handle as they barrel between low walls of concrete. The car bounces and sways through craters. The drunk at the wheel—drunk on tequila and stoned on Tijuana weed—steers with the palm of his right hand, punishing the road and the car without prejudice. He's mad at a boss who has committed a discombobulated array of atrocities against this flawless worker who now has express plans to ease his grievances with a blowjob once he gets to a bar where his old lady had better be waiting for him if she knows what's good for her. Frankenstein declines an invitation to come along. He wants to go north, toward Lark, on a state highway that intersects the interstate somewhere in this Department of Transportation War Zone. He knows his inebriated benefactor has forgotten that, so when the alley widens a bit,

FRANKENSTEIN ON THE CUSP OF SOMETHING

Frankenstein, gizzard in throat, suggests, "You could let me off right up there."

"You sure?"

"Sure!"

The station wagon slides into the wide spot as if into second base. Dust catches up from behind, tumbles over the windshield. Frankenstein steps into the gritty air. The rear seat door grunts as he opens it to retrieve his duffel bag from its nest of scrap wood, forlorn tools, beer cans, the exoskeletons of fast food. As soon as the door grunts shut, the car launches into the roller coaster of traffic. Its tires spin up more dust, bombarding Frankenstein's sandaled feet with hot chunks of busted concrete and asphalt.

So here he stands, bag on shoulder, no idea which way to go. America hasn't created a worse place to hitchhike since Iwo Jima. Jackhammers punch through the air like machine guns. Trucks roar like animals in heat. A sign warns of blasting. The earth is rubble. The Arizona outback, somewhere out of sight, will be Eden compared to this.

Raindrops on roses and whiskers on kittens but there's no hitching out of *this* spot. Frankenstein sees a long hoof ahead. Just to figure out which way to go he'll have to pick and weave his way through hundreds of yards of no-man's land. For this he turned down barfly fellatio.

The haze makes the setting sun look hung-over, exhausted, resigned to gravity. Frankenstein keeps it to his left. He climbs over barriers, skitters through lulls in traffic, almost castrates himself on the rim of a chain-link fence. He wanders to the left, to the right, back over the other way. A man in a yellow hard hat points toward a flat black glacier of fresh asphalt lined with bright orange pylons. Frankenstein thanks him kindly.

Alas, it's a highway without traffic. He must trudge. The asphalt seethes beneath his feet. It's still hot, fresh from the oven. His heels dent it. Grains stick to his sandals. He wonders about the chemical composition of smell, in this case the tar fumes wrapping around his face. Are they vaporized asphalt, the same stuff in gaseous form? Do they condense on the walls of the lung, paving them wisp by wisp? It sure feels like it.

A steam roller comes long, backwards, the driver leaning around from under a bright yellow parasol, keeping his rollers along an invisible line parallel to the pylons. It looks like a job Frankenstein could do. It would sure beat lugging a duffel bag around, looking for he doesn't know what. Given a steam roller, he'd know exactly what to do. He'd flatten asphalt. No big decisions. No fuzzy future. No getting lost. No one to persuade or impress. No arguments. He wonders whether he could get the job if he doesn't have hairy knuckles. He wonders if steam rollers have horns or if you just shout, "*Hey!*"

He trudges on. The bright black roadway, not yet festooned with yellow lines, adorned only with the orange cones so neatly in a row, lies flat and straight. Half a mile ahead, it vanishes in a rippling sheen. How far will he have to walk before he comes to traffic or a glass of water? Off to the west, maybe a mile away, dust rises in a long horizontal line. Cars flicker behind the distant brush. It's a connector road to the end of the newly paved highway. That's where he should be. Now he knows. Should he walk over there, risk rattlesnakes and an insurmountable fence? Or should he stick to the stinking asphalt? Sweat oozes around the back of his ears and drools to the upper corner of his jaw. Whatever he decides, it will be wrong. The hobnail of that inevitability presses on his brain. It makes him want to walk on hot asphalt. He wants to wrap himself in misery like a horsehair cloak. He deserves this for what he might have done.

What forces work on Frankenstein as he presses through the heat? Gravity holds him to the planet. Centrifugal force tries to throw him into space. Memories tug him backward. Hopes pull him onward. Sloth would have him stop. Habit keeps him going. Thirst figures in. Fears whisper from his dark interior. *Guilt*. The past motivates him; so does the future. His feet urge him to reconsider, but his imagination leaves them behind. Astrological energy beams down on him, cosmic rays inducing him to avoid business decisions, rethink his travel plans, watch for love from an unexpected source. Newton applies: A body in motion tends to stay in motion, but a body under a duffel bag tends to slow. It doesn't help to have asphalt sticking to your footwear.

Common sense prevails. If he stops, he'll die. He keeps leaning toward the shimmerous vanishing point at the end of the long, black road. He keeps his knees passing each other, his feet planting and uprooting themselves. One foot stands there while the other moves on ahead. Then they change roles. Like the inhale-exhale cycle of the meditating Buddhist, the movement/nonmovement of his feet hypnotizes him. He comes loose from time. His mind flies. He feels like he's got his head in a plastic bag. He becomes a former incarnation, a child of six or seven whizzing down pavement on a bicycle. Beneath him, beneath the cross bar, between the wheels, the macadam blurs to gray. The blur takes form. The pavement's cracks and pebbles and stains meld into a infinite, wriggling, molting ghost. The frame of the bicycle hovers motionless as the blur scurries by like smoke in a rush. Six or seven years old and he's seeing something no other human being has seen, he's sure of it. No one has ever noticed the undulating patterns in asphalt because no one has ever thought to look straight down while riding a bicycle. He understands why, this young philosopher, as the front wheel of his bike meets the curb at the end of the street and the back wheel rises behind him, pitching him overhand into the side of a public mailbox. As it mashes the cartilage of his little nose, the mailbox booms with the full authority of doom and the federal government. Little yellow birds circle his head, *tweety-tweet-tweet*, and five-pointed pulsars throb with his pain.

He awakens in Arizona on a black cloud below a hovering angel in a yellow helmet. She eclipses the sun, which dazzles around her dark hair in a golden halo. Two broad beaver teeth show just below her upper lip. Wayward strands of shiny black hair curl out from under her hard hat, hang around her face like feelers of kudzu. As she removes her dark aviator glasses, the furrows above her eyes flow inward and down toward her nose. She's so close he can see the dust in her nostrils. The backs of her soft fingers kiss his cheek. With the voice of a distant harp, she sings, "Are you all right?"

When he tries to speak, he finds his lips welded shut. He hasn't the strength to crack them. A moan through his nose, replete with meaning but as basic as a grunt, sears with the heat of chimney fire. He inhales with the shuddering effort of a child at the shore of tears.

Still shading his face with hers, the angel lifts his head from the back, tilts him forward to a plastic canteen. Water, warm but good, dissolves the seal along his lips. It swells his tongue, erodes through his throat, trickles to his desiccated gut. He suckles with desperation. She tips the canteen just so, neither choking him nor denying a gulp. "Easy, now," she says, elongating her syllables. "Easy."

Easy it is. He hasn't had it like this since he was three months old. The canteen issues milk and honey, and Frankenstein falls in love with a woman who's but a blur. As he closes his eyes again, the sweat on his eyelids cools. She says, "There, there," and nestles him closer. Two fingers lick his temple. He wants to weep with unutterable comfort. He loves this woman more than love should allow. He would suckle from her canteen until death did them part. He'd forget about North Dakota. He'd forget about blimps. That was a stupid idea. He just wants this woman to hold him while he takes a nap, even if on hell-hot macadam. Should she dump him here, he would die. Should she take him home, he would float on puffy clouds.

She takes him to a dusty, lime-green dump truck. With one arm around his waist, one hand to his upper arm, she guides and steadies him. He worries that he might fall again, take her down with him, break something. Her weight against him makes him no more steady, but he works an arm up and over her shoulder. She's a solid woman, solid but soft. But even her hard hat feels soft as it rocks against his cheek. He thinks of kissing it. He would.

She says, "Easy now."

It's a castle of a dump truck. It could hold a house in its dumper. She's stopped it just off the pavement, its engine running. At a slow, stammering idle, the engine barely flips open the cap atop the vertical exhaust pipe. A thin chain attached to the cap goes *chi-ching, chi-ching, chi-ching* to the humping rhythm of the diesel.

She says, "Can you make it?"

She means up the six steps to the cabin on the passenger side. The cabin's so far up, so huge, that it even has a little steel grate balcony at the door. A person could sit there and have a cappuccino at a little round table. A heat-struck person, however, might have a little trouble getting up the steps, which are actually more like a ladder at a steep angle rising across the side of the truck. Can he make it? He will try. If the heat and altitude drain his blood, he'll know what it feels like to fall off a dump truck. His angel will save him again. If he succeeds, she and he can drive their beautiful lime-green dump truck into the sunset, or, for that matter, north to Lark. For that, that mere possibility, he will assault these stairs. Also, he wants to see the inside of a dump truck. He's never touched one before, not even a regular-sized one, nothing bigger than the yellow one he used to push around a sand box, supplying his own diesel growl, squeaky brakes, whoosh of cascading coal. That truck seemed as real, in an inverse sort of way, as the one he's about to surmount now.

Her hands steady him at the waist and the elbow as he eases to the first step. As he rises, her hands, soft and solid, cup him at the waist. Then it's only his fingers touching hers for a lingering moment, not a touch of support, just a kiss of *hasta luego*.

Luego happens up in the cabin. What a place, ten feet wide, first-class seats, a picture window as vast as the great outdoors, *air conditioned*. It feels like genuine oxygen, mountain air, breath of glacier, vapor of toothpaste. Two nice people could live happily ever after in a place like this.

She rises into view, swings open her door, rolls in his duffel bag, which he'd completely forgotten. As he pulls it out of the way, she climbs in, smiling at him, gazing at him as she comes. He tries to keep his eyes from slurping over her thighs as they tighten her jeans. She's happy to have him here. He feels this. Her face, tan and burnt, exudes warm invitation. Her cheeks puff with gladness. Her two center teeth, divided by a dark gap, peek from between her lips like kids all shy and giggly. She says, "Off we go!" as if into the wild blue yonder. *Yes, yes,* thinks he. *Off we go.*

Her perfectly cylindrical arms go taut with muscles for the moment it takes to shift into drive. It's an automatic transmission with the shifter coming out of the steering wheel shaft. The steering wheel, a good three feet wide, moves easily under her quick, precise hands. She looks pleased with herself—pleased with her job, pleased with her big green truck, pleased to have Frankenstein looking at her with fawning admiration. He loves everything about this woman, the way she rolls the sleeves of her T-shirt right up to her armpits, the way she checks her mirrors, the quickness of her movements, the hint of smile that varies from just-about-to to just-did. He loves her low leather work boots, her dusty white socks, the way she keeps her shoulders back, the way her breasts don't need size to assert themselves. This is a woman who can make decisions. *Off we go.*

"Feeling better?" she asks, just glancing over at him, almost smiling.

"God, yes," he moans. "Where're we off to?"

She laughs! She sees the humor of it, the openness, the potential. She knows perfectly well that they're sitting in a truck the size of a cumulonimbus and floating just about as high and cool across the Arizona heat. The truck moves with magical buoyancy, hovering over the land, its engine just a distant hum. They could drive this thing to North Dakota, Guatemala, Patagonia, no one could stop them. It's almost as good as a blimp.

Frankenstein wants to tell her that, but he's afraid. It's a stupid idea and he knows it. But he can't think of anything that's *not* stupid. He knows that, too. He might as well pursue the stupid idea that appeals to him most. But that's a lot to explain to a beautiful woman who has just plucked him from the griddle of tarstone. She might well conclude that he deserved to pass out flat on his face in the middle of an unfinished highway. She might laugh at him.

Stupid Idea #2: Sit there like a dummy and don't say anything. Wait for her to say, "So, where're you coming from?" Wait for the conversation to wend its way to the subject of blimps, then mention casually that maybe North Dakota's where they ought to go, the two of them, to start a new life together, hired hands on a hamster ranch.

But no, he won't bring that up, not unless he can do it as a joke, a disposable test of her reaction. Besides, he's not so sure hamster farming is the right career move. He thinks he might try civil engineering, starting, perhaps, as the guy who paddles traffic along by waving a bright red flag. From there he could move up, become the guy who operates the sign that says "Slow" on one side, "Stop" on the other. From there he could move up to a steam roller and from there to co-pilot of a gargantuan dump truck.

He knows it won't happen like that. He knows fantasy from reality. He's just not sure what difference it makes what he chooses to let himself think. He'd be happy enough to take the flag-waving position and just dream about the rest.

"Hey," he says, the word bubbling up from a ticklish place, "is there any work around here?"

She looks absolutely *delighted* to hear the question. She almost giggles. "Work?" she says through a full-face smile. "You can't work. You're sick!"

He doesn't feel sick, not anymore. But she says it with such glee that he feels obliged to at least feign queasiness. With all possible melodrama, he lays the back his hand against his forehead, emits a thin, weak whine. "I needs lay me down," he sighs. "I need Mexican food and cold beer and a bath."

She laughs with feminine guffaw. "That's the cure," she sings. "We can take care of that."

The big truck swirls into an encampment of trailer offices, pick-ups, highway department vehicles, forests of stacked traffic cones, dull orange signs warning of slow traffic, men working, vehicles on the road, expected delays. The steam roller, its little yellow parasol off balance, looks like an obese, exhausted ice cream cart. Heavy dust lends everything to a kinship of earthtones. With the alacrity of a sports car, the truck tools around the little settlement. The girl's tan elbows flap as her big green steed homes in on the place it belongs, noses into a parking spot next to a low black asphalter. She says, "Atta boy," as the truck shudders with exhaustion and settles into silence.

He insists on lugging his duffel bag down to earth himself. It's up on his shoulder when she comes around the front of the truck to wrap her arms around one of his. "Come on," she says and pulls him at a bouncy pace, riding high on the balls of her feet. She tugs him toward a late model black Toyota pick-up. She gives him a little push to carry him the rest of the way. "Hop in," she says. "I've got to punch out."

While she bounces off to a dirty white house trailer, Frankenstein rolls his bag into the back of the truck and wonders if this is really happening. It certainly seems to be. As the screen door at the trailer claps shut behind her, he hopes no one inside will distract her, no one will ask her about the unauthorized tramp who climbed down from the department of transportation dump truck, that no one will invite her to a bar or propose marriage, hypnotize her, slip her a mickey, steal her away.

No one does. The screen door claps again, and the beautiful girl emerges. Half skipping, half trotting, hard hat off, hair as black as macadam, she hurries toward the truck. Her low, heavy boots kick up puffs of dust. Yes, yes, it is really happening. They are going to get in the truck and go somewhere.

For almost an hour they drive down the interstate, then down a well-paved state highway that ripples with the last of the day's heat. Her name is Wendy. His name is Frankenstein. Wendy blurts, "*Frankenstein?*"

"Frankenstein." He states it half factually, half apologetically. "That's my name."

She smiles the smile of someone with a juicy, secret thought, keeps her eyes on the road. "Frankenstein," she says, weighing the sound of it. "That's a nice name."

Wendy drives with one arm straight to the steering wheel, elbow locked. The other arm lolls on the sill of the open window. Sometimes she leans her head to the left to rest it on her shoulder. Frankenstein's stuck for words. He's uncomfortably inactive in the passenger seat. He wishes she would give him a job to do, read a map or something. Looking at him more than at the road, she interviews him. Where's he going? Where's he coming from? Why? He tells her he's coming from Seattle. He doesn't mention the bank teller, the one with the black tire marks on her linoleum. He tells her he's going to North Dakota to look for work.

"North Dakota?" she laughs. "Is that still a state?"

"What are they going to do, sell it? Who'd buy North Dakota?"

She laughs more. Frankenstein feels himself in good form. *Who'd buy North Dakota?* That was a good one.

"There's work there?" she asks, her cheeks high and tight with smile.

"I figure nobody else is looking. Who ever heard of somebody looking for a job in North Dakota?"

She laughs again. He wonders how many times he can get away with using *North Dakota* as a punch line. "What do you do," she asks, "besides sleep on highways?"

This is it. Should he mention Walter's blimp? Should he confess that he really can't do *anything*? He didn't even get enough credits to qualify as an English major. He can't use a hammer without damaging the nail and the wood around it, can't do much with a computer, never milked a cow, can't speak a foreign language, can't fix a car, has no idea how electricity works. He's a pretty good swimmer; that's about it. Now he hangs his career on a hamster ranch, a long shot so ridiculous he can't bring himself to mention it. It isn't even a long shot. It's just a direction. It's a place so far away that he doesn't have to worry about actually arriving there.

To his amazement, he says, "I travel." It sounds so cool, so perfect. And it's true.

"Wow," she says, her head rocking heavily as if on low waves. "Where to?"

He almost says, *nowhere*, but that's too easy. He finds himself saying, "*Where's* not the point." He can hardly believe it. Siddhartha himself could not have uttered anything more profound.

She laughs in a whisper through her nose. Frankenstein detects suspicion, but he's not sure. Maybe she thinks he's on parole or something. He backpedals. "I don't know where I'm going," he admits. "I just feel like moving. I thought I'd head toward North Dakota, see what happens. Maybe I can chop wheat or something."

"Chop wheat!" she hoots. She laughs so hard she has to put a hand on his leg to keep from falling over. Frankenstein's hand darts to the steering wheel, saves their lives. As he leans against her arm, he puts his head near hers, laughs, inhales with a jittery stomach. Her hair smells of fresh asphalt.

"Whoa!" she says, drawing out the vowels, sitting up straight, braking hard and wrenching the shift into second gear. For a second, Frankenstein's terrified that he's done something wrong, that he's about to get shoved out the door. But as soon as the truck stops, Wendy slams it into reverse, backs up a hundred feet, swirls the steering wheel around and dives onto a dusty road. A cattle guard fills the truck with thunder. Wendy snaps on the headlights.

Frankenstein loves roads like this, just a couple of ruts among the brush, mile after mile. The end of such roads always offers something interesting, even if nothing more than a gradual closing-in of the vegetation and an evaporation of the ruts. In this case, it looks like the road might dissolve into desert scrub. But as they sweep around to the north side of a little mountain of half-naked boulders, the headlights swing across a sloppy barbed wire fence and then a yard and an adobe house with the proportions of a shoe box. Wendy says, "Be it ever so humble," and kills the motor.

Signs of animals clutter the yard: a rabbit cage, a tire half sliced like a bagel to hold a ring of water, a chicken coop, a beehive, a rope tied to a broad, low tree, buckets old and new. A little dog barks in the twilight, up on the mountain behind the house, working his way among the boulders, finally arriving. With glee and a clap of her hands, Wendy says, "Rascal!" and bends down to receive him. Rascal's a Chihuahua mix with fluffy hair and a fox-like snout. He's missing half his front right leg. As he hobbles and yaps to his beloved Wendy, it looks as if he's coming to shake hands. As he comes into Wendy's arms, she blesses his little head with a thousand kisses. He licks her face. Holding him high on her chest, she lets Frankenstein stroke his head with two fingers. Rascal's cautious, and Frankenstein's ready to snatch his hand away, but the little dog's whippy, hairless tail twitches with tentative acceptance. Frankenstein chances a scratch behind Rascal's ear. Rascal whimpers. Frankenstein takes the stump of Rascal's right leg, shakes it and says, "Pleased to meet you." Rascal licks the butt of his thumb. Wendy beams.

Frankenstein loves Wendy, her dog, and the place where they live. The mountain seems the friend of the house. The yard flows into the desert, across a sea of stolid scrub, lapping up at the indigo horizon and its sleepy, heroic stars. A rabbit crunches something in its cage. Crickets crick. Chickens mutter in their sleep. Dung, dust, smoke, dew, and sage slide around the air, mingling with Wendy's essence of asphalt and her truck's sweet petroleum perspiration. The truck clinks as if falling asleep. Frankenstein could stand there forever, drinking in the sounds and smells, the darkness, the calm. Only one sound would be worth the loss of the near-silence, and Wendy says it: "Let's go inside."

She launches Rascal like a sixteen-ounce bowling ball. Frankenstein lays a hand over her kidney. Her arm reaches around him. Her thumb burrows under his belt. Though they're joined at the hip like Siamese twins, she still walks with that urgent, energetic bounce. He has to fall in step. At the front door, she pirouettes away from him to put her back against the heavy slats of wood. Frankenstein thinks this might be the moment to move in for a kiss, but before he's in position, Wendy's heel has thumped the door three times hard. The third thump nudges it open with a grunt. The walls of this house are two feet thick. Wendy steps backward into the cool darkness. Frankenstein follows, hands on her hips as if dancing. *Yes,* he thinks, *this is really happening.*

But a sudden light, as ragged as a cat scratch, rips open the darkness. It's a kitchen match in Wendy's hand. She has just dragged it up across the adobe wall. Until the flame settles down, she looks like the Statue of Liberty with a tired arm. With a quick, precise movement, she lifts the glass chimney of a kerosene lamp that hangs from the wall. As she touches the flame to the wick, warm light oozes across the room only slightly faster than the spreading of dawn under a thunderstorm. It oozes across a floor of rough pine boards, curls around a coffee table of tangled driftwood and ragged slate, climbs a massive chair of cedar logs, rises around a hammock strung between tree-trunk posts. The light barely washes to the far ends of the house. One end is a wall of books, the other a sparse kitchen with a simple stove, a broad, shallow sink, a counter with open shelves below, a clodhopper of an armoire that is either homemade or a survivor of the Alamo. The kitchen table is a slab of tree trunk roughly the shape of Alabama.

Wendy, her face half shadowed, half in the glow, is more beautiful than beauty. For a long moment she looks expectant, as if inhaling very deeply and slowly, but then she says, "You wanted beer, right?"

Well, he did, but not all that much. It wasn't absolute top priority. It could have waited. It occurs to him to say *I don't want beer, I want you,* but at this point, she seems to be pushing the beer more than herself. Maybe she's thirsty. In an involuntary tone of statement and question, Frankenstein says, "Beer(?)."

"Sit," she says, pointing to the split-log bench at the dining table. She clumps across the room to a refrigerator, a wide, wooden ice box that might have seen action in the Civil War. With a twist of her wrist, she unlatches one of four little doors. Her other hand pulls out two brown bottles, her knuckles gripping them at the top of their long necks.

"Old Undershirt," she says as she hooks each cap at the edge of the heavy, rustic table and whacks them down with the butt of her hand. "Made it myself."

She pours the beers into the centers of two heavy, slightly conical glasses. The head rises precisely to the lip. She looks pleased, if not outright proud, of having poured such classics. When Frankenstein holds his glass high toward the lamp, an ember-red star wavers in the brew. The reddish-brown of the beer is pretty close to the burnt tan of Wendy's cheeks. As it soaks into his throat, it's not cold but cool. It's tinged with a flavor of chrysanthemums, thick with minuscule fizz. As he exhales through his nose, he's sure he smells sage.

"Exquisite," he murmurs. He hasn't used the word for a long, long time, hasn't needed to. "*Exquisite.*" Everything is exquisite. Exquisite is Wendy, with her tan, taut body, her smiley face, her broad, shy front teeth. Exquisite is her earthy house, with its hewn furniture, its thick yellow lamplight. Exquisite is the whole situation. Though his hand grips a moderately cool glass of beer, it sweats.

He's about to reach for her, but she brings her glass to her lips and drinks deeply. Her eyes close with pleasure. Frankenstein does the same. Before he's done, Wendy smacks her half-empty glass to the dining table and says, "Mexican food."

With famished enthusiasm, Frankenstein says, "*Yes.*"

"I've got refrijoles," she says, extracting a pot from deep within her ancient ice box. She digs around more, bending to peer into the dark interior. "I've got some amazing tortillas made by a little old Mexican woman in town. I've got garlic guacamole. I've got shredded rabbit haunch with peppers that were smuggled in from Guatemala, I think." She lifts a ceramic bowl to her nose and gives the rabbit haunch a sniff. "I think it's still good."

"I'll eat it."

He would eat anything Wendy made for him. Her socks would be a sacrament. He sits at the table, watching her from behind as she ignites her gas stove, refries her refrijoles, warms her tortillas, snatches a gulp of Old Undershirt. She is so beautiful in her energy, her gracefully efficient movement. She cooks just as she drives her dump truck, same joy in the doing of it. She slides the bowl of guacamole onto the table, scoops out a finger-full, puts it between her lips. Her eyes look over toward New Mexico. Frankenstein takes a taste. It resonates with cilantro, mint, chili, cumin, basil, jalapeña, dill. He can hardly untangle the flavors.

Frankenstein says, "Your beer's the best in the world. Your guacamole exceeds my wildest dreams. Your two front teeth drive me crazy. Wendy..." He has to stop. If he gave his feelings words, they'd sound like a lie. He's dumbstruck, but his heart's wide open.

Wendy comes around the table, straddles the bench, scoots in close, curls a denim leg around his waist. He cups her shoulder blades. As her face comes into his, she brings him the smell of asphalt. His lips skate across her bulging cheek, veer around the corner of her smiling eye, home in on her temple. He presses her black hair to his face so hard it seems to leave an indentation. It moistens with his perspiration, then grows wet. It coats his face like beach sand, then drips and cools like a splash of seawater. He sputters in it as if drowning, clings to it the way a sinking swimmer tries to clutch the surface of the water, to grip the ungraspable air. She feels hard, granular, scabrous. In some strange way, she is leaving him, fading into an odd solidity. In a desperate squeak, he whispers her name.

Knuckles, hairy knuckles, tap and massage his cheek. A deep, dry voice says, "Hey...hey..." More water splashes on his face. His eyes crack open. He is lying on something that feels like a highway but smells of Wendy.

"Hey...hey...." The hand shakes his shoulder.

He's conscious now. The voice says, "Can you get up?" It tries to lift him by an armpit, but Frankenstein clings to the asphalt, at least as much as fingers can.

- CHAPTER SIX -
Life on a Pinkie

Frankenstein and a cricket sit beside Interstate 35 in Kansas. Or maybe it's still Oklahoma. The hazy blue sky, the great plain of corn stalk stubble, the straight edge of the concrete highway, they haven't changed in days. The boundary between the two states, as he recalls from grade school, is an arbitrary line, a length of latitude, not something logical like a river or ridge. It divides nothing. Neither state has something the other doesn't. Judging by the dearth of traffic, few Oklahomans have reason to go to Kansas. The two states wash together like water in an ocean. No barbed wire fence, no guard towers, no red-striped poles across the road, nobody asking the purpose of your trip or whether you're carrying any crickets.

He's sitting on the shoulder, facing the roadway, his knees raised a bit, his right arm resting on his dingy duffel bag, his shoulder blades hooked over one of the cables that keep cars from diving into the corn. The cricket's behind him, off in the grass but not far away. It's been hounding him for at least three days. He hasn't seen it—for all he knows, it could be a tiny robot from another planet—but it's been bugging him with its slow, humble *crick-creck, crick-creck* beside at least ten entrance ramps. It has nothing else to say, of course, and it has yet to hear a response from another cricket. Either it's the same cricket hopping aboard each car that stops for him, or Oklahoma and Kansas deploy lone crickets along the interstates to remind hitchhikers that they're not alone, that insects live here, too. Or maybe they're calling out to lovers who have met their maker on the windshields of cars and trucks. *Lonely crickets chirping in the wilderness.* If Frankenstein had a pen and paper, he'd write that down.

Bored to the point of desperate wonderment, he thinks it would be nice if the cricket leaped out of the dusty grass to sit on his shoulder. He wouldn't mind a cricket like that. He would talk to it, exchanging nonsense for nonsense. He'd say, "*You* know what it's like on the side of the road. If you had a Winnebago, would you stop for me?" and the cricket would say, "Crick-creck." That would be good enough. He's had less productive conversations with college graduates.

But this cricket remains out of sight, pitching its repetitious syllables from nowhere. Having heard its same word every three or four seconds for most of three or four days and nights, Frankenstein calculates that he's heard it at least eighty-six thousand times. He does his calculating in the thin layer of sand on the asphalt, tracing numbers with a bent, rusty screw. He calculates that if he spread those chirps out, he'd have 10.709838107 for every day of his life. He doubts he's heard his own name that often. He's heard the chirp so many times that he's not entirely sure whether he's hearing it or remembering it. It's synonymous with monotony. It occurs to him that even with a semi-automatic shotgun, he wouldn't be able to kill that cricket, to shut it up, but then he thinks of lighting the grass on fire. Yes, that would do it. He won't, but he's comforted to know he has a way to escape the relentless reminder that he's not going anywhere, not in any sense.

A tractor trailer whooshes by. The bow waves hit him like a soft punch. The wake rushing up at the stern whips sand against his face and tilts him slightly to the north. It doesn't matter. He's still alive, and the cricket hasn't missed a beat.

He stands up for each car, holding out the palms of his hands and probing for eye contact. Ten thousand miles ago he theorized that this nonthreatening pose would hook in more cars than the traditional thumb.

According to the theory, the image of a man jerking his thumb up and down will only set off subconscious fear. But no matter how he stands, most people drive right on by. All he's figured out is that it feels slightly better to stand there like a drooping crucifix. At least people might remember him, maybe even for days. He'll be a cricket in their minds, making them feel a little guiltier each day. Maybe someday someone will pass him a second time and get a second chance to do the right thing.

After way-too-many hours of truck-whoosh and cricket-chirp, a rusty, pale blue van pulls over. Coming up to it from behind, Frankenstein smells trouble. One brake light's out. One back tire is bald, and the other has the clean, generic look of a spare. The engine shudders in a three-beat pulse. The tailpipe wags with the effort of sputtering semi-solids into the atmosphere. Two rusty puckers in the back door look a lot like bullet holes. Frankenstein knows rides like this. They can get very complicated and take a long time. They break down, they get stuck, they need to be push-started. Short excursions to drop something at an in-laws' house end up taking hours, even days. That can be good and it can be excruciating. It depends on the in-laws.

Frankenstein slides open the side door to put his duffel bag in. Most of the space is taken up by an old queen-size mattress stuck in there at an angle, propped against the wall of the van. Beneath its sag, a greasy toolbox, a battle-weary chain saw and a tire rim sit as if under a lean-to in the rain. Frankenstein's going to come away from this ride with a dirty duffel bag. He already knows this and resigns himself to it. Worse things have happened.

The man at the wheel needs a new undershirt. But a new undershirt would be wasted on a man like this. Besides, he's not done with the one he's got. It still covers most of his broad, relaxed paunch, except in spots. The spots look to be of the same caliber as the holes in the back door. As the man works the van up through its three gears, the engine goes FUD-dud-da/FUD-dud-da/FUD-dud-da/FUD-dud-da with exhausted determination.

"So where you going?" Frankenstein asks, hoping it doesn't sound like he means *How far do you think you'll get?*

"God," the man says with an inflection of utter disgust. "It's mighty hard to say."

FRANKENSTEIN ON THE CUSP OF SOMETHING

Frankenstein knew it would be. It crosses his mind to say he's only going to the next exit. But even though he's known this man for only two or three minutes, doesn't even know his name or anything about him, he already feels in a certain way obliged. Attached. He can't just abandon ship. He's onboard for the nonce. He says, "Hard to say?"

The man wipes his forehead with the back of his hand. He has grease on three knuckles, a smear on the haunch of his thumb. The rest of his hand is neither clean nor permanently be-smudged. Frankenstein's best guess: He's not a mechanic, but he's been working on a machine. He's on his way to Wichita to get a spare part.

But no. It's not that simple.

"It's so complicated," the man says. "It's so complicated."

"I've got time. Tell me about it." Frankenstein always prefers to let the other guy do the talking.

The man releases steam, pulls on his left eyebrow, shifts his grip on the steering wheel. He finally locates the crux of his situation. With measured cadence, he says, "I…am the president…of the PTA."

"No kidding." He manages to sound intrigued. The man doesn't look the part.

"Yep." The man nods heavily, then turns it into a heavy shaking from side to side. "But it's not that simple."

Frankenstein bides his time in silence. He hopes the explanation comes to involve sex with a kindergarten teacher. He hopes he can keep saying "no kidding" with real interest.

"OK. So look. The other officers of the PTA are an unwed mother who just got her G.E.D. a couple of years ago because her kids were making fun of her. She's the treasurer. She can balance a checkbook. I'll say that for her. The secretary is my wife. She hates me. She hates the treasurer, too. She hates just about everybody. That's why she's in the PTA. It gives her a chance to hate. The vice president's a real winner. A professional educator, right? That's how she likes to present herself. What does she do? She's runs a taxidermy class. Hunters come in and learn how to stuff their kill. And she has a dog obedience school. Education, right? You say 'Heel!' and if the dog doesn't heel, you yank his choke collar. Works great on German shepherds. But it doesn't work real great if you try to apply it to, like, the secretary of the PTA, if you catch my drift."

"I catch your drift," Frankenstein says. He catches it completely. The vice president has been yanking the chain of the president's wife. Nothing good could possibly result from this.

"Right. But we're just getting started here. The treasurer's got a kid with a learning disability. He's not retarded or anything. I personally think he's probably over-bright. I mean, the kid's bouncing off the walls at school. Can't sit still. Can't keep his little mouth shut. He's in the fourth grade. So the teacher, who's an absolute idiot, has the kid go run around the soccer field about three or four times a day. To burn off his energy."

Frankenstein lifts an eyebrow, tilts his head. "That sounds like a good idea to me. That's what I'd do if I were a teacher." But he knows he wouldn't. He'd end up lashing the kid to his chair with duct tape. His classroom would rage in insufferable chaos. He wouldn't last three days. He remembers himself in the fourth grade. Duct tape wouldn't have been a bad idea.

"It *is* a good idea," the man says, raising a forefinger to the side of his head. In his ragged T-shirt he looks for a moment like the scarecrow in *The Wizard of Oz*. "Or it *would* be a good idea if the kid could just run around the soccer field and come right back without getting distracted."

Of course. Frankenstein hadn't thought of that. It sounds just like the kind of mistake he'd make. He'd send a kid off and then not notice when the kid failed to come back. He identifies with the fourth grade teacher. "Yeah," he says. "So what happened?" It's as if his own fate depends on the kid's return.

"Well, nothing really bad happened. I mean, it doesn't matter, but, like, once, the kid...see the school's next to a farm that has cows and goats. So the kid climbs under the fence and goes chasing the goats around, comes back with shit on his shoes. Another time he came back with a snake. Once he was out there lying on his back, staring at the sun. Staring at the sun! Said he liked watching it change colors. Nobody ever told him not to stare at the sun, right? So he did it."

Frankenstein vaguely remembers doing that. Only now does it occur to him that that might explain why he's always worn glasses. He never had a father to tell him not to stare into the sun. He wonders if this kid has a broken nose. He'd almost bet on it.

He's already losing track of the man's complicated story. He says, "OK, so, you're married to the secretary, who hates the treasurer and everybody else. The treasurer's got a hyper kid and the fourth grade teacher's an idiot."

"And the vice president teaches taxidermy."

"Right. I forgot her."

"Don't forget her because look at her brilliant idea. She wanted to bring stuffed animals into the school."

"Hmmm." Frankenstein thinks that might be a good idea, but it might not. He can almost guess what's going to happen.

"'Hmmm' is exactly what I said when I heard about this brainstorm. I smelled trouble. And sure enough, half the stuffed animals she wants to bring in are dead pets. She gets them from the veterinarian. For the hunters to practice on."

Frankenstein smacks himself in the forehead, holds his hand over his eyes. "Jesus," he says.

"You got it. Dead pets. And it's a small town. East Wilma. The kids know these pets. Fido. Bootsy. Jerry the Gerbil. Harry the Hamster. I don't know who-all else."

"Hamsters!" Frankenstein gets an inkling of the world making sense. With a glorious burst of inspiration, he imagines himself arriving at Walter's hamster ranch with the idea that will make them both rich: *stuffed hamsters.* If ever a rage were poised to sweep the nation, stuffed hamsters are it. America needs a pet like this—soft and fuzzy yet needing no more attention than a pet rock. No cage to clean, no holes chewed in the wall, no untimely death to deal with. A person could attach one to a sweater, deploy them in cute spots around the house, set one on a desk with its little paws in beg position. Is America ready for the hamster barrette, the hamster brooch, the hamster key fob? Stranger things have happened here. The market's certainly big enough. Frankenstein tucks this nugget away for consideration the next time he's stuck on the side of the road.

The man nods matter-of-factly. "Hamsters. Snakes. Parakeets. And of course half these animals got hit by cars, so they're a real mess…all busted open and stitched back shut. Like furry little Frankensteins."

Frankenstein winces but doesn't let on. He's going to just sit there and watch the world begin to make sense. "Jesus," he says. "You're not going to let it happen are you?"

"Let it happen? It happened! She brought all these practice trophies in and set them up all over the school. Up on shelves. Behind doors. Sitting at desks. She meant to surprise them. She thought it would bring a fond tear of remembrance to the kids' eyes. Fond remembrance and squeals of joy. That's what she said. And you know something?"

"She was right, right?"

"*Half* right. Tears and squeals. We got plenty of that. Kids were freaking out all over the place. One little girl saw her neighbor's dog in the lav, holding its little paw up to be shook. A kid heard his cat was in somebody's else's room and he started screaming when they wouldn't let him go see. A kid found a guinea pig in his desk. There was rat snake hanging from the florescent lights."

"Where was the principal?"

"The principal freaked out, too. He's this real prissy guy who keeps washing his hands. You always see him walking down the hall, wiping his hands with a paper towel. So he freaked out. Went right into his office, shut the door and started making phone calls. Called the police, but they said there was nothing they could do without some kind of paper from a judge. But court was in session or something, so no judge. Nobody knew where the vice president was. The teachers wouldn't touch the animals because they were so gross. You know, kind of half-shaved, stapled shut, little glass-bead eyes hanging out by a thread? You can imagine."

He sure can. But he couldn't have imagined the situation if it hadn't happened. How do human beings manage to get themselves into such fixes? Why can't people just go about their business? Even Ann Landers couldn't solve this one. He says, "Why didn't they tell the janitor to do it?"

"The janitor lived next door to the vice president. He knew better than to mess with her. He complained to town hall once about all the dead animals in her backyard—she let them pile up in the winter—so she turned him in for making vodka in his basement. Then he turned her in for building a deck without a building permit, and she turned him in for burning leaves in his backyard, which technically you're not supposed to do in our town, though you can because the fire marshal's a volunteer and really couldn't care less. As a matter of fact, his kid's the one who found the stuffed guinea pig in his desk. As long as we're at it, you might as well know that the guinea pig had once belonged to a girl who left the thing home when she went to college in Massachusetts. Her mother fed it wet lettuce and it died in its sleep at the vet's. Did you know that? You can't feed wet lettuce to a guinea pig or it'll die."

"Well I'll be damned."

Wet lettuce. How did this tale get down to wet lettuce? Frankenstein can't even begin to backtrack. He's completely lost. Does this guinea pig count in the bigger picture, whatever it was? The PTA? He's already forgotten half the story. But for the rest of his life, he'll remember the part about the wet lettuce. Wet lettuce sounds like the first thing he'd give a guinea pig. In the far-back darkness of his mind, he can almost see a shadow of his little self feeding greens to a domesticated rodent—not his own but somebody else's. Was it a guinea pig? Was it lettuce? Was it wet? Did the animal die? He can't quite remember. He searches his mind for other guinea pigs he may have fed. He recalls none, but his imagination conjures up a clear image of a trail of little graves stretching back into his earliest days. He can almost feel the wet, slender leaves of doom in his fingers as he slides them through the chicken wire of a cage. He envisions himself walking away, satisfied that he has helped feed the needy. Behind him he hears the nervous little *crunch-crunch-crunch.*

The man continues: "Enter the federal government."

"Uh-oh."

"You got it. The day after all this, who shows up but a federal cafeteria inspector out of St. Louis. Any school that accepts federal lunch subsidies has to get inspected by this dope on a quarterly basis. Of course he shows up on the day we've got a stuffed raccoon crammed into a basketball hoop in the cafeteria."

"Basketball hoops in the cafeteria?" For some reason it sounds stranger to have a basketball hoop in a cafeteria than a stuffed raccoon in a basketball hoop.

"You got it," the man says with an emphatic nod. "I should mention that this is a very rinky-dink school. The cafeteria's in the gym. Special ed's in a closet. The library's on a little cart that gets wheeled from room to room. The janitor's a drunk. The art teacher's a drunk but she's got tenure. But at least the kids get lunch every day. Or they did until the federal inspector showed up, by which time that hyper-berserkoid kid I told you about found out that if you toss a lime Jell-o cube into the basket net, it sticks to the raccoon's fur."

"I never knew that!"

"It's not one of your wider-known facts. And guess what else…."

The man waits for a guess. His hand scoops at the air, trying to coax an answer out of Frankenstein. "I give up," Frankenstein says. "I really do. I just can't imagine." He wonders if he'll ever have kids, whether he'll ever get suckered into joining the PTA.

"All right. I'll tell you. It turns out there's a law against having a dead animal in a cafeteria."

"Sounds reasonable, when you think about it."

"A *federal* law, mind you. Some *senator* or something thought it up. Had *absolutely* nothing else to do."

"They think of everything, don't they?"

"Everything except how to feed a hundred and eighty-three kids lunch every day. The state got involved and shut the cafeteria down, pending re-application for our permit. The kids are eating bag lunches in the classroom, which is in itself a federal offense because they have a right to a hot lunch. But the bigger problem's the janitor. He's all pissed off because of the peanut butter and Fig Newtons that get mashed into the carpets."

"This is the same guy who wouldn't take the dead raccoon out of the basketball hoop? The drunk? I say get rid of him." For just this moment, Frankenstein feels a glimmer of satisfaction that he has contributed to the situation. He has offered his advice.

But the man says, "Can't get rid of him. He's a Teamster. And a volunteer fireman. You get him mad, the next thing you know, your house is on fire."

"Which means he's a friend of the fire marshal who didn't mind if he burned leaves in his backyard."

"Those were poison ivy leaves. I should have mentioned that."

FRANKENSTEIN ON THE CUSP OF SOMETHING

"Aha!"

"Right! He burned them as an offensive attack against the lady next door."

"The one who stuffed animals. The secretary."

"Nope. The secretary's my wife. The lady with the stuffed animals is vice president."

Out of the blue, Frankenstein says, "Is she married?"

The man looks at him. "She's in her late fifties and built like a walrus. And, in case you haven't guessed, she's a little sick upstairs. Believe me, you wouldn't be interested."

"I wasn't. I meant doesn't she have a husband to stick up for her?"

"I was *getting* to that. He split a couple years ago. Ditched the bitch. Know why? Same thing as happened at the school. She stuffed his vizsla."

Frankenstein's inner reference librarian goes tearing through the shelves of his mind. *Vizla, vizla, vizla…if you can't spell it, you can't look it up.*

"It's a hunting dog," the man says. "Hungarian, I think. Not a particularly *bright* animal. This one stuck his nose in a porcupine, then ran out in the road and got run over."

Frankenstein shakes his head. History will never record these details of humanity. He imagines the poor vizsla bolting in panic, pain and perhaps an enraged sense of stupidity. He darts onto a state highway. Tires screech with the power of a pterodactyl. The dog stops, turns, scampers, changes his mind, cowers down, and *thumpity-thump*, that's the end of him. His master can hardly believe the suddenness of the tragedy. Maybe he takes a potshot at the car as it speeds away. Maybe the driver stops and drives them to the vet. At any rate, it's too late. The dog is dead. Later, the vet calls the wife, says, "Hey, you want to surprise your husband?" Maybe she did it to be nice, maybe to be mean. In a certain sense, the sense of the big picture, it doesn't matter. Unless it's the dog of a king, history will pass this incident by. It's a shame, Frankenstein thinks. Someone should write all this down. It matters.

But history depends on interpretation. You need all the facts, and then you need the stuff that matters, the stuff that doesn't fit into factual form. Such as why she stuffed his vizsla. The *Encyclopedia Britannica* doesn't have that. Frankenstein can't even imagine what topic to look under. "Dogs,

Hungarian hunting"? "Taxidermy, as psychological weapon"? "PTA officers, unusual"? Even if he got the facts straight and figured out the motives and wrote it up in some intelligible way, where would history stick this nugget of human interaction? *Miscellaneous?* If a history book had an appendix for humanity's miscellany, it wouldn't even fit on the planet. They'd have to store it on Jupiter.

Frankenstein asks, "What kind of car *was* it? That hit the dog."

"It was a pick-up truck. Belonged to my wife's hairdresser, as a matter of fact. Which figures in."

"Wow! Small world! Did he stop?"

"Oh, he stopped, all right. But look at the complication. He had a mattress in back. He bought it at a yard sale, right? But of course it wasn't just your random yard sale. It was the yard sale of the family of the girl who went to college in Massachusetts and left her guinea pig home under the tender loving care of her mother."

"Who fed it wet lettuce."

"*Bingo.* And it was *her* mattress. The *daughter's* mattress. This guy with the pick-up truck used to go out with her. It was a major scandal. He was twenty-seven. She was seventeen. In fact, that's why they sent her all the way to Massachusetts to go to school."

Frankenstein smacks himself on both cheeks, making his mouth pop. "He bought his ex-girlfriend's mattress!"

A big fat smile pushes the man's cheeks up high. "Close but not quite. He *stole* the mattress. They wouldn't sell it to him. They saw him sniffing it. When he asked them if they'd take five dollars, they told him to get lost. He thought it was a matter of price, so he said OK, ten, which was the price on the tag. They told him to get lost again. He said the hell he would. The price said ten dollars so they had to sell it to him. It was his constitutional right. He threw the money at them and heaved the mattress into the back of the truck and off he went."

And ran over the vizsla of the husband of the taxidermist vice president of the PTA, setting in motion the final stages of marital disintegration.

"That's not the end of it," the man says insistently, keeping his eyes on the road but pointing his pinkie at Frankenstein. "That's not the end of it at all. The people still wanted their mattress back. So they got a court order. An *injunction* or something. The sheriff goes and gets it. And what do you think?"

The man waits. It's guessing time again. Frankenstein thinks hard, imagines the mattress of a lovelorn bachelor. Maybe he framed it and put it on the wall. Maybe he made an altar of it, an altar to the god of panmixia, the almighty Kink.

The man turns and leans in close. He squints hard through one eye. Frankenstein watches the road, the man, the road, the man. In a whispery growl, the man says, "*It was smeared with blood.*"

Frankenstein's aghast. History has taken a turn to the gruesome. He should have expected it. In the vicious small-town swirl of human urge, something had to crack. With a crazed taxidermist at the center of things, blood was inevitable. Just as barbers of yore bled patients to relieve fever, blood had to burst from the pressure cooker of East Wilma, OK.

But then the man reveals that it was only the vizsla's blood. The dog had lain on the mattress as it died in the back of the pick-up. No doubt the taxidermist's husband had sat back there, easing his faithful companion into the afterworld on a fragrant mattress that lovers had left softly dented. The man probably spoke reassuring words as he plucked porcupine quills from his best friend's snout. "Hold on, buddy," he surely said. "Everything'll be all right."

But everything wasn't all right. The poor dog died in pain and humiliation, its master abandoned his wife, the forlorn lover lost his mattress, the family got back something too disgusting to touch, and then their guinea pig died. Frankenstein wonders if they have lawyers in East Wilma. He wonders if he should inform the ASPCA about this place. Animals don't seem to last long there, and a pack of talented attorneys could probably get these people to sue themselves out of existence.

Frankenstein, resorting to his practice of repeating someone's last three words, says, "Smeared with blood!"

"Yep. And who do you think gets held responsible?"

"It should've been the guy who stole the mattress." Frankenstein would have made a great judge. Sometimes he thinks that. Other times he's sure that in that capacity he would fail most miserably. In a slow flash as surreal as a dream, he imagines an irate jury tossing him out of a courthouse. He rolls down the marble steps and into the street. A bus honks at him. He sees himself slogging out of town, duffel bag on his shoulder, his black robe drooping with the weight of a job done poorly. He's already sorry to have declared the mattress thief guilty of something he didn't really do. It wasn't his blood.

The man overturns Frankenstein's decision. "Nope," he says. "It wasn't him."

"The truck driver, then?" He isn't declaring guilt this time. It's just a suggestion.

The man says, "Nope."

"The taxidermist's husband?"

"Nope."

"Not the dog, I hope."

"Nope. Not the dog."

That's all the suspects Frankenstein can think of. Who else could it be? The girl who went to college? The prissy principal? The drunk custodian? The fire marshal who didn't care? The federal cafeteria inspector?

Just then Frankenstein remembers the funny little holes in the back of the van, and just as he turns to look back at them, he sees the mattress. *Of course. Of course.*

"Not *you*," he gasps.

Mouth clamped shut to a cynical slit, the man nods.

"But why *you*?"

"I…am the president…of the PTA."

Frankenstein turns to look out the windshield. The highway goes straight to the vanishing point, a distant ripple of heat waves. He feels himself and the president of the PTA riding a flaming comet toward infinity, destiny hurdling absolutely nowhere. The tires go *th-thud, th-thud* over the cracks in the concrete.

"You probably didn't know all this was going to happen when you signed up for the presidency," Frankenstein offers. He's hoping to hide the fact that he's still confused.

"Hey, I never signed up for this," the man says. "I am *not* a responsible individual. Never meant to be one. In fact, that's how I ended up with the job. I was fishing when they elected me. I didn't go to the meeting, so at my wife's behest, they elected me. I might add that a) it was not fishing season and b) I don't have a fishing license. I was committing at least two illegal acts. And on top of that, I was out there with the taxidermist lady's husband, which meant of course I was drinking bourbon, which is probably illegal in a row boat. Without a life preserver on. By all of which I mean to say that I'm not a responsible person and never should have been elected to the presidency."

"But it happened."

"It happened, and maybe I deserve it. I don't know. But this mattress..."—he sneers and jerks his thumb toward the back of the van—"it should definitely *not* be my responsibility."

"But there it is." *Following us*, Frankenstein thinks.

"There it is. Responsibility. On its way to St. Louis. And me in charge. *God damn it.*"

In a tone of uncommitted amazement, stretching out the vowels, Frankenstein says, "St. Louis." For the first time in his life, he wonders who Saint Louis was, what he did, why they named a city in Missouri after him. He imagines his kind benefactor, president of the PTA, being canonized, patron saint of bedroom furniture, for his martyrdom in East Wilma.

"I caught hell all over town," the man says. "It was me who finally got the stuffed animals out of the school. I just went and did it. I threw them all in the Dumpster, and not gently. Their owner got all pissed off about that. They were her property. These former pets. That's what she kept saying. Her *property*. My wife went ballistic when we got a bill from the lady for $8,981.52, which I'm sure is just a number she made up. And of course the kids got mad, too, seeing Bootsy and Fido and whoever the fuck else getting chucked into the garbage, which means all their parents got mad. About the only kid who didn't give a damn was the treasurer's kid, the hyper kid who threw the Jell-o on the raccoon. I boosted him up to the basketball hoop so he could get the coon out. Of course I had to hold him up by his little fanny, which got the principal all bent out of shape. His mother got all bent out of shape because I made her kid touch a dead animal. And right in the middle of all this, the family with the mattress calls and wants *me* to come get it."

"*You?*"

"Sure. Of course. The president of the PTA. Who else would they call?"

"Sounds weird to me."

"What it was, was, they wanted to donate it to our annual auction. They just wanted to get rid of it. But they didn't want to throw it away...."

"But wasn't it covered with blood?"

"Naw, not *covered*. It just had a little on it. And it's a *real* good mattress. Look..." The man reaches around, slaps it a few times. "Some kind of high-tech whoopty-do titanium coils or something. Practically new."

Frankenstein gives it a feel. It's firm and smooth and not bad looking. He'd sleep on it. He gives it surreptitious sniff, but he's too far away to tell if it smells like her. Or the boyfriend or the vizsla. If anything, it smells like the chainsaw and toolbox underneath. He says, "So you're taking it to St. Louis."

"Right. Because my wife hates these people."

"The mattress people."

"Right. She hates them because they organize German beer fests, and she's Polish."

"You mean like from Poland Polish?"

"Hell no. Her grandparents on both sides were Polish. Her father organizes Polkathons in New Jersey and Pennsylvania. So she's vowed to hate Germans all her life. Germans and all things German. Especially German beer fests because they compete directly with Polkathons, which if you ask me are the same damned thing. At the beer fests, they drink beer and dance. At the Polkathons, they dance and drink beer. It's nothing worth starting a goddamn war over."

"She wants to start a *war?*"

"She would if she could." The man snorts with a sudden amusing thought. "Maybe that's what she's up to. Because you know what she wants me to do with the mattress? Give it to her hairdresser."

Frankenstein knots up one eye, tilts his head. "Her hairdresser," he says, stating the fact, hoping the man will remind him how the hairdresser fits in.

"That's right. And he's all hot to trot. Wants the smell of his sweetie-pie back, vizsla blood or no vizsla blood." Eyes squinted, the man holds the tips of his fingers at his nostrils, French-style.

Frankenstein remembers. The hairdresser ran over the dog. He says, "So you're going to let him have it?"

"You nuts? If he gets ahold of this mattress, I'm puppy chow."

"And if you don't let him have it, your wife kills you."

"In a nutshell, yes. She will grind me down. She will drive me to an early grave. And I'll look forward to it. I'll crawl in and lie down and think, 'Thank God almighty I am dead at last.'"

Frankenstein can see it happening. The van pulls into the cemetery, parks at a nice new grave. The hole is perfectly rectangular, the proportions of a bathroom door. Beside it stands a classic mound of fresh earth, a pyramid of clay on a bed of topsoil. The engine of the van sputters a low cloud of blue exhaust across the cemetery lawn. The woman at the wheel, shoulders broad and rounded, hair of gold, holds a cigarette between two wrinkled knuckles of her right hand. A man eases himself out of the passenger side. His hairy gut bulges from under his T-shirt, which seems to have more bullet holes in it than before. He doesn't look back. He trudges to the grave, lowers himself to all fours, turns around, climbs in backward. The van pulls away—*FUD-dud-da/ FUD-dud-da/ FUD-dud-da/ FUD-dud-da*—and the grave overflows with a sigh.

"So what are you going to do in St. Louis?" Frankenstein asks.

"I'm going to hand the federal fucking cafeteria inspector the papers which, if they're all filled out right, will force him to rescind his condemning of our cafeteria. That's step one."

"Yeah?"

"Step two was supposed to be 'Turn around and go back home.' But you know what I say to Step Two? I say *fuck it*."

"*Fuck it*," Frankenstein says as if both agreeing and needing to think about it.

"Fuck it. Fuck-it-fuck-it-fuck-it-fuck-it. I'm not going back home. Handing the cafeteria inspector these papers is the last responsible thing I am ever going to do. Then I'm going to sell this mattress for what I can get for it, and then I'm heading for Kentucky."

"Ken*tucky*," Frankenstein says, hitting the second syllable hard.

"Kentucky. Blue Grass State. Land of thoroughbreds. I just want to get a job on a high-class horse farm and shovel high-class horseshit all day long. Because you know why? Because did you ever think how an atom and the solar system are the same thing, just about?"

As a matter of fact, Frankenstein *has* thought of that. He's just never figured out what to do about it. And he *never* saw the connection with Kentucky. He never even thought to look.

The patron saint of bedroom furniture continues: "They have the same structure, right? Something in the middle and littler things orbiting around, right? So how do we know that Earth isn't just an electron in an atom that's just part of a molecule that to us looks like a galaxy? That the whole universe as we know it is just the tip of a hair on the ass-end of a flea which is huger than anything we could ever conceive of? Huger than the universe. I mean, it makes *sense* when you think about it."

"Sure does."

"And meanwhile, a'course, some little molecule on the end of my finger..."—he holds up his pinkie, marks the tippy-tip of it with his thumb—"...is a whole 'nother universe to a bunch of people so teeny-weeny we couldn't possibly imagine them. They're down there looking up through teeny-weeny telescopes and thinking, 'Wow, look how big the universe is' and they can't see halfway across my fingernail."

With fathomless wonderment, Frankenstein shakes his head. The man from East Wilma is stuck between imponderables. He's torn as if by proximate gravities. He's afraid to go home yet unafraid to venture forth on the capital of a used mattress. He's taken on a town's responsibility, yet he's abandoning it. He's in despair; he's charged with hope. He's guilty; he's innocent. He's wrong; he's right. He cares and he doesn't care. He's tethered; he's free. He's aware of what's going on, but what's going on is bigger than he by far. He's doomed...he's doomed.

He shakes the tip of his pinkie at Frankenstein. "There's some tiny-ass East Wilma down there," he says, "and everybody thinks everything is sooooo fucking important. They're all bent out of shape over...what?" With tight lips he makes a quick high-pitched spitty-farty noise. "Nothing," he says in a rough hush. "*Nothing*."

Frankenstein could have told him that, but all he's going to say is that he likes the idea of shoveling manure for a living. He wonders if he should suggest looking for a job in a planetarium. He turns to look out the side window. Oklahoma, or Kansas, rushes by, quite still at the horizon yet a rippling blur at the guardrail. His cricket's still out there, he's sure, still hidden, infinitesimal and alone. He's ready to hear it again. He practically wants to. *Crick-creck, crick-creck.* It's something to think about.

- Chapter Seven -
The Hamsters of Lark

Frankenstein continues up Interstate 29, turns left in Fargo. It doesn't take long to cross half of North Dakota. People are super friendly here. They'll give a guy a ride just because he looks like he needs to get somewhere. Frankenstein has that look. When he holds his palms out, he makes them look heavy. Creases between his eyebrows hint that maybe he's rushing to a loved one before she expires. They ask him—they *all* ask him—where he's headed. He tells them Lark. They all make a sound like a dog waking up to a half-dreamed noise. Then they say, "Lark?"

Frankenstein says, "Yep. You know anything about a hamster farm out there?"

And they say, "*Hamster* farm?"

"Or hamster *ranch*?" He can't remember what it said in the article in the airplane magazine. The farther west he gets, the more he worries about it. Nobody knows anything about a hamster operation in Lark. Frankenstein starts to worry.

But one guy says, "I didn't think they had *anything* in Lark. Prairie grass. Rocks. Buzzards."

FRANKENSTEIN ON THE CUSP OF SOMETHING

"Yes," says Frankenstein, "I believe buzzards are a problem there." With that one word, the man has raised his spirits above the threshold of hope. But it's hard to ask a follow-up question. Maybe he's too tired to think right. Maybe he read too much Shakespeare in college. He's embarrassed to hear himself say, "What do you know of the buzzards of Lark?"

The man—an overweight purveyor of accessories for mobile homes ("pumps, furnaces, standard porch assemblies, anything you want")—didn't catch the accidental poetry of the question. He just says, "I don't know. I just remember somebody saying something about it."

"It wasn't a guy who shot buzzards from a blimp, was it?"

The man chuckles up phlegm from his blubbery torso and says, "No, I don't reckon it was."

They drive through five or ten miles of North Dakota before the man asks, "That what you're looking for? A man who shoots buzzards from a blimp?"

"Well, sort of." Frankenstein's ready to back down from this one. The man doesn't need to know his true mission, that he wants a job shooting buzzards from a blimp. But he tells the man about the article. He makes sure to mention that he read it on a jet. "It had a picture of the guy and everything," he testifies.

"Hamsters," the man states. "You'd think I would of heard about something like that."

Trying to sound knowledgeable and prepared, Frankenstein says he needs to get out at exit 27, then go south. His map's a little vague, but it looks like the road to Lark might be dirt all the way. Twenty-five miles down that road, where it intersects another road, there's Lark. From there he'll have to ask directions.

At exit 27, as Frankenstein steps into the Dakota cold, the mobile home accessories salesman says, "Good luck."

Frankenstein says, "Hey, good luck to *you*." He's glad he's chosen a career in hamster protection. He really hopes it work out. He can't imagine a life spent flogging mobile home accessories across the prairie.

Exit 27 is probably the quietest exit he's ever been at. Once the car has pulled away, Frankenstein hears nothing but wind. It sears him with chilliness. If it weren't for the wind, the day would be downright decent, full of sun and brisk air. It's not real cold, just a hint of the winter to come. He's never heard anything good about North Dakota winters. He wonders what hamsters do when a blizzard strikes. He guesses they burrow into the ground, snuggle up with each other and hibernate. Which, now that he thinks about it, eliminates the need for a buzzard-shooter or hired hand of any sort. He guesses it's going to be seasonal work. That wouldn't be so bad. Maybe he'll just save his money and spend his winters in Cancún.

But there's no Cancún for Frankenstein unless he finds Walter's hamster ranch. He scans the vastness of the unmarred sky. Way, way up there, half a dozen specks float as slowly as planets. *Buzzards*, he's sure of it. They're cruising for hamsters, or maybe just digesting possum in the ozone. He imagines the clear beads of their eyes searching for movement two miles below. He imagines the beady black eyes of nearsighted hamsters searching for movement above. He imagines Walter's sharp blue eyes squinting upward, downward, assessing the situation with wisdom and courage. He imagines himself taking a potshot at a buzzard and blowing a hole in his own blimp, the blimp flailing around the sky with an exhaustive flatulation until it falls in a limp rubber heap, himself half trapped beneath it. He imagines the buzzards circling in, the hamsters scampering from their shadows, leaving Frankenstein behind.

If he actually lands this job—in all reality, he doubts he will—he's going to be careful. And thankful. He'll do a good, conscientious job. He won't complain, not even to himself. When he leaves, Walter will wish him well and regret the loss of a worker and a friend. In their own little way, his hamsters will cheer him. He can picture their little hats flying into the air. It's OK for him to imagine such a thing. He's all alone at exit 27 in the middle of North Dakota. It's just him and the cold wind of the west. If he wants to entertain himself with an image of hamsters in alpine hats with pheasant feathers, he gets to.

And if he wants to get to Lark, he needs to walk. It takes him three hours to figure this out. Not one vehicle has come off the interstate or gone by in a northerly or southerly direction. Exit 27 was clearly inspired by the federal government, which must have made a comprehensive study to determine a perfectly useless place to lay a couple million dollars' worth of concrete. So he walks. The road is a carpet of crunchy red stones. They look like ceramic shards of broken pottery. The road has no pavement, power lines, guardrails, or yellow line down the middle. The only sign was the one at the bottom of the exit ramp: left to Lark, right to Hannover. The road to Hannover was clearly the road more traveled—paved at least. Frankenstein feels pretty good heading the other way.

In an hour or so, the interstate's out of sight. He figures he's walked three miles. He sits on the side of the road, his back to the wind. The side of the road is right down at prairie level. He looks into the spotty grass and thinks about North Dakota. He'd always pictured it planted border to border with wheat. This particular stretch of it looks like it might be good for deer, antelope, desperate cattle, nothing more. The cattle wouldn't be too happy. They'd have to poke around rocks and bushes to find tufts of grass. They'd find enough, he figures, but they wouldn't have the life of cows in the plush pastures of Wisconsin. They couldn't just stand there and eat.

Frankenstein wouldn't mind eating a little something. He wonders if there's any kind of eatery between here (nowhere) and Lark. He doesn't think so. Unless he comes across an apple tree or something, he'll have to walk twenty-five miles before he eats again. He decides to take it as a test. To get the best job in the world, he has to prove himself. He has to walk all the way on the faith that Walter needs him and that he has something to offer to Walter. He has little faith on either count, but he suspects that a twenty-five-mile hike will have an effect on things.

So Frankenstein keeps walking. To keep track of distance, he tries counting paces. Within a few hundred yards, he loses count. It's hard to think in the constant buffeting of the wind, its soft drum in his ears. He tries to estimate time by the position of the sun, but either it never seems to have moved, or it seems to have jumped quite a distance while he wasn't looking. Even then he can't remember from where it jumped or how far back he was before it jumped or what percent of the 180-degree arc that jump represents. All he can do is keep walking. The measurement of time and distance, he tells himself, doesn't matter. He has to concern himself with only two things: either he's arrived or he's still on the way; either he walks or he stops. It's like being either quick or dead.

But as he walks, he becomes concerned with other things. How much farther should he walk before he stops to take a rest? If the place had landmarks, he'd tell himself to keep going until he reached such-and-such a telephone pole. If he had a watch he could walk until such-and-such a time. In the lack of such goals, he has no objective reason to stop. He's always tired, always ready for a rest. And when he's finally reached the spot where he just has to stop, the question is how long to stay there. He could rest all day. He pulls his feet from his rubber sandals, takes off his socks and blows on his soles. They are the only warm part of his body. He blows on his soles and imagines an old water pump on Walter's front lawn. There he will bathe his feet. Bathe, hell; he's going to anoint them. The thought makes them ache even more. The more they ache, the more he's sure Walter will give him a job. Either that or the other way around.

He isn't really expecting to get a job, he tells himself. He just wants to see something interesting. He adopts this as a formal position after what feels like about twelve and a half miles. At *least* twelve and a half miles. Maybe fifteen. More than halfway. He's almost there.

An hour after sunset, the wind fades away. Frankenstein's ready for bed. Bed this night will be a blanket on prairie gravel in a nook among tufts of tall dry grass. Frankenstein doesn't care. He's so tired, with feet so sore, he'll sleep as soon as he's horizontal. If a rattlesnake comes along and bites him, so be it. He's used to that kind of thing.

He does his plastic bag trick. It's a white shopping bag that smells of the tangerines he bought in Nebraska. It has a small hole in the bottom, so it doesn't contract against his face the way it should. The slow rhythm of the crinkle is fine, however, and soon his ears pulse like nauseated kettledrums. But when he inhales deeply, fresh air slips in through the little hole. Pretty soon he's getting nowhere, so he removes the bag and tucks it under his blanket.

It's darker outside now. As the night seeps out of the ground, Frankenstein's day-deep layer of sweat becomes a veritable glacier across his body. He's freezing. Having no other blanket, he pulls out his alternate pair of pair of pants, lays them along his legs like a custom-made blanket. He lays a shirt across his torso, the wrists crossed at this sternum. He lays his duffel bag on his chest and hugs it like a trunkless lover. He doesn't notice precisely when the indigo sky turns to black and the first few bold stars get lost in the awesome blaze of galaxies. Teetering on sleep, he tries to absorb the beauty of the sky and wishes he had someone to whom he could say, "Isn't it beautiful?" He wonders if there's a God, grapples with the concept of infinity, wrestles with the impossibility and inevitability of nothingness, imagines his mother at that moment honing her toenails after a long bath, her wet hair pulled back tight against her scalp, her stereo playing show tune after show tune, her mind's eye ranging around the house in search of a germ or an errant sock her son may have left under the couch. He can almost hear the clipped syllables of her irritated voice reminding him how much the lawn needs mowing, how bad his room smells, how she can't possibly keep a house clean all alone, and then he's asleep. If he dreams, it's only about sleeping on crunchy ground.

During the night, he hears an animal chewing. In a delirious state of semi-sleep, he's sure it's a bear. All he can see is stars. He tries to move. He can't. He tries to shout, but his mouth is clamped shut as if by rigor mortis. The only sound he can make resembles that of a constipated bear. He decides to die. He just hopes it won't hurt too much. Quite likely, no one will ever find his bones. He thinks that's probably good. Maybe someone will find his duffel bag. They'll find some unfinished letters to his sister, some dirty underwear, a toothbrush wrapped in toilet paper, a dwindling supply of toothpaste, perhaps a pen or pencil, a sock or two, T-shirts crusty with sweat, three or four road maps, an empty canteen, some matches, a fork. He doubts anything in there has his name or address on it. He lost his wallet under a horse jump in a pasture where he slept in Utah, he thinks. For a long time he carried a piece of paper with his name and his sister's address on it, just in case, but he lost that, too. Now he can't decide if that's good or bad or whether it even matters if he's been eaten by a bear, then buzzards, then ants and flies, then microbes. He draws no conclusion before he falls back to sleep.

He awakens chilled and stiff. He tries to sleep more but can't. He tries to get up but can't. He tries to think of a reason to get up but can't, not until he remembers Walter's hamster ranch. He has not come to North Dakota for comfort. He is here, walking to Lark, with every intent of suffering.

Stiff and hungry, he sets out to the south. The stiffness and the hunger wear off as the sun rises. Progress today is different from yesterday. He doesn't think about it. The wind builds as the sun rises. Frankenstein just keeps going. It seems to be a little past noon when he reaches a crossroads, a paved highway running east and west, tapering to a point at each horizon. A sign with arrows indicates Carson to the right, Flasher to the left. Nothing aims toward Lark. This, he assumes, is it, and there's nothing here. Just prairie grass, red pebbles, warm wind, a couple of buttes beyond walking distance.

Fingers to his forehead as if in salute, he scans the entire horizon, turning slowly like the center pole of a merry-go-round. He scans around again. No buzzards, no blimp. If Lark is the standard Midwest township, it's a mile square. If the crossroads is at the center, he's no more than half a mile, or half a hypotenuse, from Walter's farm. If the blimp were out there, he'd see it. If buzzards are indeed a hazard of the business, they'd be circling the place. But there are no buzzards and no blimp, and nobody in North Dakota has heard of a hamster ranch. The place does not exist. He's sure of it, and now that he thinks about it, he was sure of it all along, ever since the airplane where he read about it. Like everything on TV, the radio, magazines, any medium but the most local of newspapers, it was all made up. Walter's hamsters are as much an artifice as Santa Claus, lottery winners, atomic bombs, orgies, and the President of the United States. Nothing's real but the broken grassland from here to the horizon. Frankenstein's only slightly satisfied to confirm this long-held suspicion. At the same time, he's crushed, beaten down, all but smothered with the weight of a world free of all but the mundane here-and-now.

This isn't the first time Frankenstein's had to fish all three sides of an intersection. He's been stuck in spots like this before. Sometimes it takes two days to catch a ride. The theoretical waiting time extends indefinitely. His tradition is to lie down in the center of the intersection, arms out, legs spread, face to the sky, eyes closed, as if tempting a car to come along. This worked the first time he did it. A car arrived within minutes. He barely rolled out of the way in time. The car slowed down just enough to let him live, but then it just kept going. Still, he suspected the ritual cut down the wait by several hours. This time he doesn't care. He just wants to lie down. He wants to fall asleep and get run over. He remembers now that he forgot to pack up his plastic bag. It's blowing around North Dakota somewhere. This makes him feel even worse. He could really use it right now. He's never felt as bad as this, not only lonely but far, far removed from everyone. Lying there, the back of his head against the black highway, all he can see is blue. He's pretty sure, now, that there's no God up there, so he finds it odd to feel himself saying, "Hey, remember me?" He can barely hear the words because the wind just slaps them away.

- Chapter Eight -
Frankenstein at Sea

Frankenstein gets a job picking strawberries, he and half the population of Central America. All day he squats along with these short, chirpy people. They seem to regard him with suspicion but not with hatred. The once or twice he tries to talk to somebody—just small talk, in English, about the heat, the dust, the sore back, the acrid odor of fertilizer—they do not respond. His pathetic supply of Spanish, remnants from high school, sounds like a parody. He says "*¿Como está usted?*" to a teenage girl in a droopy, frilly dress that might be right for a party, but her answer is something more complicated than, "*Bien, gracias, y tú?*" She's mad about something, that's all he knows, but it doesn't stop her from plucking strawberries at an astonishing rate. Alongside her, Frankenstein is an incompetent. She bends from the waist and flicks up strawberries as if they lay loose like pebbles. Frankenstein tends to mutilate the fruit and yank the plant from the ground. He has to keep shifting position, now bending at the waist, now sitting on his heels, now advancing on all fours. He picks one strawberry to her fifty, and he eats about half of what he picks.

OK: so he wasn't born to pick strawberries. He knows that now.

FRANKENSTEIN ON THE CUSP OF SOMETHING

Exactly what he was born for, he doesn't know, but at least he has eliminated one possibility. In fact, as he thinks about it—that's one good thing about strawberry picking, plenty of time to think—he can probably eliminate the picking of *any* kind of fruit or vegetable, except maybe the kind that grow on trees. He adds that profession to those of the car wash attendant, dog kennel assistant, gravel shoveler/ wheelbarrow operator, put-sausages-in-a-box guy, wintertime gas jockey, and waiter, all professions which he has tried without pleasure or success. None caused him to tarry in his travels for more than a few weeks. He has also rejected, without even bothering to try, dentistry, proctology, sales, nuclear waste disposal, artificial insemination of cattle, and anything that demands the wearing of a uniform.

Though fed up with plucking strawberries, he's too embarrassed to drop his meager collection and stalk back across the field to the main office. He thinks maybe he'll slip away as soon as he's worked his way back down a row that passes back that way. He'll limp, he thinks, maybe hold his gut like he's got appendicitis. Or he'll stand tall and spank off his hands as if he's finished all he meant to do. He'll take his pittance and go on a fruit diet for a day or two.

No, not fruit, he thinks as he spits out his last gob of semi-ripe strawberry. Maybe he'll go on a clam chowder diet. Or onion rings. Maybe he'll go to the police, confess a crime and live off gruel until they figure out they've got the wrong guy. Strawberry pickers get to have thoughts like that. Useless thoughts and free strawberries are their only fringe benefits. He entertains himself with another one: He emigrates with the Mexicans, follows them to a wondrous land where sub-minimum wage can buy stuff. He builds himself a bamboo hut, wears a serape and a sombrero, learns to play one of those big mariachi guitars, serenades a rich and pretty señorita who looks a lot like the girl who wouldn't talk to him in the field. He marries her, then finds out her big, fat father owns *the very strawberry farm where he and his* compañeros *used to work.* He picks seven quarts of strawberries before he regains full consciousness, thanks mostly to a bee that stings him on the tip of his forefinger. Were it not for that bee, he might have had the old man bitten by a rattlesnake, thus allowing Frankenstein and his sweet señorita to liberate this whole farm and turn it over to *el pueblo*. He is cheered, revered, and elected *Presidente de México*. He manages to hold that image while sucking on his swollen finger and squeezing a very salty tear out his left eye.

By day's end, Frankenstein feels like a sun-dried tomato. He has earned $32.04 in take-home pay. Alas, he has no home to take it to. After waiting in line to get to a spigot outside the main office, he dumps handfuls of lukewarm water over his head and neck. It doesn't help much. Dust has settled into his pores, mixed with sweat and dried to specks of adobe. His hands, wrists and forearms, riddled with strawberry harpoons, are mottled with a blotchy rash. His brain has dehydrated and his stomach doesn't feel so good. He has reached the end of his career as a fruit-picker. He's ready to retire. Without saying *adios* to his Latino friends, he balances his duffel bag on his right shoulder and walks away.

He passes miles of strawberry fields, finally comes to an interstate but can't bring himself to thumb a ride. Just beyond the exit ramp on the other side, the Forty-Niners Motel hunkers under the last heat of the day. It offers clean rooms, satellite TV with X-channels, and a swimming pool, all for $29.29. He's sure there's a catch, but he's also sure that a swimming pool would feel *awfully* good. He imagines himself soaking up half the water and leaving the rest looking like a mud puddle. He imagines the cool press of clean sheets. He imagines sleeping all night without rolling over, without slapping at mosquitoes, without collecting dew. It's only $29.29, with maybe a little tax thrown in. Anything less than $32.04 is worth it. He'll break even for the day. Abandoning his ramp, he moseys fast for the motel.

It feels good to tap the little bell at the front desk. He hits it again for the pleasure of the sound and the weird sensation of beckoning a person. What he gets is a woman with frizzy white hair who's straight from the middle pew of a Baptist church. She says, "Yes?"

"I'd like a room." His voice is both friendly and desperate. To himself he sounds like someone in a movie, someone used to checking into hotels, someone for whom bell hops hop. He lays one forearm along the counter, leans on it, half facing the woman, half facing the door he just came through.

"Way-el," the lady says. "We have room 42-B. How's that sound?"

FRANKENSTEIN ON THE CUSP OF SOMETHING

She's not originally from around here. Frankenstein guesses Alabama, maybe southern Georgia. She's not somebody he'd want to argue with. He says, "Forty-two-B sounds perfect." A bra size comes to mind. He entertains himself with that while she fills out a little form.

"Sign right here," she says, turning the form to him and pointing to a blank line.

Frankenstein signs. The lady snaps the pink copy from the little form and says, "That'll be $39.68."

He *knew* it was going to be $39.68. He knew it back at the interstate. He knew it in North Dakota. He could have guessed within a nickel. His face flashing hot, he moans, "But out front it says $29.29!"

"That was *before*." She says *before* in three syllables, and she tilts her head at him as if he is to catch her drift.

Imitating her drawl, he says, "Before *what*?"

"Before we changed the price."

He should have known better than to ask, and he now knows better than to argue. Logic would bounce off this woman like bullets off Godzilla. But Frankenstein's been around the block a few times. He knows that where logic fails, emotion may break through. He drapes sadness and exhaustion across his face and pulls out the envelope that holds his pay. Pouring its three tens, two ones and four pennies onto the counter, he says, "I was hoping I could get a room for this much." He fans the cash so she can see it all. "Thirty-two-o-four."

He sees her feel sorry for him. She looks at the money tenderly. "Way-el," she drawls. "If that's all you've got...."

It isn't *all* he's got, but it isn't a lie to let her think so. His eyes shift into begging-puppy position.

"I guess we could let you have Room L," she says. "It's not being used."

"If it's $29.29 and within walking distance of the pool, I'll take it."

The woman fishes around an overcrowded coffee can, then spills its contents onto the counter. "Room L," she says as she extracts the key from a pile of nails, rubber bands, old pens, paper clips, matches and dusty coins. "It's all yours, but the pool's empty, I'm a'fraid."

"Empty? How come?"

"We drained it."

She *does* have a certain control of logic, he thinks. She can sure stick to the irrefutable. For nothing more than a few moments of amusement, he leans in and asks: "Whatdja drain it for?"

"Well, we thought we ought to after half of it evaporated."

"Evaporated!" Frankenstein hasn't thought about evaporation since elementary school. It just hasn't been a problem.

The lady says, "It sure takes its toll."

Now that he thinks about it, he himself has been evaporating all day. Strawberries have done to him what this motelier has done to her pool. He feels half evaporated and fully drained. The next logical question is why she doesn't fill the pool with more water, especially given the recent increase in the price of a room. But just as he's wondering the obvious question, she asks him the equally obvious: Would he like to see the room?

Yes, he would. She leads him through a sliding glass door, past a stained and dilapidated pool that looked like it wouldn't hold water even if they didn't drain it, past a row of rooms that end with A, under the balcony of the rooms that end with B, around the corner to a single room with a junior-size Dumpster at its door. There's no L on the door, but the key opens it. It groans as it opens inward. Must and dankness billow out, but it's cool must and humid dankness. The lady turns on the light.

It's a regular motel room except that it smells a little funny and has no window. Frankenstein's slept in worse-smelling places. He can live without a window. In fact, it might be kind of nice to tuck into a little burrow that's free of sunshine. The double bed, oddly low within an almost square wooden frame, is a luxury he'd all but forgotten. The bathroom's right there for him and him alone. It even has little bottles of shampoo, hair conditioner, moisturizer, little bars of soap wrapped in paper, a shower cap, a cloth for shining shoes. All of this stuff will leave with him, of course, even the toilet paper, all but three or feet left behind in the name of decency. It's his due. At the same time, it's a treasure he had forgotten to expect. He feels rich as the lady closes the door on him. The steel door shuts with hermetic finality.

Frankenstein strips. The white from under his shorts and T-shirt gleams alongside the tan and dust of his exposed skin. It looks like he's

FRANKENSTEIN ON THE CUSP OF SOMETHING

wearing a weird little set of pajamas. He settles into ten inches of bath water. Though too shallow for true comfort, it feels pretty good. He soaks for a while, then takes a shower, then lathers himself all over again, top to bottom, stem to stern. He does the shampoo, the hair conditioner, the moisturizer. And then he goes to bed. This is what he's paying for, and he's going to get his money's worth.

He topples face-first to the bed like a felled tree. With a splash of surprise, he realizes it's a water bed. He groans with pleasure as the little waves massage him from below. He doesn't even have to make the effort of breathing. The movement of the water moves him just enough to push air through the sag of his mouth. If Room L is this good, he wonders, what's going on in the other rooms?

This is too good to sleep through. He turns on the TV, uses the remote to click through the 60 channels, all of which seem to be showing sports, local news, business news, documentaries about snails, sitcoms about half-wits sharing inside jokes, nonsensical music videos, religion, and commercials upon commercials upon commercials, all of them urging, urging, urging, urging, urging. And the x-channels cost extra.

He'd rather look at the dark than watch TV. He lies atop the bedspread, head on the cool, spongy, pillow, his arms and legs spread wide so the air can dry the last nooks of his body. He likes being clean and on a bed and in a locked place. He wouldn't mind always having a place like this. A *home*, he thinks. Not that he's never been in one. He lived in one for over twenty years. And it's still there. And he supposes he could go back. He just doesn't want to. He doesn't know why. The very thought makes him antsy. As soon as he imagines himself in his own bed in his own room, he imagines himself packing up and leaving, getting away for vaguely the same reason that he couldn't stand the television. At home, there's just nothing on. It's one channel, one show, a perpetual Procter & Gamble advertorial-docudrama called *Frankenstein's Mother*.

But he isn't getting his money's worth just floating in the dark. Rising and falling with the swells of his bed, he gropes around and around the bedside lamp, his fingers rioting around the base, shinnying up the shaft of it, wiggling up under the skirt of the lamp shade, finally closing in on a little button accessible only to children and contortionists. He twists the button around and around, turning a little night light on, then the regular light, then making it brighter and then off and then on and then the bright light and brighter then and off and on. Whew! He collapses back on the bed. He's ready for another shower. *Technology*, he thinks. Whatever happened to the good old pull-chain? Down for on, down for off—you always get what you haven't got.

Still, he's glad he didn't have to start a fire with flint and a pile of dried grass. As he thinks about it, he realizes he's probably poised about halfway between the dark days of the cave and the bright and shining future when you'll need post-graduate degree just to turn on a light. Things could be worse. He shouldn't get so upset.

Appreciating the light, he rolls to one side so he can search the little night table beside the bed. The upper drawer has postcards featuring the Forty-Niners Motel under a blazing sunset, a local phone book, brochures for a petting zoo, a ghost town, a trolley museum, a dinosaur park, and under it all, a brochure for God, a fat and moldy Bible with "Donated by the Gideons" embossed on the cover in faded gold.

Frankenstein figures he can give the Bible one more shot. Maybe this time it will make sense. God's word will complete the jumbled jigsaw puzzle of his mind. It will bring him to his knees. He will genuflect and weep. He will have purpose and certainty. That purpose, he's pretty sure, would have to be the life of a full-time man of the cloth. He can't imagine how any true believer could do less. If there's a God, his strawberry-picking days are *really* over. He's a priest and a prophet, and if he can ever find the applicable paragraph, he'll even go for celibate. He decided all of this a long time ago, well before closing his eyes and opening the Bible to roughly the middle, the chapter of Isaias, whereupon he cast his eyes on Chapter 36, and he found it confusing:

> *And it came to pass in the fourteenth year of King Ezechias, that Senmacherib King of the Assyrians came up against all the fenced cities of Juda, and took them.*
>
> *And the King of the Assyrians sent Rabsaces from Lachis to Jerusalem, to King Ezechias with a great army, and he stood by the conduit of the upper pool in the way of the fuller's field.*

FRANKENSTEIN ON THE CUSP OF SOMETHING

And there went out to him Eliacim, the son of Helcias, who was over the house, and Sobna, the scribe, and Joahe, the son of Asaph the recorder.

And Rabasaces said to them: Tell Ezechias: Thus saith the great king, the king of the Assyrians: What is this confidence wherein thou trustesth?

Or with what counsel or strength dost thou trust, that thou are revolted from me?

Lo thou trustest upon this broken staff of a reed, upon Egypt: upon which if a man lean, it will go into his hand, and pierce it: so is Pharoao kind of Egypt to all that trust in him.

But if thou wilt answer me: We trust in the Lord our God is it not he whose high places and altars Ezechias hath taken away, and hath said to Juda and Jerusalem: You shall worship before the altar?

Frankenstein doesn't get it. These are the words of God? All he can think is, *So what?* What is he supposed to do? Not trust the Pharoao of Egypt?

He flips to Deuteronomy. *Thou shalt make strings in the hem at the four corners of thy cloak, wherewith thou shalt be covered.* Nearby it recommends that if his bride can't prove her virginity, she should be stoned to death. That sends him into Exodus in search of the Ten Commandments, but he misses by a page and reads, *He that curseth his father, or mother, shall die the death.* He pokes into Genesis. *I am the Almighty God: walk with me, and be perfect....Abram fell flat on his face.*

Frankenstein drapes the Bible over his nose. He wouldn't be caught dead in a fringed cloak. He tries to imagine throwing stones at a hypothetical wife, but the image blurs and withers before he can get it into focus. He tries to recall actually cursing his mother, but he doesn't think he did, not technically, not legally. He doesn't think he knew any swears the last time he saw his father. But he can sure see himself trying to do right and falling flat on his face.

He returns the Bible to its nest of brochures and closes the drawer. He'll have to find God elsewhere. Meanwhile, maybe what he needs to do is call his sister. After about five attempts, he figures out how to dial long distance on the motel phone, but apparently it's not going to be the collect call he was attempting. Before the first ring finishes, Little Tom answers.

The boy can't guess who it is. When Frankenstein gives him the answer, he just says, "Hold on." His footsteps pound into the distance. He thumps on a door—the bathroom door, Frankenstein's sure of it. He can see it all. He can also see the dollars wafting from his pocket like the souls of the dead on their way to heaven, never to return.

Suzie Creamcheese arrives all breathless but perky. She was indeed in the bathroom, but not for any of the usual reasons. She was trying to bathe a baby groundhog who got sprayed by a skunk. She says, "Where are you now?"

"In a hotel, taking it easy. On a waterbed."

"In?"

"California."

"Cool!"

But then he doesn't know what to say. His mind is filled with a vivid resurgence of himself in sandals and a fringed cloak, stoning a beautiful but sullied señorita while his mother comes after him with a battle ax because she mistook a sneeze for a common curse. The image is as useless as that of himself as president of Mexico, but for the moment it clouds out the possibility of conversation.

She seems to suspect trouble in the silence. Hesitant, she says, "So...what's up?"

The cloud thins. Frankenstein says, "I can hardly tell anymore." He's pressing on his temples with his thumb and longest finger. The palm of his hand presses his eyes shut.

"Uh-oh," she says. "Dipping into the controlled substances, are we?"

"Nope. I wish that were it. At least it would *explain* something. I just can't *think* straight anymore, and there's no reason for it."

Not only can he not think straight, he can't even think why he's telling her this. It isn't even true. Except maybe a little.

"You sound tired," she says.

She always knows. In his mind he reviews the places he has slept these past few weeks: in a half-built house, under an old school bus parked in a meadow, in a barn from which he shoveled petrified manure for two days, in a hospital waiting room, in the back of seat of a stranger's car, under a bridge that crossed an interstate, under a boat on a trailer, in pastures and fields, behind hedges and bushes, on grass, sand, assorted stone, plain dirt, here and there. Every afternoon, without thinking about it, his eyes looked sharp for places to tuck himself. The last bed he slept in was at the grubby little apartment of a semi-professional, totally inebriated hockey player, and technically it was not a bed but a couch, and the TV was on all night.

"I think that's it," he says to his sister. "I'm beat."

"You should visit Mom for a while. Recover a little. Rest. You know?"

"Maybe I will."

And maybe he won't. His sister knows this. He doesn't have to say it. They both know what she means when she says, "Good."

Frankenstein senses a gulf between himself and his sister. Though they're on opposite sides of a continent, he can almost see the waves and swells of a vast sea between them. She's way over there somewhere and drifting farther. He's over here and going the other way. The waves between them are slow and high, dark beneath a pattern of thin foam, not whitecapped yet but uneasy. He can almost see this, almost hear the lonely swish, as he stares dully into the darkness of the phone.

"I don't know what to do," he says. His lips, heavy and a little numb, move of their own accord. He could cry right now if he let himself. "I don't know where to go. I don't know what I'm doing."

"What you need is a *purpose*."

"Yes, that would be fine. I think I'll run right out and get one."

Decent pay for migrant workers comes right to mind. Regulation of the motel industry. Little shelters for hitchhikers at interstate entrance ramps. The Nation-in-a-Blimp idea. He wouldn't mind starting some kind of foundation for homeless puppies. But what does she want him to do? Go to the door, open it up, spot a purpose and pursue it? He could go to the door all right, open it right up, but he has no idea what comes after that. He hasn't seen a purpose in months, maybe years. He can't remember the last time. And what would he do if he came across one? All he knows is what he learned in college, which wasn't much and certainly hasn't proven useful. He can't type straight. He can't handle a weapon. He can't tell other people what to do, and when other people tell him what to do, he does it wrong. What good would a purpose do? It would just be one more thing to screw up. What could be worse than finding something worth doing, then screwing it up? He'd much rather screw up things not worth doing.

To break the slick of silence he's laid across the sea from there to his sister, he says, "Maybe I should chain myself to a nuclear power plant."

"That would kind of be avoiding the issue, wouldn't it?"

Sisters know these things. How do they do it? Is it all women or just sisters? All people or just women? Is it everyone but him? Frankenstein wonders but doesn't know how to ask. But he does manage to say, "I don't even know what the issue *is*."

His honesty surprises him, and he's rewarded with soft words. She says, "It's out there somewhere. You'll find it." The sea's not as wide as he thought. The waves aren't so big, and the water's pretty warm.

Shortly after hanging up, Frankenstein hears people move into the room next door. Their room shares the wall at the head of his bed. He doesn't try to, at first, but he can hear them. They are busy people. They close and open the bathroom door several times, run water, rip open the Venetian blinds, open and close drawers, turn on their air conditioner, thump around, talking the whole time. He can tell when one of them flops onto the bed. He hears small shoes clunk to the floor.

Now he's trying very hard to hear—just out of curiosity. Nobody's getting laid over there. It's a woman and girl, no doubt a mother and a daughter. The girl is whining and arguing. The mother's voice thrusts and parries with exasperation. He wonders what she looks like and where her husband, if any, is. The little girl sounds about ten years old. That makes the mother thirty or thirty-two or so—a little old for him but within the range of possibility. Not that he has any reason to worry about it. He's not going over there, and she's not likely to come around the corner to knock at the door near the Dumpster. He's certainly not going to see her swimming in the empty pool. Still, he wonders.

He really shouldn't be trying to listen, he knows, but what's it going to hurt if he puts his ear to the wall? He's sure the Bible doesn't have any shalt-nots for this. He doesn't need to check. He's just curious what it's like in somebody else's motel room, somebody else's family.

So he kneels at the head of his bed, leans against the wall and sets his ear against it. It's a little hard until the waves die down. He can hear the people next door but not clearly. They're definitely having some kind of childish little argument. He remembers a trick from years ago, maybe from a science class, maybe from TV or a comic book. He gets the glass cup from the bathroom, presses the bottom of it to the wall and inserts his year in the open end.

It works. The words take shape in the glass just in time for him to hear the mother say, "*No!*"

The girl pleads, "But you *said*."

"I said you could have a Princess of the Light special meal number two. That was it. Period."

"But the princess meal *includes* a medium soda with a free thirty-two-ounce poly reusable Princess of the Light sport cup. It's *free*."

The mother seems to be shouting from the bathroom. She says, "Nothing's free."

"But it *says* free. It said it on TV! It says it right on the cup!"

The mother does not respond. She's concentrating on her bladder. He can almost hear it. Then there's a flush, and she says, firmly, finally, back in the room, "It's free if you order a large fries."

"That's what I said! *Free*."

"You can never finish a large fries, and the last time you tried to drink thirty-two ounces of Coke you threw up in the car."

"It doesn't have to be Coke. Just a soft drink. *Anything*. It could even be ginger ale if they had it."

"How about water?"

"*Gross*."

"Try it next time, you think you're so smart. Order a Princess of the Light special meal number two with large fries and a medium water, see what you get."

"They don't serve water there."

"Right. Because it's free. And nothing's free."

The little girl doesn't take long to say, "But how can it be free if nothing's free?"

"Because if you ask for it, that's what they give you: nothing. And it's free. OK?"

"But I *want* it!"

And Frankenstein wants to go over there and grab the little twirp and tell the mother, "Let me have her for a while," and he'll take her out in the desert until she really, really, *really* wants a glass of water, even if its not in a thirty-two-ounce poly reusable Princess of the Light sport cup.

But that wouldn't work. It would constitute child abuse, though in Frankenstein's opinion, a quart of caffeine and corn syrup constitutes plenty of child abuse in itself, and whosoever advertises it and puts it in a poly sport cup featuring a multinational cartoon character ought to be forced to pick strawberries for a day. If Frankenstein were king of the world, he'd have things straightened right out.

But he's not king of the world. He's Frankenstein, almost broke and totally alone, either not sure what's right or afraid to get up and go do it. No purpose, however simple or clear-cut, will ever suit him. He wouldn't even qualify for junior assistant duke of the world. He wouldn't qualify for life guard of the Forty-Niners Motel. When the mother and daughter thump their door shut as they go out, he's sure the mother will succumb to the relentless whine and corporate onslaught. The girl will get her quart of soda and cherished cup. She will be momentarily satisfied, and by the time she gets out of junior high school she'll weigh two hundred pounds.

Frankenstein lies down and gets to thinking. He thinks about the other people who have spent the night in Room L. What remains of them? Do their cheek cells still sift within the pillow? Does a stratified micron of breath coat the walls? Do their eyebrow mites mingle in the bedspread? Do their germs loiter in the bathroom? Do the fading echoes of their moans and conversation still ricochet around the room? Do pockets of carbon dioxide and methane linger in places where the vacuum cleaner never goes? Do invisible fingerprints grace the phone, the doorknobs, the Bible? Do their smells comprise the mustiness? Have the swells of the waterbed absorbed their weight? Does the moisture of their emotions coat the surface of things? Do their thoughts still hang in the air? Do memories link the room to the minds of hundreds of inhabitants? Do these people carry each others' mites and molecules? Does a certain gravity draw some of them back? Have human eggs been fertilized in the rolling waves on which he now floats?

FRANKENSTEIN ON THE CUSP OF SOMETHING

When he thinks of how much archeologists can deduce from shards of pottery and chips of bone, he wonders how much future investigators might be able to learn from the human detritus in Room L. They'll examine microscopic flecks of his scat and determine that his diet consisted of nothing but strawberries. They'll assess his sweat and determine the depth of his concern. They'll measure the remainder of his ripples and know that he did not sleep well. They'll follow his fingerprints up the lamp and from them derive a rough estimate of his IQ. Their super-enhanced cosmo-powered cathode ray whoopty-do infrared heat detector will photograph each of the eighty-odd positions in which he tried to find comfort. They'll pick through the sludge in the sink drain, do a carbon-14 test on his plaque, and they will conclude that the wedding ring they found in there would not have fit around his knuckles. They'll examine his scuff marks to determine the make of the tire from which his sandals were made. They'll deduce the pages he read from the Bible. On the floor where his duffel bag lay they'll find the dust of Texas, Oregon, Maine, Canada, the Carolinas, Lark. They'll wonder, who was this guy? What was he doing? Where was he going? They'll figure all that out, he's sure. But no matter how fancy their machines and brilliant their ability to deduce, when they try to detect his purpose, they're going to find a darkness as deep as a cave with nothing inside worth a goddamn thing.

- Chapter Nine -
To Whom It May Concern

Dear Abby:

I just read your interesting recent column in which Suspicious In Tennessee complained of a husband whom she thinks is abusing her pets. (For reasons I shall not go into, I was especially sad to hear of the dreadful demise of her hamsters.) There's no doubt that the husband is the culprit, so before I get into my own personal problem, let me say, with all due respect, that your recommendation that Suspicious confront her husband with direct questions just isn't going to work. Either he's not the type to confess, or if he does, she's not the type to do anything about it. You should write again and tell her to abandon the son of a bitch and for God's sake take the cat with her.

Not that I'm an expert in such things. I'm not an expert in anything, especially marital relationships. I suppose if I read your column I'd know a lot more about how to handle the many situations human beings get themselves into, but I'm kind of on the road at the moment, and I have scant resources for newspapers. The world's just been having to get along without me. On the occasions when I happen to be in a diner that has a house copy of the local paper floating around, I do a bit of catching up. This explains my current situation. It's barely dawn in this little Montana town. I slept on the back porch of a mortuary last night and got up early so as to not be caught by the mortician, who no doubt is a bit jumpy about finding inert bodies at his door. So I dragged my sorry butt on over to this sorry diner, where the early morning crowd consists of a bunch of old guys at the counter drinking coffee, smoking cigarettes and making smells like maybe there was one thing they forgot to do before they left home this morning. They do not make me feel wanted here, but here I am.

Like you need to know that, right? I'm sorry. If I were writing this on a computer, I'd go back and delete that. It's too much to scratch out, so I'll just leave it. If you choose to run this letter in your column, please leave that part out. Also, there's no real need to mention that it's written on the back of a place mat dotted with coffee and smelling of a damp old dish rag.

You can leave out as much as you want, but I feel like I have to include it all or you won't know what I'm talking about. The guys at the counter figure in, but I'm not sure how. I guess they're just an indication, a symbolic indication, of where I am, i.e., the outer bowels of nowhere.

I've been bumming around for a couple of years now. I don't know why, but I just keep going. I hitchhike. A lot of nice people pick me up. All the rotten ones just drive on by. That's one good thing about this way of travel. And the ones who stop, I've just realized, all sound like the type of people who would write to you. Or I guess I mean they have the kind of problems that you specialize in. A guy in Florida, I think it was, said he hadn't had a conversation with this wife in over thirty years and he didn't care. He was going for forty. An old lady outside of Birmingham hired me to drive her to Knoxville because she wanted to drink the whole way, which she did, in the back seat, snorting off bottles of vodka she had in a cooler. She was rich from winning a lottery, but she had cancers—that's what she said, cancers, in the plural—so she decided to just drink herself to death. She was going to see her brother, who had lost both legs in World War II and never married. A guy in Iowa was a bartender who got thrown out of his own bar by a bunch of gay guys because it was a gay bar and he wasn't gay and didn't like them, but it was the only job he could find and he was desperate for a variety of reasons, so he took the job but couldn't help but insult his customers, which he didn't really mean to do, but he just couldn't help himself, like, once, he said, he slid somebody some awful mixed drink that was pink and said, "Here you go, toots," and the guy got all huffy. To somebody who just asked for a beer he said, "You sure you can handle it?" It got so that everything he said was taken as an insult, even when he asked some guy if he wanted a straw. So one day they dragged him over the bar and threw him into the street. It was broad daylight, so half the town saw, and pretty soon the whole town knew, and all he could do then was leave. The only reason he picked me up was so he could ask me for enough gas money to get him to Des Moines. He should have written you a letter. You'd know what to do. If you sent a letter to "Bounced in Batavia," they'd know who it was for, but they wouldn't know where he is, so don't bother.

The whole country's got this kind of problem. I haven't met one person who hasn't got himself or herself painted into some kind of corner. Maybe other kinds of people just don't stop for hitchhikers, and I guess I can't blame them. Why take a chance on a stranger if everything's going your way? But still, how happy can they really be if they're afraid to take a chance on helping somebody?

None of this really relates to my personal problem, except maybe indirectly. I'm not sure because I'm not sure what my personal problem is. Compared to everybody else's, it must not be much. But at least they know what theirs is. A guy gets bounced out of his own bar and the whole town laughs at him. That's his problem. The solution: Des Moines. Easy. But I went to Des Moines with him, and you know what? It didn't solve my problem. Not in the least. In fact, I went into an employment agency to see if there was any easy work around. By easy I mean anything I know how to do. They asked me what I wanted to do. I said I didn't know, and all of a sudden, out of the blue, I start choking up. Like crying, almost. I tried to say, "Just dig a hole," but all I did was squeak. I couldn't talk. The guy said, "Look, why don't you come back later?" which of course I didn't, no more than that bartender could go back to Batavia.

Do you care to tell me what to do about that, Abby? Or is that a problem for Ann Landers? Or Dr. Joyce Brothers?

FRANKENSTEIN ON THE CUSP OF SOMETHING

Look what happened in New Jersey. A lady comes along and picks me up. In her car, I mean. She says her coins told her I was OK, meaning I wasn't going to rob and rape her. I certainly couldn't argue that fact with her. Her coins were dead on. She was about sixty but looked about fifty, and I think she was trying to be half that. She was very thin and wide-eyed and dangling all over with turquoise and jewelry made of wood and shells and bones and stuff. This lady believed in absolutely everything: pyramid power, crystal power, astrology, herbal cures, the Tibetan Book of the Dead, tarot, everything. It was the I Ching that checked me out and said I was OK. I guess she must have driven past me once, pulled over, tossed her coins, checked out the triads and then come back and got me. She guessed my astrological sign right off the bat but then said it was pretty weird because Virgos don't usually hitchhike. "You should be an accountant," she said. "You should get a nice suit and a nice shirt with plenty of starch and some black shoes and a job in a big company, the bigger the better, and a desk that you can keep clean, and then you'll be happy."

I said, "Oh, OK." Like yeah, right. Me in a big company. I pictured myself up ahead on the side of the road, wearing nothing but a neck tie, big brown wingtips and tight socks that came all the way up my calves.

But then she says, "What's your rising sign?"

I told her I didn't have the slightest idea. She asked me my birthday and what time I was born. When I said I didn't know the time, she said she could already tell I was probably a Mars rising but could be a Uranus, depending on a lot of things, some of which were important, so I should ask my mother. I said I would do that for sure next time I saw her, which I didn't say might not be for a long time. But then she said, let's call her. Next rest area.

I didn't say a thing. I figured any lady this flaky was going to drive right by the next rest area and forget all about it. But she didn't. She pulled up to this pay phone that's right at car level.

"My nickel," she says. Her nickel was a number off a credit card, which she punched right in and then asked me my mother's number. I couldn't think of anything to do but tell her. I figured that as long as I didn't have to talk to her, so what? Not that I'd really *mind* talking to her. I just didn't want to. Not yet. If you knew my mother, you'd know what I mean. Sometimes you need to take a break.

The lady listens to the phone for longer than it should take. I count nine pieces of jewelry in her right ear. She's got heavy peach fuzz all around her lips. It was kind of back-lit by the sun. Her lips moved as she listened. I was thinking about kissing those lips and how much I wouldn't want to. Then she hangs up the phone with one finger and says, "They changed your area code."

I don't know why that was such a shock, but it was. It hit me right in the heart. It was as if they'd moved my hometown to Yugoslavia.

But they hadn't. They'd just changed my area code. The lady called information and got the new one, which I've already forgotten. Three weird numbers, that's all I remember, like a code they'd give to Newfoundland or someplace else that nobody calls.

Anyway, the lady re-dials the credit card number and my phone number again and all of a sudden she's got my mother on the line. She says, "Hello, Mrs..." and she looks at me over the top of her bifocals.

I thought the best thing to do would be to say *Frankenstein*. The lady just kept looking at me and then repeated the name in slow syllables. As you might imagine, it kind of freaks some people out. But my mother heard it and started saying something, and little by little the lady stopped looking at me and started listening to my mother, who talked for a long, long time. I could hear her quacking away, and barking, in a ceaseless flow. I'd say it wasn't until about ten minutes later that the lady finally said, "South of Nutley."

Which I guess was the main thing my mother wanted to know, that and what the woman said next: "Dawnita."

Then my mother had a lot of stuff to say, tons of stuff, stuff I'll never know. Dawnita kept nodding and saying, in long, knowing, drawn-out tones, "Aha!" and "Oh *really?*"

So it was no longer me and a lady who gave me a lift. It was my mother and her old buddy Dawnita against just me. They knew something I didn't, and whatever it was, it wasn't good. It was my mother's version of me, which I'm sure was a whole different person from the one sitting there in the car at the pay phone at the rest area in New Jersey. I was a regular person until Dawnita got my area code figured out. Things had been just fine.

Somewhere in the middle of half an hour of *oh really's* Dawnita broke in with, "Oh, and what *time* was he born?" followed shortly by, "*You're kidding?*" and, in a while, "Are you sure?" When the hanging-up process started, Dawnita had to keep saying, "OK, I'll tell him, yup, I'll tell him, yup, yup, OK, I'll tell him, right," and finally, "Good-bye."

As soon as she had the phone back on the hook and the window on its way up, I said, "What?"

She said, "Nothing. Give me your palm."

She held her hand out, waiting for mine. What was I going to do, get out of the car? I gave her my left hand, palm up. She flattened it out like a wrinkled letter, lifted it up to the sunlight and studied it at an angle down through her glasses. One little fingernail—she had the thinnest fingers I've ever seen—traced a slow line from my wrist to what I guess is called my second finger. It was so slow that I wondered if it wasn't sumptuous, too. I still don't know. But if it was supposed to be, why would she say, "You've definitely got some problems, and it looks like they're going to last a long time and they're going to get worse before they get better."

Which, as you know, my dear Abby, is advice that applies to absolutely everyone who does this "Earth" trip. And not only does everything get worse before it gets better, everything gets better and then gets worse. Am I not right? Up and down, up and down. That's about all you can count on.

You can put that little piece of advice in your column if you want. And just once I'd like to see you write, "I'm sorry, but absolutely nothing can be done about your problem, so stop worrying about it." Tell them Frankenstein told you.

Back to Dawnita. She had my hand in hers and my palm tingling, and I knew exactly what she was full of. The crack in my palm could not possibly reveal my worsening situation. But while I didn't believe her, I had a desperate need to know what was going to happen. Was she predicting "worse" in the sense of stumbling over a cliff, or "worse" in the sense of getting loster and loster until I slowly die of hunger and arthritis in a sleet storm at the end of an interstate where no one ever goes?

So I said, "Tell me what else."

Dawnita was holding my thumb like a handle. It looked big in her little hand. With the pinkie of her other hand, she traced a line west to east across my palm. "Love," she stated. "I've never seen it come in at such a weird angle. You're in for a doozy."

Suddenly I felt the way I'd felt in the employment agency in Des Moines. Maybe not as bad, but I knew better than to try to talk. Love was on its way, but it was going to be a doozy. I hadn't really thought about how nice it would be to be in love. Still, the doozy part smelled like trouble. Did she mean doozy at a weird angle in the sense of menage a cinq? Or, as I most feared, in the sense of an affair with an older woman with nine ear rings? Or what? And anyway, doesn't love always come in doozies? How would you know it's love if there's no doozy about it? In other words, Dawnita was speaking in meaningless generalities, and again, I wanted more.

"Doozy?" I squeaked like a little frog.

"That's all I can get out of a palm," she said. "It isn't too specific, but look…" She poked at the crucial intersection and peered at me over her glasses. "That's your doozy blip right there."

Sure enough, where the two lines crossed, a tiny starburst of cracks shot out. I always thought those cracks were from when I had a job operating a wheelbarrow for a week. I had a blister there. But if that blip meant love, I was in for a momentous event. I closed my knuckles around it and pulled my hand in close to my liver.

"What else?" I asked.

"If you really want to get specific, I have to throw your cards. They'll tell us everything."

Smart fellow that I am, I knew I could say OK with the certainty that she'd never be able to deal tarot cards in the front seat of a Ford subcompact that looked like it had been made in one of Asia's smaller nations and assembled in Rhode Island. But then at the same moment she and I saw the picnic table under a tree whose branches reached in over the chain-link fence that divided the rest area from the wilds of New Jersey.

What was I going to do? Tell her no, drive on, please? It was her car. She was the boss. If she wanted to tell me about my problems and my future, I guess I had to listen. But I *hate* that kind of stuff, you know? I don't believe in it, but whenever somebody tells me my fortune, I keep remembering it. I actually start to count on it. I was already counting on things getting worse and me falling in love. Now Dawnita wanted to get specific.

I did something for Dawnita that I've never done for anyone else, ever. The picnic table benches were wet, and she was wearing a nice white translucent dress that wasn't meant for getting wet. So I sat in the wetness for her. I blotted it up with the seat of my pants. I itch just to think about it. At first she didn't know what I was doing, but when I made a sweeping gesture for her to sit in the dry spot, she fluttered her fingers over her heart and said, "Oh, my!"

I suppose I shouldn't have done that. I think it gave Dawnita the whole wrong idea. To make matters worse, I then spread my jacket across the table so she wouldn't get her cards wet. So while she's dealing the cards on one side of the table, I'm on the other side, slightly cold and scrunching my buns around because of the itch.

"Think of a question," she says. "Anything that's on your mind."

Now, Abby, I have so many questions in my mind that I can't possibly untangle any one of them and flatten it out on the table to be dealt with. I couldn't think of a single one. So after a dramatic pause, I just nodded and said, "OK." If I had a question, it was "What kind of idiot am I to be doing this?"

She instructs me to shuffle the cards and cut them twice so three piles lay face up on the damp denim of my jacket. She says, "O-ho" for the first, "Hmmmm" for the second, and "Wow—interesting" for the third. It was then that I noticed the smears of light pink lipstick on her canine teeth. Both of them. *Hmmmm*, thinks I. *Interesting*.

Card-wise, I had no idea what she was talking about. I had a hard time paying attention because every time she said something, my mind just took off thinking about something else. The whole thing smelled strongly of what a dictionary would call nonsense but what my mother would come right out and call bullshit.

Yes, my mother. She wouldn't say shit if she found a lump of it between her teeth, but at some point in her life, bullshit became an indispensable linguistic tool. She uses it as far more than mere opinion. The word is a pronouncement, an irrevocable judgment. And I think that's what she would have said about these tarot cards. I don't remember what Dawnita said, but it was stuff like "a strong man who you respect as a down-to-earth spiritual leader will encourage you to seek new paths to a kind of celestial freedom." That's not what she said. It was just stuff like that—abstract and way, way up there in the clouds, like cosmic fog. She lost me completely, and I felt guilty about it. She was trying to help me (I guess), and it went right over my head. I kept thinking *bullshit*. Unlike my mother, however, I didn't say it. I mean, why not just let bullshit *be*? Coming from Dawnita, it was *nice* bullshit. It was pleasant. I daresay it was even loving. It was a gift from her: twenty minutes of prediction and personality assessment, none of it true. But I didn't really care. I liked Dawnita. I liked her *conviction*. I liked her outlook. And I think I liked the way she was paying attention to me, the way she seemed to care what was going to happen to me.

As she peeled off the cards, I kept listening for signs of love coming down the pike. One card I remember had a woman, seated, blindfolded, her back to the sea, a sword in each hand, blades to the sky, her white toga stretched a little tight along her thighs, and I thought, *Maybe that's her*. She sure looked interesting. I don't remember what Dawnita said about that card, but it had nothing to do with love. Then along comes a guy face down on the ground with ten swords stabbed through him. "A plan gone awry," Dawnita says. "Don't worry about it." Along comes a crippled guy and starving girl in a snowstorm outside a church. Dawnita just says, "Hmp," and moves on. Along comes death on a horse. Dawnita says, "It's not what you think," and goes on to explain why, which of course I did not understand, except that she ends it with, "Because look..." and she turns over the next card, which says on the bottom, "The Hanged Man." But they haven't hanged him the way they hang regular people, maybe because he's wearing pantaloons, tights and yellow slippers. He's upside down on a cross, hanging by one foot and looking less than concerned. "*That's* me," I say, tapping the card with a finger. "Right?"

"Your mental outlook, yes."

"The mental outlook of a crucified buffoon?"

"*No.* The mental outlook of a person who has surrendered desire, ego and cleverness and cast his fate to the winds." She looked at me over the tops of her bifocals. "OK?" she said. "Ready to start believing?" She had her fingers around the next card.

I tilted my head left and right. I was ready to believe, ready to disbelieve. I was glad to believe in the blindfolded girl in the toga and disbelieve death on a horse, and I could go either way on the crucified buffoon. One thing for sure: I wanted to know what was on the next card, as if it might answer the question I hadn't asked.

I don't remember what was on the next card. Whatever it was, it didn't make sense and it had nothing to do with love. It was upside down, *reversed*, as Dawnita called it, so it meant the opposite of whatever it was that I didn't understand in the first place about the question I hadn't asked. I hardly paid attention to the explanation because I was so intensely wondering why I was so intensely caring about something I didn't believe in.

And then she's got her fingers pressed against the back of the next card on the deck. "Last card," she says. "The final outcome."

Going for a joke, I say, "Gulp," and pull my collar out to let imaginary steam escape.

No laugh. She looks me deep in the face while she waits for me to settle down and get serious. And I *do* get serious. We're both frozen for the time it takes to inhale and exhale. A mourning dove in the dark of the dripping woods beyond the chain-link fence hoots its single, sad note twice. As if having received a go-ahead, Dawnita lifts the card, rolls her hand over to reveal it, slides it onto the table and with palpable satisfaction says, "Bingo."

Bingo in my personal circumstances turns out to be a rather depressed-looking guy in a red cloak with a staff in his hand, walking away from eight golden goblets stacked unevenly, three on five.

Dawnita says it again, very quietly this time, with burden: "Bingo."

The burden is the one of all who have no reason to stay and no place to go, the burden of moving on.

"These cups are your family, your relationships, your emotions," Dawnita says, audibly satisfied with her certainty. "And that's you walking away from them. They haven't satisfied you. You are wearing red, the color of urge and desire. You are restless. You have disentangled yourself, abandoned a hopeless situation, taken off on a journey of discovery, looking for answers, for something that satisfies you, something that *means*."

"But *everything* means." What I really meant was that everything *seems* to mean something if you look at it hard enough. My itchy buns and the mourning dove (of all birds!) hooting in the woods and the color of Dawnita's Ford (red, wouldn't you know, and freckled with rust) could all mean something if you thought about them long enough. But do they mean what you think they mean? There's the interstate, *highway of life*. Here's the wet picnic table, *sacred altar of family foodstuffs*. Or maybe the highway is a tentacle of cancer reaching across the land. Maybe the picnic table is the life raft of the weary. And here's the tarot cards, describing a drifter to a T. Or maybe they mean the United States should have pulled out of Vietnam sooner. Maybe they mean I should abandon this picnic table and never look back.

But I don't say any of that. I let Dawnita take my meaning wrong. She says, "Right!"

My buns itched too bad to argue. I wanted to get up. I wanted to go somewhere. I was glad to see we'd reached an agreement even if it was based on a misunderstanding. I wanted to leave it at that. I wanted to give Dawnita a detachedly passionate kiss and wave good-bye as she drove off in her little red car.

Which is basically what happened. Yes, I kissed her. No, I didn't lick her canines. Yes, I waved good-bye, and so did she, out the half-opened window, her turquoise bracelets jangling in the breeze. And there I stood, once again all alone on the side of the highway, chilly in my wet jacket, itchy in my wet pants. I raised my right hand to the side so drivers could see my palm, but I was looking at the palm of my left hand. In the whoosh and buffet of a passing semi I found my doozy blip. It was about halfway up the line where things were going to get worse before they got better. I saw nothing to indicate whether love was going to hit me before, after or during the disaster that lay between me and the good life. The blip stood on the line quite like the way I stood on the side of the road, halfway

FRANKENSTEIN ON THE CUSP OF SOMETHING

between nowhere and nowhere else. I should have asked Dawnita, but by that time, she was already miles away. Not that it mattered. If it's carved in your palm, it's written in the stars. There's nothing I can do about it. Right? What do you think?

Sincerely,
Marooned in Montana

- CHAPTER TEN -
Things Get Worse

It takes about two weeks for Dawnita's prediction to start coming true, or so it seems to Frankenstein. He's eastbound on a state highway across southern Illinois, going back to look for a letter to his sister. He's sure he left it in the crotch of a bench in a booth at a truck stop and which he would not want anyone, not even his sister, to read. He's in the front seat of an old station wagon driven by a lady built along the lines of a snowman. She's got tons of stuff to say, none of it relevant to Frankenstein. It's blabbety-blabbety-blab through an endless field of corn.

Her little daughter's in the back seat, hanging over the front. She's kind of humming to herself, maybe trying to drown out her mother's unrelenting blabbety-blab, maybe learning to blabbety-blab herself. After a while, she's got her chin on Frankenstein's collarbone. Her hums vibrate clear across his neck and up into his jaw. When her mouth moves to sing "la-la, la-la, la" or something, it shoots a ticklish thrill through his chest. When her head rocks to the rhythm of her secret tune, her brown hair brushes against Frankenstein's ear. It smells sweet and clean. He's glad the girl's mother doesn't notice and doesn't know how much he's liking it, even though he's liking it in a sublimely innocent way. He's ignoring the mother and drinking in the sensation of the girl's sensuous little chin. As the girl pauses between songs, an inexplicable warmth seeps into his heart. Until she coughs, he doesn't realize that the pocket of his T-shirt is filled and sagging with the better part of the little girl's breakfast. The girl barks with a strangulating cough, gasps a chestful of air, then wails into Frankenstein's ear. She's got breakfast gook running from her mouth and nose.

Mommy panics, whoops, slams on the brakes, swerves all over the place, abandons the steering wheel to plunge into her pocketbook for tissues. Frankenstein grabs the wheel, brings the car in for a landing even as the wet warmth seeps through his shirt and with surprising rapidity forms a trickle down his chest and belly, under his belt and down his hip. As soon as Mommy gets the girl mopped up, she notices Frankenstein's thumb hooked in his shirt pocket, holding it out from his torso. With sympathy and a little pleading in her voice, she says, "You probably just want to get out right here, don't you." Though he'd much rather continue to a place with water, he gets out. The lady drives away. Just getting his shirt over his head is a disgusting trauma. Even though it's his only shirt, he pulls it over a speed limit sign, puts on his jacket and walks away. *Good,* he thinks. *Things are getting worse already.*

Later that same day, a tentacled black cloud that reeks of evil comes along and stones him with hail, lashes him with icy rain, stings him with wind-borne grit and leaves him caked with adobe. *This is not worth it,* he thinks in the thick of the onslaught, but he survives and feels better for it.

Still wet, his quivering titties sore against the cold denim of his jacket, he gets picked up by an well-kempt, eastbound Jesus freak who won't take no for an answer. Jesus loves Frankenstein. If Frankenstein doesn't want to burn in the forthcoming apocalypse, which, according to the Bible on the dashboard, is right around the corner, he'd better get down on his knees and pray. Only briefly wondering if this love is what his doozy blip's all about, he decides hell's worth the quick sin of a lie. He says he believes. But the man won't take yes for an answer. He wants Frankenstein to prove his love. He wants Frankenstein to pray with him, knees to the pavement, both their hands on the Bible, right there on the shoulder of a well-traveled highway. Frankenstein looks at the blur of the shoulder as it hums by at precisely fifty-five miles an hour. He'd much rather see it as a blur than as specific pebbles, grains of sand and the mottled texture of asphalt, the discernible details of a standstill. The last thing he wants to do is stop and kneel on it, not even for the thirty seconds it would take to transfer his limited sins to Christ. He especially doesn't want to do this in the hail and lightning storm they are passing through, the same one that hit him just an hour ago. As soon as they pass out of it and break into miraculous sunshine, the apostle says, "Are you ready?" His super-blue eyes look both offended and hypnotized. He holds his right hand palm up as if expecting Frankenstein to place an answer in it. Frankenstein has no answer. He *is* kind of praying, however—praying that God will give him firm, gentle words that mean no. God doesn't. The driver slows and eases onto the shoulder. Sand showers at the underside of the car. Watching his rearview mirror, the man says, "Are you or aren't you?" Now Frankenstein knows the answer. God has delivered. He gets out, pulling his duffel bag with him. He says, "Thanks for the ride." The man says, "Christ be with you," and drives away, leaving Frankenstein once again in the middle of nowhere.

The hail storm catches up, hammers at him again, worse this time. He hitchhikes like crazy, his duffel bag on his head to protect himself, hail rattling off him and everything around him, but nobody stops.

When the sun comes out, his pants and jacket steam. His skin, steeped, feels Precambrian, itching and stinking with primitive forms of life. He imagines his pores sprouting with microscopic proto-fungi and primordial slime. No wonder nobody stops. They can see his smell from a mile up the road. So at the first hint of sundown, he packs off into the field of wet, chest-high corn that has been devastated by the storm. Respectful of the crop, he bends around the stalks to avoid injuring them further. He creeps deeper and deeper, getting as far from highway as he can. He doesn't want to hear it. He doesn't want to smell it. He doesn't want to remember it or dream about it. He wants to become at one with corn.

He stops at a place where a breeze sets everything rustling. He rolls out his blanket and snuggles into the damp trough between the rows. The corn leaves form a beautiful, riddled thatch between him and the purpling sky. As the air cools, he buttons his jacket from neck to waist. He sleeps soon, settling in for a peaceful ride through the night. He feels a certain warmth in his gut. When he rolls over, a rat squeaks hard once, struggles between his gut and his jacket, in desperation sinks its incisors into the soft flesh just under his lowest rib.

Jerking awake, Frankenstein, having no idea what the pain is, screams and curses and punches at himself as the rat struggles to escape. As it breaks free between buttons, Frankenstein yanks up his jacket to look for the source of the excruciation. He still isn't awake enough to recognize the sharp green blades that curl around him like scimitars. He can hardly breathe against the pain, and he can't see a thing through tears in the dark. All he sees are blue-white orbs and squirms of pink lightning. The wound hurts worse than anything has ever hurt before. It radiates from his toes to the back of his tongue. It's bleeding, and before he knows what to do about it, he's got blood smeared all over his hands and face. Half crying, still cursing, he squeezes the little wound with his fingernails, then with his jacket, then with the first thing he can tear from his duffel bag, a pair of underwear that's far from sterile but no dirtier than everything else in there. Through teeth clenched hard he keeps crying, "*Jesus*," and "*Jesus God*," but he mixes those laments with the crudest of vulgarities, none of them meaning anything but pain. His diaphragm tightens so hard against it that his stomach convulses. Acid rips into his throat and laps at the back of his mouth. He collapses onto his blanket and wails softly, one arm clutching his pain, the other across his face. His teeth grip his sleeve as hard as they can without breaking. His gut flutters. His nose huffs and snorts. He finds himself blubbering, "I want to go home. I want to go home." And that's all he wants to do, all that matters in his life now. He wants his mother to put a little bandage on his rat bite. He wants to lie in a bathtub, up to his neck in clean water. Then he wants his mother to tuck him between clean sheets and let him slowly die of rabies, tetanus and gangrene. He deserves it and doesn't care. He just wants to get it over with.

As he waits for morning, he starts to shake. He thinks maybe he could stop, but he doesn't want to. His teeth clatter with hollow resonance. His stomach keeps heaving. Snot dribbles out his nose. He wipes it with his denim sleeve and doesn't care. He just keeps whimpering and thinking about home. The pain in his belly keeps mutating through a cycle of stabbing, aching, throbbing, wrenching, burning and stinging. It feels like the rat got inside him and is still in there gnawing around. It's slavering around his bowels, nosing up his throat, skittering helter-skelter through his ventricles, scampering pell-mell up his spine and nesting in his cerebellum. Stricken with this, gangrene would be a godsend.

It's barely dawn when he gathers up his blanket and stuffs it into his duffel bag along with a lot of dirt. One elbow pressed low over his rat wound, he stumbles toward the highway. Corn leaves slice at his muddy, bloody face and sprinkle him with dew. His bag rips a swath through the stalks, but Frankenstein couldn't care less. He's going home. Maybe he'll drop by the truck stop to look for his sister's letter, but if it isn't sitting right there where he left it three days ago, *Fuck it.*

He looks like shit on the side of the road. He feels like it, too. If a twister came along like a celestial pooper-scooper and sucked him up off the face of Illinois, he wouldn't blame it a bit. Still, the two cops who come along in a Ford aren't a pooper-scooper he's happy to see. He's standing there by his duffel bag, one hand still out for cars, one in his jacket pocket, pressed to his rat bite. The cop car slows and parks right in front of him, its frantic red-white-and-blue lights flashing like something eager to kill him. When the doors open, he knows he's about to meet the Wilmington police. How bad can Wilmington police be? The last time small-town cops picked him up, they gave him a ride to city limits. They were pretty cheerful about writing him out a summons which they said he wouldn't have to pay until next time he visited town, which they sincerely hoped would be never. Frankenstein wrote a little letter to his sister on the back of that ticket. If he ever needs to go back to wherever the hell it was, the ticket's at his sister's.

Two Wilmington cops get out and saunter toward him. One swings a nightstick just the way cops do in old movies. The other has a hand casually hooked over the gun in his holster while his other hand rather awkwardly tries to tuck in his shirt. Both men are smiling a little, chewing gum with their back teeth and wearing sunglasses. The one with the nightstick has lips as thin as blades of grass. The other seems to have twice his share of lip. Frankenstein wonders how they might have worked that out. Thin Lips gives a tight little nod and says, "Morning," but Frankenstein can't get a word through his teeth. If he could, it would just be "Yes."

"Could we see some ID, please?"

Frankenstein's been through this before. He lost his ID a long time ago. He's never figured out where to get another one. Until he does, he loves saying, "I'm sorry. I don't have any identification."

Thin Lips smiles in a way that would almost look shy if didn't carry such undertones of nastiness. "None at all?" he asks.

"'fraid not. I lost my wallet in Utah."

"Well you're a long way from Utah, son."

Frankenstein doesn't like the tone of that, especially from somebody no older than his sister. He knows he's a long way from Utah. He's a long way from everywhere. He's in the middle of Illinois. He thinks he's bleeding, too. Either that or sweating up a trickle. He says, "Yes, sir."

"Well then why don't you just tell us your name?"

"Stein," he says, standing on constitutional principle. "Frank Stein." He hopes they ask for a middle initial, too. He hates this cop stuff. They always ask his name, but it never seems to matter what it is. He thinks he might still have the tattered wad of a traffic ticket from California somewhere in his duffel bag. He thinks it might even say Frank N. Stein on it. They might take it as an ersatz ID, but it isn't the best identification document for a situation like this.

Fat Lips smiles with half his mouth and draws a leather-covered notebook from a little holster. "Cute," he says. "What have you got for an address?"

"None."

"Oh, really?" He chuckles a few bubbles of breath. "Free as a bird, are we?"

"I'm kind of between addresses at the moment. I hope there's not a problem with that."

"Actually, Frank," says Thin Lips, his eyebrows humping up over his sunglasses as if for a peek, "we have a problem with where you were last night."

Frankenstein can't help but turn his head for a quick look at the cornfield. It's a wreck from the hailstorm. Why does he feel he's going to get blamed for it? He's not sure he should confess sleeping on what was undoubtedly private property, but that leaves him with little to say. He's not sure if they already know where he slept or if they think he was somewhere else. He remains silent.

Fat Lips says, "You holding something there in your pocket, Frank?"

He doesn't have a chance to say he's got a nasty little rat bite in there. Before his knuckles come to daylight, Thin Lips's nightstick jabs out as if to pin the pocket shut. It *really* hurts. Blue-white orbs burst in Frankenstein's eyeballs again. Of its own volition, his hand jerks out of the pocket, grabs the stick and pulls it off his wound. Before he lets go, before his vision returns, one cop or the other swings a foot out to kick him hard behind the knee. His kneecap explodes with black-red blood and pink lightning, and the lower half of his leg topples end over end into the corn field, or so it feels as he crumples toward the asphalt. Before he finishes that long journey down, the nightstick swings into his groin, knocking at least one testicle clear up to his throat. Before he can open his eyes, Fat Lips straddles him, pulls his head back by the hair and pokes the barrel of his gun up into the soft underbelly of Frankenstein's jaw. Thin Lips has a gun drawn, too. He grips it in both hands, pointing it directly at Frankenstein's eyes. His holds a manly stance, his pelvis thrust forward as if that has something to do with the situation. He hollers, "Freeze!"

Frankenstein's frozen, all right. He can't even inhale. To his own surprise, philosophical reflection, like bliss before death, overrides his pain and fear. Still, he isn't thinking exactly straight. Looking up into the dark barrel of Thin Lips's gun, he thinks, *So this is rape.* Then he wonders what might keep these men from killing him. They certainly could. They're clearly up to the task, and they obviously aren't here to issue a summons for hitchhiking. *The law,* he thinks. *They won't kill me because they're afraid of the law.* That's all that stands between him and what these men want to do. But of course the man who's sitting on him and pushing a semi-automatic into his neck is an agent of that law, and so is his friend with the pelvis. Both of them are behaving more like cops—

TV cops—than any cops he's ever dealt with. The one on his chest smells a lot like sweat, fart, chewing gum and whiskey. *Things are going to get worse before they get better.* He doesn't need tarot to figure this one out.

- Chapter Eleven -
Frankenstein's Guttersnipe

These jolly cops share an inside joke. With Frankenstein in the back of their cruiser, cuffed and lying there like very dirty laundry, they're free to giggle in the front. They drive along in the silence of men who have been awake all night, but every few minutes their mirth breaks out. It starts as a suppressed chuckle, but as their breath runs low, it turns to an inward gasping followed by a spasmodic guffaw. It's infectious. Frankenstein, curled up on the seat, hands painfully behind him, is crying, but he gets a little urge to laugh along with his captors. The urge only makes him cry more. He tries to do it quietly. They're laughing at him, he's sure, and they'll laugh even more if they hear him whine.

They're about one-quarter crocked—under control but feeling fine. Frankenstein wonders how they can get away with such a thing. Surely the police are public enough that someone would notice and render them some consequences. He supposes that might happen. Until then, he's under arrest. Or at least he hopes he is. They haven't read him his rights or even told him what he did. They haven't even asked him for a real name. They haven't blown the siren, and he suspects they aren't using their flashing lights. Maybe they don't think he's worth it; maybe they're on their way to an isolated spot for a little fun and games. By the time they get caught, if they ever do, it'll be too late for Frankenstein. He'll be in the bottom of an old quarry, weighted down by twenty-odd slugs of lead, listed as disappeared, last reported in Utah.

The only slightly comfortable position he can find is on his knees on the floor of the car, his head and shoulders on the seat. He feels helpless and pathetic in this position, but it gives him a certain sense of solidarity. How many millions of prisoners have held this position, waiting for the verdict, the truncheon, the guillotine, the bullet in the back of the head? And of course that's just what they got. Frankenstein doesn't know what he's going to get. The best he can hope for is something soft to wipe his nose on. He thinks about his duffel bag in the trunk of the car. He feels sorry for it, as he would a pet. He imagines it shivering with fear. He tries to remember if he's got a plastic bag in there.

When they stop, he doesn't even get up to look out the window. When they open the back door, he doesn't lift his head. When they say, "Come on, fella," he doesn't move. When they grab him by the armpits and haul him out the door, he barely opens his eyes. He's got snot dangling from his chin. It seems to be in his mouth, too. It feels all gummy and wet. He surrenders himself to all this. If they want to kill him, it's OK. They'd be doing him a favor.

But all they do is guide him across the dirt parking lot and through the back door of a little police station. It's in a little downtown area, between a diner and a hardware store. It reminds him of the dog kennel he used to clean—same dustiness, same heavy steel door, same concrete floors.

And the pens aren't much better. People get steel bars instead of chain-link fencing. They get a stainless steel cot on the wall instead of a stainless steel bowl on the floor. The place smells of urine rather than dog doo. Dogs, as he recalls, get a little flap door through which they can go outside. People don't.

Trusting cops that they are, semi-inebriated and blustery with confidence, they remove Frankenstein's handcuffs at the door to the cell block. They tell him to go on down and pick out a nice cell for himself and close the door behind him. One of them waits while he takes the three or four steps to the cells. One on the right, one on the left. He looks at them both. They're identical. Neither is any less a jail cell than the other. Frankenstein looks back at the door to the cell block, if indeed that's what this stupid little two-holer is called. The cop's still standing there, though he's paying more attention to this buddy than to his prisoner. They're still giggling about their little secret. So when Frankenstein steps into his chosen cell, he doesn't close the door, not all the way. What are they going to do? Sue him?

No. In fact, they don't even come close the door. They don't even notice. They go on giggling and snorting for a while. Then Fat Lips takes an absented-minded look, turns away and lets the cell block door thump shut.

Jail isn't *quite* so bad if you can leave your door open a gotch. That's all it takes to make Frankenstein feel a *lot* better. Not real good, but better than real bad. He likes having pulled a fast one, even if not a real fast one. If he feels like it, he can switch cells. He can take a little walk up the aisle and back. He could stand on the lower bar of the door and take a little ride. But these are urges for the future. Right now, he just wants to lie down and cry.

Even without a pad, sheet, blanket or pillow, the steel cot is better than a wet cornfield. His cry is a good long full-bodied sob. His head hurts, his rat bite aches, his testicles throb, and he can barely bend his left knee. His throat is sore from crying and his nose is sore from being wiped with denim and the leatherette seat of a cop car. His stomach's a real mess, a famished maelstrom of bile. He blubbers into his jacket sleeve. He just wanted to go home. He didn't do anything wrong. Why does God hate him so? Should he have kneeled on the road with the Jesus freak? Would that have changed the rat to a Swedish girl, the cops to a string quartet? Even in his anguish he can't pretend to see the power of prayer. It wouldn't have worked. If there's a God, He hates him. If there isn't, well then it's the whole fucking universe.

All of a sudden he stops crying. He's all dried up. He just wants to sleep. An eternal coma would be perfect. For the first time since infancy, he craves his thumb. Rolling over to face the wall, he slowly bends his knees and brings his thumb up. It fits right in, curving perfectly along the roof of his mouth, the knuckle locking nicely behind his front teeth.

FRANKENSTEIN ON THE CUSP OF SOMETHING

Thumbs were meant for sucking. Now he knows. It tastes good, a personal salty-sourness, and the sensation of outward pressure on the skin and thumbnail is a new one. He kind of likes it. This could become a long-term habit, especially if he's going to live in a jail cell. Who's to stop him? His mother? He's not even going to tell her where he is. He can suck his thumb all he wants. He might even keep it up for the rest of his life. It might help the hitchhiking, a nice, clean thumb, white as a bone, wet as a frog, glistening in the sun for all to see.

Frankenstein releases thoughts of the Swedish girl and the string quartet. They seep down the inside of his skull like Novocain. He's read pornographic letters by guys who claim to have been picked up by beautiful sluts, and he supposes it could happen. He has never, however, heard of a string quartet driving up, red-white-and-blue lights flashing while everybody piles out, sets up and plays a little Mozart for the itinerant. Rather than whack his nuts and kick him in the knee, they'd ease him into a recliner, soak his feet in herbal water, and dip his clean thumb in German chocolate. Then they'd play "Eine Kleine Nachtmusik" a couple of times and give him a ride to the nearest truck stop. That would be so much more efficient than throwing a guy in jail. If Frankenstein ever gets elected president, he's going to propose a law that requires all cops to carry and know how to use a musical instrument. The country could use a president like him. He just needs to call a little attention to himself. But here he is, sucking his thumb in a small-town hoosegow.

Apparently they don't serve breakfast in this hoosegow, and Frankenstein wonders if lunch time hasn't passed as well. He'd relish a gruel sandwich. At the same time, he wouldn't mind starving to death. He wonders how long you have to go before the stomach stops gnawing. Maybe a hunger strike would gain him some mileage, though he can't imagine in what direction. Wondering whether chewing gum counts in a hunger strike, he pats down his pockets. The cops have already done this and relieved him of matches and a dollar bill he kept for emergencies, a pencil stub, and a bit of letter, all of which they just tossed toward the cornfield. His twenty or so dollars of disposable cash ended up in Fat Lips's pocket. He still has some coins and...*yes*...two dusty sticks of gum in an inner pocket of his jacket. He unwraps one and slides it onto his tongue. For lack of other possessions, he saves the foil and wrappings for emergencies.

He rolls to his back, rests his head on his hands and chews for a while. Chewing gum is a little more interesting than not chewing gum, but the sugar gives him the energy he needs to get really bored with his little cell and his hard cold cot. He gets up, slowly stretching his knee and the skin around his rat bite until he's standing almost straight. Just because he's not supposed to, he wants to leave his cell. With all due trepidation, he eases his door open and takes a step out. Nothing happens. He takes another step. He remembers the nightstick. He doesn't want to get caught doing this, but for some reason he's doing it anyway. Walking quietly on the outer edges of his feet, he creeps to the big gunmetal door that leads to the outside. He presses his ear to it, hears nothing. He tries the doorknob. It turns—a little…a lot…all the way around, and around again. That's enough for Frankenstein. He creeps back to his cell and pulls the door almost shut. That's when he thinks to check out the latch. The cell door has kind of angled latch that lets a door shut and stay shut. Once it's shut, only a key will open it.

Frankenstein chuckles just a teeny-weeny bit. For nothing more than pointless pleasure, he's going to fuck up his jail cell door. As if merely remembering this trick, he gets the gum foil he just moments ago saved for an emergency. Making it up as he goes, he shreds the foil, then takes his gum from his mouth and mashes the foil into it. With his pinkie he pushes the latch back into the door and crams the dense gum wad into its little hole. The latch stays in but looks kind of shaky. He closes the door *just* enough to keep the latch from popping out but not quite enough for it to connect with its socket. His theory is that once the gum dries, the latch will stay stuck in. Only an actual key would really lock the door. Frankenstein lies back down. His heart pounds very hard but he feels pretty good, at least a wee bit better than before. He's in jail but his door is not locked.

A long, long time after that—after dark, Frankenstein figures—noise comes in the back door from the parking lot. It's a lady screeching. A quick series of thumps and bangs hints at a struggle. The cell block door flies open with a kick. It's Thin Lips hauling in a whore. She's handcuffed but fighting hard and cursing up a storm. She sounds a little drunk and very riled up. Her captor grips her very thin arm in his meaty fist. He puts spin on her struggles, letting her slam herself against one wall, then the other. Somehow he keeps a cigarette in his mouth during this waltzy little operation. Frankenstein leaps up and gently pulls his cell door shut all the way. The latch holds but the door looks locked. With a final pirouette, Thin Lips swings his prisoner through the door of the other cell and kicks it shut.

"Bitch," he says, taking his cigarette from his mouth. He looks at Frankenstein in an almost man-to-man way and tilts his head at the girl. "Crackhead," he says. "Have a pleasant evening."

Frankenstein, face to the bars, says, "Hey, do you think you could get me a little something to eat?"

"Fuck you, asshole."

And with that, he's out the door. And within half a minute, he's back. This time he's got a toddler, a skinny little girl in pink shorts. He just opens the door and swings the girl in by one arm. The girl's crying and clawing at the hand that holds her, struggling like an animal caught by the tail. When her little teeth nip into Thin Lips's wrist, he shakes her onto the concrete floor. "Mommy's down there, ya little shit," he says, and he's gone before the door swings shut.

Mommy's still screeching and swearing and slamming her walls. She grabs her bars with both hands and with her whole body yanks and shoves at them. It looks like aerobic exercise except that between screeches she sounds like she's being electrocuted.

Frankenstein can't tell what race she is. Bathed and primped, she might look white. Left out in the sun, she might look a light shade of black. She looks like she might have a little Hispanic in her, too, but she could be Ukrainian for all he knows. Her hair's short and matted in something like dreadlocks. Her sunken cheeks and bone-thin legs imply a life of cocaine, and her cut-offs and tie-dye T-shirt imply a dirty desperation The little girl picking herself up off the concrete floor hints at the product of it all. She's whining loudly but not in the tone of a kid who's terrified or feeling the pain of bare knees scraped on concrete. It's just a whine of utter misery, maybe of a kid who needs sleep, maybe of a kid who's had one too many of life's rat bites.

She doesn't go to her mother. She gets up and toddles hard to the door. She smacks it five or six times, as if mad at it, then stretches for the knob, then puts the top of her head to the door and whines with frustration. She doesn't seem to notice her mother screaming and huffing and yanking at her bars.

Frankenstein, afraid to open his door until he's sure Thin Lips won't be coming in, says, "Pssst, hey, little girl." He reaches through the bars and snaps his fingers as if calling the attention of a cat. "Little girl, little girl."

The little girl doesn't hear, and her mother makes no notice of him. Frankenstein claps his hands and whistles. "Little girl, hey!"

This time she notices. With a hard sniffle, she sucks in her whine. Frankenstein says, "Come here." He squats down and puts his arms through the bars at a lower level. "Come here, kid. Come sit with me." He shows her the palms of his hands.

The girl looks at him with wavering eyes. They're dark but glistening with tears. She says, "*No*," in a tone of protest, and her little head shakes with vigorous insistence.

"It's OK," Frankenstein coos. "I won't hurt you. Come over here so Mommy can see you." He wiggles his fingers a bit, imitating bait.

But Mommy can't see much of anything. She doesn't seem aware of Frankenstein or her daughter. She's a volcano of anger, cursing with immense energy, still battling with her walls and bars as if by desire and necessity she might rip them open.

Frankenstein hollers, "Hey, lady! Stop it, wouldja? You're scaring the kid!"

At least he gets her attention. Still heaving at her bars, she screams, "Fuck you! Fuck you! Fuck you! Fuck you! Fuck you! Fuck you! Fuck you! Fuck you!"

He shows her the palms of his hands and from his lowly squat tries to look harmless, innocent and bereaved. It does no good. She doesn't stop. *Fuck you* is all she's got to say, all the words she has. Like the bark of a dog, they're laden with unarticulated meaning, two syllables speaking volumes.

The little girl goes into a hard whine and stamps her feet in a standstill jog. She's wearing pink sandals. She doesn't know where she is or what to do about it; she just knows she hates it. She hates it but has no idea what else there is. Frankenstein understands her completely. Pleading this time, stretching his fingers toward her, he says, "Little girl, come here. Please. It's OK. I'm your friend. Come here."

She pouts out her lower lip to think about it. The pout verges on both hatred and hope. When Frankenstein says "Please," again, it isn't for her as much as for himself. He doesn't want this little girl to hate him. She probably hates everybody else in the world. He can imagine the kinds of men she's known. He doesn't want her to hate him the same way. "*Please*," he says. "It's OK," but the pout breaks into a sneer as the little girl stamps her foot and says, "*No*."

Frankenstein can't take it. He can't stand to see the poor little thing out there alone, her mother berserk, no one to touch her or help her. With both hands he opens the door of his cell. The little girl clutches her forearms to the center of her chest, screams, "*No! No!*" and inches backward.

When Mommy sees his cell door open, she screams, "You keep away from her, motherfucker! Motherfucker! Motherfucker! Fucking motherfucker!" She shakes at her bars like a crazed ape and keeps screaming.

With a calming gesture, Frankenstein says, "Shhhh, be cool. I'm not going to hurt her. Little girl..." He reaches out. The girl backs up. Frankenstein inches forward. He can't be playing games out here. He keeps saying, "It's OK, it's OK," as he creeps forward. When he reaches her, she just scrunches her eyes shut as if to squeeze him from existence. He takes her by the shoulders, lifts her to his chest, puts one arm under her and wraps the other around her back. He kisses her hair and hugs her as hard as he can. To his surprise, she doesn't resist. She's as limp as someone asleep. She smells of dirty laundry, maybe a little urine. Her mother keeps hollering motherfucker, motherfucker, motherfucker. Frankenstein touches the girl's cheek with a soft, dry kiss and strokes her hair. He whispers, "It's OK, it's OK," and gently twists himself to the left and right, giving her a little ride. "It's going to be OK."

But OK's the last thing it's going to be. The girl has scabs on her face and a broad scrape across one eye. He can feel more scabs or scars on her bony little shoulder blades. A thought like an evil cloud with tentacles looms into his mind. This girl went limp when he picked her up because men have been fucking her. Once he had her, she just turned herself off. She's been beaten and abused, fucked this way and that, no doubt continuing a family tradition passed down from her forebears. Her mother is screeching inane vulgarities, and Wilmington's finest have dumped her on the floor and called her a little shit. Three years old and she's in jail. OK is the last thing this girl's going to be.

    Except she's sitting on Frankenstein's arm, leaning on his chest. She's flaccid and warm. Her little pink sandals are dangling on her feet, bouncing weakly against his waist as she rides his gently jouncing arm. He hums a non-song into her scalp, maybe the same one that yesterday's little girl hummed to him before she threw up in his pocket. With his vast hand, he pats the full breadth of her back. She sounds a little hollow. When he holds his hand against her, he can feel her tiny heart kthump, kthump, kthumping. She isn't a little shit. She's Frankenstein's little girl, his thirty-pound ragamuffin doozy blip. She is indeed going to be OK. No one will ever hurt her again, and nothing else bad will happen to her, not as long as Frankenstein's alive.

- Chapter Twelve -
Frankenstein's Little Lam

In a technical sense, Frankenstein has broken out of jail. His cell's over there and he's not in it. He feels pretty good about this, a little bit cool. It's the kind of half-true stuff that makes up life's great unwritten curricula vitae. Someday he'll casually mention it at a party. He'll swirl his martini and tell some eager-eyed young thing, "Oh, I know about busting out of the joint, all right. I think it was out in Illinois somewhere…."

On the other hand, he has a long way to go before he's bait for the bloodhounds. He isn't in, but he's far from out. He's out enough to qualify for a beating but too in to hitch a ride to somewhere else. And he's got this little girl sitting on his arm, draped over his chest, maybe sleeping, maybe only making believe. There's no going back into the cell because he'd have to leave her out in the cold. He could no more peel away her warmth than he could rip out his heart. He could not stand to hear her cry. Asleep on his shoulder, she snuffles with each exhalation. That's the sound he wants to hear.

So there's no going back to the cell because love is love, and there's no going out because jail is jail. Frankenstein's stuck in purgatory.

He considers a compromise: he'll go into the cell and leave her on the outside, but he'll put his arm through the bars so he can hold her. But that wouldn't work for long. Sooner or later the cops will come back and take her away from him. They'll drag their little shit out the door and dispose of her. She'll end up with Ms. Crackhead's ex-boyfriend or going through an archipelago of foster homes that do it for the money until she finally ends up in the dim, sticky hovel of somebody who does it for the fun.

Frankenstein can't think of a way out. He's just outside his cell door, patting the girl on the back, rocking his body like a cradle, hoping that if someone comes to the door at the end of the cell block he'll have time to put the girl down and slip into his cell.

Maybe the situation will resolve itself. Situations tend to, at least for him. No matter how long he's stuck on the side of the road, a ride comes along. No matter how boring, drunk or obnoxious the driver, sooner or later he lets Frankenstein out. Rain never falls forever. Illness evaporates. Food always comes along before death by starvation. Most of life, for Frankenstein, is a matter of waiting for things to resolve themselves.

But this guttersnipe situation isn't going to go away. Oh, he supposes it *could*. The police could resolve it for him. They could walk right in, throw him back in his cell, punch him in the rat bite just to teach him a lesson, and remove the girl from under his wing. He'd never see her again. Maybe he'd spend the rest of his life crying, but the problem would be resolved.

The little girl's mother has resolved her personal situation in much this same way. She is crying. Still holding the bars of her cell, she has sunk to a deep squat. Her head dangles between her arms. Frankenstein has never heard anyone cry quite like this. It's an almost mechanical boo-hoo-hoo. It's the final stage of something, the last of a dying weep. When she's run out of boo-hoo-hoos, she'll ride the last of the endorphins into a stupor of despair. Frankenstein's been that route. He knows she'll survive. She'll have to do a few years in prison, or she'll go back to doing what she used to do, whatever it was; maybe with a daughter, maybe without. Whatever her fate, she'll survive, even if she has to die to do it.

The right thing to do at this particular moment seems to be to go sit outside Mommy's cell and see what she's got to say. Grunting like an old man, holding a cell bar with one hand, balancing his girl on his arm, he gets his sore knee out from under him, folds a crease along his rat bite, and lowers himself to the floor. *Ahhhhhh.* The girl keeps snoozing, as limp against his shoulder as an understuffed pillow.

He has sat in a sour puddle of alcohol fumes, a low cloud of acrid leftover smoke. He reaches into the cell and lays a hand on the woman's thin forearm. She doesn't look up, but her boo-hoo-hoo softens to a ragged whine. Frankenstein strokes her arm between the wrist and elbow and says, "Hey, lady."

She doesn't look up. He can't see her eyes, just the mop of her limp dreadlocks as she cries at the floor. "Lady," he says as kindly as he can, "it's not going to get any worse. Maybe everything's going to turn around right here. Hey, look at your little girl. She's asleep. Aren't you glad? She's off in never-never land. Must be pretty good, huh?"

He thinks he can feel little scars on the woman's forearm. Flea bites? Needle marks? Suicide attempts? He wonders if he can catch a disease, touching her like this. He thinks maybe her skin's a little yellow. Maybe he feels a little fever. He retracts his fingers a little, lets just his knuckles rest on a place that looks a little less infected, near the back of her wrist. Poor thing, he thinks. He can't resist reaching in further to put the back of his hand against her cheek, to check for fever, but as soon as he touches her, she shakes him away like a fly. Frankenstein takes his hand back, cups it around the back of the little girl's head.

"You want me to get her out of here?" he asks. Of course there's no answer. He keeps talking, to himself more than to her. "I mean hypothetically. If I could. Suppose I could walk on out of here with her. Would you want me to?"

That just gets her crying hard again—maybe that, maybe the lack of narcotic, maybe just the rotten way life is. Bawling, she rolls away from the door and pulls herself into a fetal curl. Now she's *really* miserable. Frankenstein hasn't helped a bit, him and his hypothesis.

One thing's for sure: it's getting mighty hungry in there. He hasn't eaten since the day before, and not much then. He bets the little girl is hungry, too. He gets up. He figures what the hell. He stalks to the end of the cell block and tries the door. The door knob goes round and round. But when he pulls on it, glory be, the door opens.

Now it's really time for a decision. He can actually walk out of this place. Nothing hypothetical about it. He looks to the left. He looks to the right. The cops are to the left, beyond a short corridor. He hears a short squawk from a two-way radio. He smells a cigarette burning, a metallic odor of old radiators, and an underlying reek of coffee warmed to sludge. To his right, just three steps away, is the door to the parking lot out back, the door through which he came into this place.

Frankenstein backs up a bit, softly closes the door. His snuffling guttersnipe is truly asleep, but one of her little hands has risen to hold his biceps. He has never felt a lighter, softer, weaker touch. If a butterfly melted onto him, it could be her hand. He wants very much to feed her, to make her hair smell of rainwater, to see her skip rope while she sings nonsense that rhymes.

First, food. He's not going to break out of jail and make a getaway. He's going to walk out the back door and go over to the diner and sit this girl in a booth and feed her some breakfast. Protein, he thinks, already planning the menu. This girl needs scrambled eggs. Bacon. Orange juice. Chocolate milk. If she's still hungry, he'll introduce her to oatmeal with a puddle of butter in the middle and honey drizzled around like the petals of a flower. That's what he's going to tell the judge when he gets caught. He's going to sound like the Little Engine that Could, and Did, before it got caught and hauled back to the slammer by the scruff of its neck. If that happens, so be it. When his little girl gets ripped from him and thrust into the cruel world of social services, she's going on a full stomach.

So Frankenstein walks on out. Three giant steps and he's standing in a gravel parking lot that smells of motor oil, dust and diner fumes. The diner exhaust fans roars softly at the near side of the parking lot. The sunlight feels very, very good on his face and hands. So much for purgatory. The little girl awakens with a start, leans away from him, looks around, not confused or scared but quite aware that she's in a new place. Frankenstein says, "Hungry?" She just rubs her eyes the way small children do when they wake up. He says, "Let's go eat."

He carries her on over to the diner, steps right onto the sidewalk and goes right up to the front door. It's a heavy wooden-framed screen door just barely high enough for him to walk in without ducking. He ducks anyway. The door slaps shut behind him with a classic, mellow whack.

The diner's a tiny place that might have actually been a railroad car. It must have been built back when everyone was smaller. The little booths could only hold skinny starving people of the Depression era. The stools at the counter were made for the short. The space behind the counter and the grill allows for only the most slender of cooks. An old sticky coil for catching flies hangs over the grill, heavy with the dead and a coat of condensed grease. The exhaust fan roars a little more softly in here. In its backlit blur he can see the gook of a million meals.

It must be the cook banging pots and running water in a back room. A waitress smokes at the end of the counter. She looks at her two new customers, doesn't seem especially happy to see them. She's too old, and maybe too hung-over, to jump right up and give them a cheery hello. She's stringy, even wiry, from a lifetime of lugging platters back and forth, forth and back. Frankenstein nods a greeting and slides his girl into the bench of a booth, then slides himself into the other side. He reaches for a menu. The girl reaches for the salt shaker, a classic little polyhedron with a dented top and grains of rice inside. The rice is as amber as the waitress's teeth. She whacks the salt shaker on the table, rattles it across the bone-white Formica, shakes some salt into the air.

"Careful there, kid," Frankenstein says. "Here comes the bouncer."

As if delivering a brick, the waitress says, "Coffee?"

"Yes, please!" He's surprised to hear himself say it so cheerfully. "And bring my friend some chocolate milk."

"Anything else?" She's looking out the window as she says it.

He hates this kind of waitress. He feels plenty enough like a pain in somebody else's ass without a middle-aged underachiever driving it home like a ten-penny nail. He has requested chocolate milk for a child. She should bow, remain silent, retreat backwards, fetch the sacrament and deliver it with two hands, genuflecting as she comes. Frankenstein says, "I'll have a tall stack, and her royal shortness shall have scrambled eggs, bacon, home fries and toast."

"Kind of toast?" Her voice is a wiry as her blue-veined forearms.

Though he doesn't like her, she touches his gut at a particular place inside. She's asked these questions a hundred thousand times, and she's got at least fifty thousand to go. She's tired of it. The sacredness has worn thin. She knows Frankenstein's going to order raisin toast while he's still deciding whether to give the girl white toast, because nobody argues with it, or whole wheat because it's better for her, or raisin toast because she's such a kid, so cute. Why not? Her mother's a drug addict! For God's sake how bad can raisin toast be? He says, "Let's go for the raisin toast," and the waitress says, "OK."

She's a very bright child, this little girl. Without guidance or demonstration, she has figured out how to untwist and remove the top of the pepper shaker. She has discovered the concept of pouring a solid and the effects of gravity. With an expansion of the hands and a sound like wind through a belfry, she has created a universe of black galaxies across the golden nebulae of Formica.

"Nice *going*," says Frankenstein. "Now who do you think is going to clean that up?"

The girl looks at him with the blank wonderment of a baby who recognizes talk but doesn't understand it. She also looks like she's deciding whether the tone of his voice calls for tears. Tears are the last thing he needs right now. To shift her attention, he holds one finger vertical before her face and says, "*Watch*."

With that finger he draws a clean line through her universe of black stars. She looks at the line and back at Frankenstein, still not sure what's going on. He says, "What's your name?" He wants to write it in the pepper. Then he'll teach her to do it. This is the first step toward Harvard.

But she just keeps looking at him, her eyes at a hypnotic stare, her little mouth open as if for extra oxygen. She's old enough to talk, but so far all Frankenstein's heard her say is "no," back in the jail house. During all that commotion, she didn't even say, "Mommy."

"What's your name?" he asks again, now a little afraid she doesn't know or maybe even doesn't have one, or that she has one and he'll never know it. Surely her mother, no matter how fucked up, no matter how lost in the hot blizzard of dope, knew that she'd had a baby and that the baby needed a name. Someone would have asked her, and she would have said something. No mother ever, ever neglected to give her baby a name, and that name had to have some kind of significance. It was her own mother's name, or the name of a friend, or a happily Irish name or seductively exotic name or just plain name that's just nice and sweet. The name would tell Frankenstein what the mother wanted the girl to be. Knowing that, he would know the mother.

"Como se llama?" he asks, just tossing out sounds for the girl to hear. "Como tally voo? Sprechen zie English?"

But she's already tired of this. She abandons him. She puts a finger to the pepper and draws a tentative line. She makes a noise like a little truck as she plows a thin white trail through her little speckled universe. Frankenstein just watches. His heart sags. He's as far from understanding this little girl as he is from understanding earthworms, hot-shot lawyers or some Chinese kid on the other side of the world. What does he hope to accomplish with her? He doesn't know. He's busted her out of the joint, so he hasn't been a total failure—not yet. If he can pack a little food into her, that's two points for him, zip for the enemy. He thinks a little self-esteem might help, too. He dotes fondly on her artwork in the field of pepper. "That's pretty good," he says. "I like it! What do you call it?"

"Nuffin'."

The girl's a nihilist, he's sure of it. Her first two words were *no* and *nothing*. He's going to tell people that fact someday when she's grown up and running around in black attire, pontificating vaguely on the darkness of art, the black holes of our beliefs and the cruel yawn of the cosmos.

"Looks like the tunnels of an ant farm," Frankenstein notes. The artist doesn't look up. She doesn't know an ant farm from a hole in the ground. But she will. Frankenstein's going to get her an ant farm. The deluxe model, if there is one.

Along comes the coffee and the chocolate milk. The waitress says, "Tcht," at the mess, but the mess is nothing compared to what comes next. Eager for her chocolate milk, the girl reaches fast—too fast for her little hand to turn around to grab it. Her knuckles hit it, and over it goes. A wave of brown milk washes away half her universe, forming a pepper-crusted puddle the shape of South America. The snake of the Amazon cascades into her lap. Peru washes onto Frankenstein. A liquid lizard lurches for cover under the napkin dispenser. Frankenstein leaps up, and the little girl cries, "*Oh no!*"

It's another sacred moment, the blessing of the restaurant table. Frankenstein could kiss the moment. "It's beautiful!" he sings, hoping to stop her from crying. The tears are wavering in her eyes. Her lower lip, as tiny as a baby slug, pouts out and quivers. "You did a good job! Look how it spreads across the table like a…like a…like a what?"

Like spilt milk. The girl tilts her head back and howls like a cheap car alarm.

Frankenstein says, "Shhhhhh!" but the little girl doesn't want to be interrupted. She has spilled her milk and intends to cry about it. When he reaches out to touch her, to get her attention, she throws his arm away, grabs the ketchup bottle and sweeps it spinning into the puddle. It sloshes milk all over the place, over the edges of the table, onto Frankenstein's legs, onto the girl's pink shorts and white shirt, onto the floor.

The waitress stomps over with a scowl and a rag. Frankenstein apologizes like crazy, tells her to let him clean it up, but she seems not to hear. She swipes madly at the table, making it clear that this incident is but a symbol of all that is wrong with the world. She has known it for years, but no one has ever bothered to ask. Frankenstein keeps telling her to leave it for him, he'll be right back. He pulls the girl from the booth, tucks her under his arm like football and heads for the restroom.

There's only one to choose from. The door opens hard and creaky against a powerful spring. It's a tiny place, barely enough room for an old toilet and a grimy sink. The door can't even swing all the way open without hitting the toilet. In a crapper like this a guy could move his bowels and wash his face at the same time, except the greasy little soap dispenser's empty and the only thing resembling paper towels is a warped roll of toilet paper on the back of the toilet.

Holding the door open with his foot, Frankenstein sets the girl on the edge of the sink, wets down the chocolaty part of her shirt and tries to wring it out while she's wearing it. Her crying tapers off to a whimper as she watches this operation. He tries to dry her shirt with a wad of toilet paper, but it disintegrates into clots of fuzz. He has no better luck mopping off the front of his pants. He's dabbing the girl's sticky belly with a cold wet pad of folded toilet paper when he hears the slap of the front door and the short squawk of a two-way radio. By the sound of the man's bark and growl he knows it's Fat Lips. In terror, he pulls the little girl against himself, feels the wetness of her shirt against his bare chest. He doesn't know if he's holding her to protect her or himself. He doesn't know what he's going to do when Fat Lips comes to the door, nightstick drawn, sneering with anger and a need for vengeance. He doesn't know whether to hand over the girl or hide her behind the door or fight back or just run for it. He doesn't know anything. He's afraid of his own fear. It paralyzes him, wraps him as tight as a mummy, and all he has for protection is a three-year-old who smells of chocolate milk and old laundry. She senses his fear; he senses hers. She's as afraid of the man squashing her as she is of the unknown threat from outside.

The radio squawks again. Fat Lips's heavy footsteps pound to the back of the diner and scuff right on by the restroom. All Frankenstein sees of him is his nightstick and his gun as they waddle by. Fat Lips opens a back door for a few seconds, growls "God *damn* it." Frankenstein, smart for a change, swings away from the sink with the girl in his arms and squeezes around behind the door. At the same moment, the door booms open, bams against the toilet, and Fat Lips snarls, "Son of a *bitch*." Frankenstein just stands cowering into the corner, his eyes shut tight, the girl clutched to him so hard she can't breathe. He can see the nightstick coming down on the back of his head, can hear that crack of his skull and feel the explosion of ache. When the door bangs shut, he almost faints with the pain that didn't come down.

As he presses his face to the top of the girl's head, he wants very much to say her name. If she doesn't tell him her name pretty soon, he's going to have to give her one. At the moment, hugging her too hard in the corner of a dingy crapper, he can't think of a name that would in any way fit her. The name her mother gave her probably doesn't fit either, but he very intensely wishes he could repeat it three times into the soft curls of her hair.

Like the last half-hearted grumble of a receding storm, the front door of the diner slaps shut and the wheels of an urgent car spin gravel and chirp onto pavement. Frankenstein opens the restroom door, sets his girl on her feet, and walks her by the hand toward their table. He can't breathe, but he figures breath can wait until he's passed the waitress and resumed the appearance of a normal life. But before he's halfway, she says from behind the counter, "Just a minute, there."

He pretends not to hear, as if that might wipe away the question and all it means. He just slides his girl into the booth and swings himself into the bench on his side. He looks out the window as a blessed minute passes. He doesn't turn around until she says, from behind the counter, "I think you'd better take these to go." She's holding two Styrofoam containers. As if carried by a dream, he and his little girl are transported to the counter and the waitress and the containers of food. Somehow the waitress drags his eyes off the containers and up to her own eyes. He sees a wateriness, maybe in her eyes, maybe in his, maybe in the air. He takes the food with two hands and can't say a word without choking up. "Don't let the bastard catch you," she says. "I mean it." Frankenstein can only shake his head, and only a little. "Go out the back door," the woman says, tilting her head toward it. "Stay off the roads."

Frankenstein can't help but set the containers onto the counter and reach over to take the woman's face in both hands. He leans way over and presses a kiss to the wrinkled corner of her lips. The wateriness is definitely in his own eyes, and now there's some on her cheek. She has Frankenstein by the back of the head, almost clinging to it. With a wiry squeak she whispers, "Send us a postcard, would you? From wherever?"

- Chapter Thirteen -
A While in a Willow

What a nice waitress. She has packed up the breakfasts that Frankenstein ordered and tossed in enough packets of fake maple syrup, fake honey, fake butter and fake jelly to last for many fake breakfasts to come. He knows why so much of it. It's energy, enough fructose to power two fugitives from Illinois to the Rio Grande. It's something an inveterate mother would know. She also tossed in a nice little picture of Alexander Hamilton. How could she have done all this so fast? How could she have known what he needed and had it ready to go within seconds after Fat Lips left the diner? A quarter century of diner service hadn't been wasted on her. She'd learned a little something. Some people are street-smart. Some are diner-smart. Anyone working next door to the Wilmington police department was probably used to prisoners coming in for a quick bite. They probably broke out of the place two or three times a week. If they all ran out the back door of the diner and kept off the roads, they probably ended up right where Frankenstein and his little girl are, under a cavernous willow at the far end of a cornfield, down in a bit of a dell still damp from the storm of the day before. That's all that scares him at the moment, that someone has done this before.

The sunlight trickles through the leaves of the willow in a flickering summery blend of yellow and green. The leaves pull cool air from the earth. In the circumference of brush, cicadas whine with the heat. Some kind of bird tweedly-tweets like an airhead explaining an enigma. Frankenstein sat in such a place at some time in his deep youth, he's sure. The place is redolent of freedom and the security of solitude. The earth and air smell the same as they did back then. Maybe that same bird was sitting nearby, giving the same explanation.

The pancakes are gummy but good. They taste a little like the United States Treasury building, circa 1910, but it's nothing a little make-believe syrup and grapish jellyoid can't hide. The sweetness hits his cavities like cattle prods, but he's sure glad to have it.

He's sorry he poured syrup on his protégé's scrambled eggs. It had seemed a good idea at the time, energy over protein, but now she's all sticky. Unlike him, she was unable to use a bent willow twig as an eating utensil. She just fingered the eggs into her face. The syrup collected a mask of food particles and dirt all the way up to her eyebrows. It looks like a little mask of Greek tragedy.

"Alexander Hamilton," Frankenstein says, showing her their entire stock of legal tender. "He got shot in a duel. He started the federal reserve or something. Not in that order. Looks like Mozart in a stiff wind. And that's about all I can tell you about him."

He's not proud of his ignorance in this area, hadn't even thought about it until just now. He knows just four facts about a guy important enough to have his picture on one of Frankenstein's favorite notes. Yet in four sentences, he has depleted his entire body of knowledge on a great American, and here's this little girl looking like she wants to know more.

"Ever seen the hitchhiker on the back?" he says, flipping the bill over. "Right over there on the side of the building. On the sidewalk. See him? He's…hey…he's gone. Somebody must have picked him up!"

The little girl looks at him like some kind of an idiot. "You know what a hitchhiker is?" he asks. She just keeps looking. "You have to stick your thumb out like this…" He forms a fist with his thumb sticking out and tilts it at the right angle. "Let me see you do it."

She does it. It's a little awkward for her, and her thumb isn't much, just a thin little inch coated with dirt stuck to syrup. "You're going to be good at this," says Frankenstein. "Nobody's going to drive past a little girl with her little thumb stuck out. Too bad we have to stay off the roads."

Roads or no roads, the girl needs her thumb cleaned. Face, too. If anybody sees her like this, it'll be a reflection on him—as if he himself weren't disgusting enough to be rescued by a squad of emergency mothers. If they get arrested again, he's going to hide his face behind his hat, just like the Mafiosi on TV—except he hasn't got a hat.

The closest thing to water in this leafy hideout is the dew on some broad leaves of skunk cabbage. Frankenstein picks one, carefully balances the moisture on the upper side, moves fast to press the leaf to the girl's face. She recoils but he gets most of her face wet enough to wipe it clean with his jacket. He does the same for himself. It's the first time he's washed his face since well before he waded into that cornfield, the one with the rat. He feels somewhat better despite the smell of skunk cabbage and a disgusting new smudge on his jacket.

He checks his rat bite. It's as ugly as only a rat bite can be. The bite tore up a flap of skin that looks like maybe it could be stitched back into place—either that or snipped off before it turns gangrenous. The wound isn't bleeding, but it looks like it could if it wanted to. It hurts just to look at it, the jagged little rip in the blue-gray pool of a bruise. Frankenstein wonders about gangrene. He knows less about that than he does about Alexander Hamilton. He knows it happens and that the cure is amputation. Then there's rabies. The last he heard, back in the fifth grade or so, the cure was umpteen injections into the belly with a needle six inches long. Tetanus maybe he won't get. He's pretty sure he's been vaccinated, though that, too, might have been back in the fifth grade. Maybe he needs a booster or something. His mother would know. He thinks maybe he'll give her a call if he comes across a pay phone not too near a road. Somehow he'll have to explain why he needs to know. Maybe he'll tell her it's for a job application. Or an adoption agency.

As if an adoption agency would even look at a guy who's foaming at the mouth and needs to have his abdomen amputated, a guy crusted with dirt and smelling of skunk cabbage, no known address, assets just barely in the double digits, with his own adoptee, a little girl for whom he will soon need a very good lie.

Though in the heart of pleasantness, under this upwafting willow, Frankenstein senses doom encroaching. He has leaped into the realm of disaster. He cannot possibly succeed in the high crime of abduction. The punishment is life, the capture inevitable. He will not get far. Heading for the state border only ups the stakes to the purview of the FBI. Can Frankenstein outfox the FBI? He cannot. He knows this. But his little girl is ruminating scrambled eggs. She is cleaner than she was when he found her. She is not crying. To the contrary, she is mumbling with a certain cheerfulness, as if she has a tale to tell or a song to sing but no words for either. Either that or she has words only of her own making. They satisfy her need to speak. Frankenstein says, "Why don't we just tell them *you* kidnapped *me*. You're a *kid*, right?"

She looks at him, which is all he wanted. He wanted her to hear his words. Somewhere he heard that this is good for a kid. She can't understand the words, he figures, but she can sense the tone. She stops chewing, looks into his eyes for a second, then returns to her eggs.

"I bet you know all about cops," he says. "I figure we're better off without them. I say we go cross-country to Baltimore. You want to? You and me. We walk all the way. We get there and then we figure out what to do. How's that sound?"

She says something of indecipherable urgency, a little squeak of a bark, something that calls for a lip-smack of eggs, something not quite angry, not quite friendly, not quite having anything to do with Frankenstein and definitely having nothing to with Baltimore. It was more like a lesson to her eggs, teaching them their place in the world. *Wham: I'm the boss.*

Frankenstein says, "Hey, let's have a little more eating and a little less fooling around." He's surprised to hear himself say it, even more surprised at how easy it was, as if the words had been perched just outside his front teeth like a wad of chewing tobacco. He's also a little sorry for saying it, but he's starting to get antsy. A posse could be closing in on them at this very moment. A farmer's wife could be reporting suspicious characters who meet the description she heard on the radio. Somebody might be gearing up the bloodhounds. The Wilmington SWAT team might be boarding a helicopter, cocking their weapons, pulling on their death masks, sharpening the glints of their eyes while Frankenstein waits for a little girl to finish playing with her food.

So he sets himself up at the trunk of the tree, leans back against it, lifts the girl and positions her in his lap. Once again he knows exactly what to do. He loads his twig fork with scrambled egg and says, "Here comes the little airplane!" He even makes the little flying airplane noise as it swoops in to deliver its payload into her little hanger. She grins with contentment, squeezing yellow egg through the gaps between her teeth.

"Here comes another one! Chew! Chew! Chew! Rrrrrrrrr-yyyyyeow!"

Frankenstein botches the last landing as his midriff contracts against the frigid blade of a bayonet in the kidney, the blunt invasion of a bullet, the steely incisors of a rat, fangs of a snake, the dead-bone finger of the law. In a blue flash of fear, he invokes the name of Jesus with a wicked curse and arches away, dumping the girl to the ground, losing a precious blob of egg. Tears shoot to his eyes so fast he can't even see who or what stabbed him. It's still there, though, around behind him, low, positioning to strike again, circling around the back of the tree, scampering, yes, scampering, it's something that stabs and scampers. The little girl shrieks with fear, clings to Frankenstein's leg and backs off as fast as he does, around the tree backward until he shakes the brine from his eyes and sees that it's a dog, a just plain gray dog more scared than he or the girl. It's cowering away from them as fast as they're cowering away from it. Its bony gray tail twitches at the end like a rattlesnake's and its head presses sideways to the ground, cringing into the litter of willow leaves. One rear leg folds away to expose its belly and row of black teats. *Kick me*, it says. *Kill me. Gut me. Eat me. I am but a worm in the path of your merciful wrath.*

It's a miserable, dusty, greasy, scabies-scarred, tick-laden, lump-ribbed mutt of the absolutely lowest common denominator, a patch of ragged fur the color of an overcast sky. And it's got tuberculosis or something. It keeps coughing and choking and hawking at globs of death that just won't come out.

Frankenstein holds his little girl away as he sizes up the invasion. This dog has not come to attack, but it's not something a person should want to touch. It was her cold and snotty nose that poked Frankenstein at the waist. The sting of the spot has settled into an itch that won't be scratched with anything less than an industrial disinfectant. Frankenstein has an empathetic urge to embrace this pathetic creature and tell her that everything's going to be all right, but who would believe such words from a guy like him? Not even the most gullible, flea-ridden, scum-dog in the world—and here she is, wagging just the tippiest-tippiest tip of her tail in a quiver of guilt and fear. *Kick me. Kill me.*

"Look," he coos to his little girl as she struggles to escape from his arms. "It's a puppy dog! And a *nice* one by the looks of her. I wonder what her name is?"

He doesn't want his little girl to be afraid. That's lesson number one, up there ahead of more eating and less fooling around. But he doesn't want to actually say it. He wants her to figure it out—the only way anybody really learns anything. He wants her to sense that the best thing to do with fear is pat it on the head and give it a name.

"Cleopatra," he says. "Want to bet?" He's tickled with the irony.

Frankenstein sees himself there, groveling in the dirt, living filth, hoping for mercy but expecting a kick. He doesn't need a neon sign to point it out. If it isn't him today, it's him tomorrow. This dog hasn't arrived at random. It could have been a spiffy little Shih Tzu, and it could have come out of the bushes and into the life of someone who owns a couch. But here it is, his own reflection cowering as if to change itself into the lowest kind of dirt. It's a message Frankenstein doesn't want and a dog he doesn't need.

What the girl needs is to see the dog eat from his fingers. Then she will lose her fear. The dog needs it too—the food and the loss of fear. And Frankenstein needs to feed the dog. He needs to help. This will make everybody happy. So with his forefinger he lifts a bit of egg from the ground and extends it toward the dog as if pointing with his finger upside down. The dog's tail twitches faster than ever. Her eyes roll away but her head moves toward him. She coughs, paws at her snout and coughs again. It's a top-of-the-throat cough, a rasping exhalation that can't quite get something up and out.

"Wow, wow, wow," the dog moans. "Ooooo." It grovels forward, chin to the ground, still hawking. The little girl tries to climb out of

Frankenstein's arms, but his elbows pinch her at the waist.

"Here you go, girl," he says to the dog, wiggling his finger. "You can have it. It's for you."

Then the dog does something strange. Just inches from Frankenstein's finger, she opens her mouth wide, rolls over and coughs up a honk. And then he can see it, something in the roof of her mouth—a flat chunk of bone, three fingers wide, wedged between her teeth. She hawks again and probes the bone with her blotchy tongue.

That's him down there on the ground, in desperate need of help. He's going to have to insert his finger into the domain of rabies, tapeworms and bites. He vaguely recalls his mother or a teacher or somebody telling him never to put his hand in a strange dog's mouth, but he has no choice in the matter. It must be done, and no one else will do it. It crosses his mind that he could dispatch the problem with a good kick to the ribs, send it scampering back into the bushes, but he could no sooner do that than he could kick his favorite waitress. Thinking of her and bearing in mind the need to keep the universe in balance, he sends his finger into the hot, damp cave of dog slime and disgust. The bone's really jammed in there, an amazingly tight fit against the roof of the mouth. Frankenstein has to grip the dog's dusty snout to hold it firm. The girl in his arms clings to him as if she might climb inside and get away. The dog gags and involuntarily puts a paw to his wrist, but Frankenstein keeps at it. The bone chunk's slick with spit. He wedges a fingernail under it and then the tip of his finger. It holds fast as the dog struggles to get away, but then it loosens and comes away, out of the mouth and down to the ground, all gooey and glistening.

The dog whines with relief. Her whole body squirms with ineffable joy. She licks Frankenstein's fingers, at first in a gesture of thanks but then with relish. It's the salt content of his personal grime, he can tell.

"See what a good dog?" he says. "She's kissing my fingers."

She's also leaving clean spots on his hand. It may be a swap of grime for dog spit, but he's heard that wounds heal faster if a dog licks them. Dog spit may well prevent cancer, AIDS, scurvy, and atherosclerosis. Frankenstein's going to find out. If he lives to be a hundred and twenty-something and people ask him his secret, he's going to tell them about

Cleopatra. If he dies next week, well, it's his own dumb fault. He can accept that. It's worth the risk—so worth it that yes, he's going to let Cleopatra lick his rat wound, if she will.

Trick one is to get his little girl out of his arms and into the circle of Cleopatra's friendship. The girl is getting tickley-nervous, almost giggling but still afraid. Frankenstein draws the dog toward him, luring her on with his fingers. As she comes within reach, the girl extends her tentative fingers. Frankenstein can see the giggle in her eyes. She pulls her fingers back a bit as Cleopatra's tongue laps at them, but they stay within reach. Soon the tongue is gently swabbing down the girl's knuckles, palm, wrist.

Frankenstein slides the girl to the ground, opens his jacket, and turns his wound toward the dog. "Here, girl," he says, touching the edge of the bruise with his finger. "Easy, girl."

Cleopatra knows what to do. There must be something about an infected rat bite that tempts a dog. Her rough, meaty tongue laps across the wound. Frankenstein inhales sharply, and his retracted belly quivers against the sting. It's a curative pain, he can tell. He suffers it until he has to breathe again. He scratches Cleo behind the ears as he expresses his thanks. The little girl strokes Cleo's back with just the center of the palm of her widely stretched hand. "Eeeeeasy, girl," she says in her little foreign language.

They are the first words she has spoken, and they are an echo of Frankenstein. He strokes her hair with one hand while the other strokes Cleopatra. "Good girl," he says. "Good dog." He feels like crying. He'd go ahead and do it if he weren't a fugitive so far from Baltimore.

It's time to move. In a better world, they could just camp under this willow forever. But this is Wilmington; just about anyplace would be better than here. Frankenstein says, "Come on, Toots," and hoists the girl to his shoulders. She holds his hair. He holds her ankles and the straps of her pink sandals. Cleopatra, panting, wagging, looks up at them. He snaps his fingers and turns toward Baltimore. Cleopatra is his dog. He is Cleopatra's man. She follows as he crouches through the curtain of willow. Toots parts the weeping branches as if they were her hair and laughs as Frankenstein rises into the sunlight.

- Chapter Fourteen -
Holding on Tight

Frankenstein, Toots and Cleopatra are walking to Baltimore. They stay off the roads. They walk through so much shoulder-high corn that the world starts to look oceanic, rippling with Caribbean green and swishing with Sargassian loneliness. As Frankenstein breaststrokes and dog-paddles through the leaves, little Toots, high on his shoulders, rides through the air like the fin of a shark, the figurehead of a ship, a bottle with a note inside. Sometimes she yanks at his hair and says "Giddyup," and her little pink sandals spur him in the upper slats. He wonders where she learned to say giddyup to a horse. Somebody has played horsy with her. She knows exactly how to do it. Maybe her life wasn't as bad as he assumed. Maybe she had an uncle or a neighbor with a sense of kindness. Maybe her mother went through clean periods when she had the time and inclination to trot her daughter up to the corner for a pack of smokes.

A haunting thought returns: He shouldn't be taking her away. Who is he to assume he's rescuing her from something? Maybe her scars just came from her tussle with the Wilmington police, her scabs from normal tumbles and accidents, her original fear of Frankenstein from a child's instinctive aversion to strangers. Maybe her mother was going to sober up in jail and emerge a new and recovered woman. Maybe she'd be doing it for her daughter, the one and only person in the world who mattered to her, a daughter now gone and, unbeknownst to her, headed for Baltimore on the back of a poor pale nag who probably won't make it out of Illinois.

But yes, he will make it. Nothing is going to stop him, and until he has better evidence, he's keeping this girl where he knows she's safe and satisfied. If someone wants to argue about it at some later date, he'll decide what's best for her. He'll make the decision. It feels good to know this. He feels like a real man

Groping through the corn of the sea of Illinois, Frankenstein wonders what the cops and local citizenry are on the lookout for. He wonders if they're working from a description (Caucasian male, five-foot-nine, scrawny, filthy, dumb look on face, eyes the color of good sod), or whether they've tried to describe him to an police sketch artist. The Lips Brothers never took his mug shot or even his fingerprints. They're identifying him with an alias. He doubts either Lips, Fat or Thin, can remember his finer features. They might not even remember the little girl they so ignominiously tossed into the cell block. As for Cleopatra, she's probably on some dog warden's most wanted list but described as nothing more than a "mix."

It isn't easy to walk through wet cornfields. The soggy topsoil sticks to the treads of his sandals, forms massive weights that he can't kick off. The leaves of the corn stalks slice at him, and mile after mile looks exactly the same. Toots falls asleep across the back of his head, but Frankenstein trudges on. He's a bit surprised and tremendously relieved when he breaks out of a field and onto a dirt road that runs north and south. He doesn't care that Baltimore is to the east. He turns left.

And pretty soon they come to a railroad track running more or less east and west. To Frankenstein it looks as good as an interstate. In fact, if a train happens to come along at a dead crawl, he just might jump on. He's always wanted to hop a freight. It's high on his must-do list, right up there riding an iceberg, bathing in the fountain of the Taj Mahal, peeing into an active volcano, and parachuting from a very high altitude. Now he's going to have to do all those things with a kid on his back. He smiles. His little

FRANKENSTEIN ON THE CUSP OF SOMETHING

Toots is going to have a very, very good life if she learns to hold on tight. Lesson One might well be a dawdling eastbound train.

Good question: Would he do it? He doesn't know. He certainly would if he didn't have responsibility on his shoulders. Its heels are kicking him gently in the ribs and humming something that probably doesn't have a song. It's just a repetitious cadence of five hum-bursts—hmm-hmm, hmm-hmm, hmmmmmmm—over and over, a soft wash of the brain as the humdrum scenery slogs by. Would he do it? Would he hop onboard a slow-moving train, Toots on his back and holding on tight? He might. He might not. He wishes he could decide ahead of time, but he knows it's going to have to wait. He hopes the first slow train's a long one because it's going to take him a while to decide.

He limps along in uneven steps. He can't work out a regular pace that applies to railroad ties. He's either mincing along like a geisha or tilting headlong with giant steps beyond his gait. He tries walking on a rail and wonders why he can't—why he *still* can't. He never could. He imagines himself high above Niagara Falls, no safety net, the fate of the entire world...no, the entire *galaxy* depending on his crossing, but that doesn't help. He still falls off—as he has fallen all his life, ever since he was a little boy and wanted to be an Indian. He'd heard how Indians get to work on skyscrapers because they can balance on I-beams. Since then he's been falling off logs and fences, even garden hoses, cracks in sidewalks and lines painted on playground asphalt. He's never gotten any better at it. He's no more like an Indian now than he ever was, except that now he's got the equivalent of cowboys chasing him. On the other hand, he's way ahead of the cowboys, and he's no worse at walking rails than he ever was. He can still go four and a half steps before his hips and arms go into pandemonium and Toots squeals, "Whoooooa!"

This is no way to walk to Baltimore. Frankenstein, pricked with a quick and sudden twinge of guilt, speeds up his pace. It doesn't matter if it's awkward to step on a tie, then gravel, then gravel, then half a tie, then a tie. He has a thousand miles to go. To make things worse, the tracks seem to be veering to the north. He tries to ignore the direction. There's nowhere else to walk anyway. He ignores the rails that taunt him from the left and right. He just watches the gray gravel and black-brown ties blur by as his feet swing into and out of his view. He feels a little like a train, huffing as the ground goes by in a smear. He finds himself whispering, to the cadence of his gait, "I *think* I can, I *think* I can, I *think* I can...."

His freight grows heavier, and soon it begins to whine. She's getting hungry. He wonders how he knows this, by what genetic memory he senses the primal basics of child-rearing. He also feels the first glimmer of desperation. While he himself could lie down and let himself starve—or so he's fond of imagining—he would steal to feed his Toots. He would kill.

Or so he likes to imagine. He can almost see himself in a fight to a finish over a Quarter Pounder with cheese, him against some starving bum who needs it less than he, he the daddy with a kid. Not that he has any idea who or what he's supposed to kill, let alone how. He just supposes he could. He supposes he could kill a squirrel if he could get one to sit still while he mustered up his gumption. But could he kill some poor sap over a bag of potato chips? He doubts it. He knows what he would do. He'd stand there and look at the potato chips until the guy finally tossed him one. Or he'd convince himself that potato chips just weren't for him.

Treading awkwardly from tie to tie, he looks at Cleopatra, who's sniffing out the lead, leaving no whiff uninvestigated but not pausing long for any. She is expendable, he knows. When the time comes to part, he will have to leave her with a pat on the head, a shake of the paw, a tear, an apology, perhaps a quick little kiss to the side of the snout. He will remember her forever, and she will go on to do whatever it is dogs do until the dog catcher gets them or they get run over. Maybe she'll remember the guy who pulled a bone from her palate; maybe she'll just worry about food and, twice a year, sex. And, if she's lucky in love, babies.

Frankenstein's got himself a baby and didn't even have the pleasure of insemination. Again he thinks back to his little girl's mother, this time mulls her over as an object of desire. Hm, yes, maybe, he thinks. Maybe if she were sober, a little intelligent, a bit better kempt, a little meat on her bones, maybe if she smiled at him and said something sweet...*maybe* he'd think about it. If he *had* to. For the kid.

He sure wishes he knew how that woman felt about her daughter being whisked away. Maybe she didn't give a damn. Maybe she gave a great big damn. Maybe she gave a damn but knew someone else should raise her kid. Maybe she thought Frankenstein was a typical jailhouse scuzzball who had nothing but foul intentions for the girl. He certainly looked and smelled the part. If the woman knew his good intentions, she'd surely approve. She'd know the girl could not hope for a better embrace. A horsy ride all the way to Baltimore! Could a kid ask for more?

She could ask for a bathroom. "Uh-oh," isn't enough of a clue. Frankenstein doesn't figure it out until he feels the warmth spread across the back of his neck. That's the end of the horsy ride. He swishes her to the ground and in one fluid movement yanks her shorts down.

"*Squat*," he urges, and he does it to show her how. Down she goes. She performs a perfect little pee smack-dab on the Illinois Central. Her eyes are wide, like those of a girl who has just felt the first twinge of sexual pleasure. Or so it seems to Frankenstein though he has never seen such a thing. He wishes he hadn't thought it. He imagines the scene recreated in court: *And then, your honor, he yanked her pants down and squatted in front of her.* Wouldn't it be a fine time for Thin Lips to show up? Or a train.

Now she's got to walk, at least until they find a place to wash her pants, which now droop almost to her knees. They walk and walk and walk. Sometimes Frankenstein throws her over his shoulder like a flaccid rifle. When one arm gets tired, he shifts her to the other. Pretty soon both arms are quivering with exhaustion, so he throws her over both shoulders like a yoke. Then his kidneys start hurting. He puts her on her own two feet. They walk and walk and walk. They sit on a rail and rest. The steel is hot enough to dry her pants. Then they walk and walk and walk. The cornfield on the right ends abruptly at a road and a field of grass that might be a cow pasture. They walk and walk and soon come to chain-link fence that surrounds a schoolyard. Kids are playing on an area of asphalt behind the school, too far away to notice Frankenstein and Toots. Toots, however, notices them and wants to see. She tugs him down the embankment to the fence, grabs it with her little fingers and pokes her nose through. He does the same. The kids are sure having fun over there, laughing, giggling, chasing each other, kicking a ball around, swinging on swings, assaulting the slide, attending to a project in the sandbox.

Sadness soaks Frankenstein's heart. She seems to know that her business is over there, in the playground with the other kids. She coos something interrogative but unintelligible. She points at the kids with her tiny forefinger.

"School," says Frankenstein, squatting down and pulling Toots to sit on his thigh. "Someday when you're big enough, you can go to school, too." He feels very paternal saying this. Also very stupid. He's glad no one else can hear. It occurs to him that he has finally found someone who won't say, "Yeah, I know," to anything he says, at least not for ten years, by which time maybe he'll have learned something worth knowing.

He knows at least this: In a few minutes, all those kids are going to hear a whistle. They'll sweep across the lawn like fall leaves in the wind, then squeeze into a line. They will be told to be quiet. In a while, hungry, they will shush each other, then proceed to the cafeteria, a magical place that will reside in their little brains for the rest of their lives. They will remember the smell of the fiberglass trays, the resonance of the little plastic bowls of canned food, the doughy cafeteria ladies ladling out glops of nutrition. They will eat in a room awash with glee. They will come away satiated and sticky.

Toots will have this someday. Frankenstein will see to it. She will be happy.

Frankenstein's listening for the trill of the time's-up whistle, so he almost explodes when he gets punched from behind by the honk of a train coming through. It rumbles at them from the direction they just came. It honks again. Frankenstein, kneeling, holds Toots to his chest, both arms around her. Her little hands rest on his forearms, cool against his heat. The massive diesels, two of them, mutter by, shaking the ground, honking yet again. Then come empty coal cars, not quite silent but not loud enough for their size and power. They limp over a gap in the rail, *k-thunk, k-thunk, k-thunk*. They're going just a little too fast for Frankenstein to hop on even if he were alone. There's no choice about it, not this time.

The k-thunking cars hide the sound of children galloping until they have almost reached the chain-link fence. They have come to see the train but they have found a man, a child and a dog.

The train keeps rumbling by, but the kids are looking at the strangers, the hobos, and the hobos are looking at the kids. No one speaks in the rumble and clunk of the train. Frankenstein finds himself wishing he could pass Toots through or over the fence. He would love to thrust her into their embrace. He could almost give her up for that. Almost.

They are a beautiful flock, these children, dressed as colorfully as jungle birds, with faces as different as those of as many different breeds of dog. Each gawks in his or her personal, unselfconscious way. The feeble kid with the runny nose neglects to sniff. The chunky, bully-looking boy has forgotten that he's in charge. The chubby girl has become a quasi-cognizant palm tree. The runt, by chance, has fallen to the fore, frozen like the marble-muscled steed of an Italian fountain. The loudmouth, whoever it is, is mute. The girl with the major schnozola has become eyes the size of radar dishes. The class clown has been rendered a silent philosopher. The valedictorian has been struck dumb.

Thus stood the Indians when Columbus landed. Thus stood the pilgrims when Squanto emerged from the woods and addressed them in English. Thus stood Michael at the burning bush. Thus will stand Earthlings when the first aliens arrive. Thus stand Frankenstein, Toots and a dozen children at a chain-link fence in Illinois.

The rumble and clunk of the train finally passes, fading around a bend to the north. Just as the children emerge from their trance of stupefied curiosity, the jungle-tweet of a whistle ropes them in. It takes them a second to break from the odd vision of a bum and a toddler at the railroad tracks, but then in trained reaction they turn and take off, again like autumn leaves in a wind that has shifted.

Toots calls out in her secret language. Now Frankenstein knows that "Glaydanbleet Nyawayoo," means, "Wait! Come back!" If the kids understand, they ignore it in their quest for lunch

Frankenstein wants to cry out, "Glaydanbleet Nyawayoo," too, but he chokes on it. It swells at the bottom of his throat, tries to punch its way up, all wet and heavy. He swallows it back. It's all he's had to eat since morning.

Toots shakes the chain-link fence and calls to them again, not pleading but demanding. Tears glob out of her eyes, enough to make her cheeks wet from nose to jaw. Frankenstein picks her up, holds her very tight. She twists to look back at the school.

"Oh, my little Toots, my little Toots," he says, his eyes getting salty. "We'll get you in a school We'd find some kids for you. Come on, let's go look for some kids."

So he carries her back up to the train tracks and swings her back up to sit on his neck. Now he walks fast. He swings his elbows high, practically swimming with them. Toots clings to his hair. Wherever he's going, he going to get there fast. Cleopatra notices the shift into high gear. She no longer sniffs things. She trots with dead-mind purpose.

It seems soon that they find themselves passing a residential neighborhood. It begins as a concrete block building the back of which has no apparent purpose beyond the storage of generic junk. They pass a place that might be a mechanic's garage or a junk yard, its backyard cast-offs slowly dissolving in weeds and weather. The next building, he can tell, is a gas station, and the next is some kind of store. They pass a dead house, its back porch succumbing to the pull of vines, and then a nice house, inhabited, and then a series of ranch-styles with yards, lawns, swing sets, barbecue grills, the occasional ankle-deep kiddie pool. The houses are on the other side of a chain-link fence half grown-over with Virginia creeper.

They come to a very inviting house, a house of children. Stray toys and accouterments lie strewn across the shaggy grass of their backyard. Frankenstein counts three bicycles, each a distinctly different size. A sandbox looks as if it has exploded guts of plastic buckets, little shovels, trucks and cars in rust and primary colors, assorted litter and household utensils that would be useful in a world of sand. Somebody abandoned a little fire engine, the kind a kid sits in and pedals. Somebody else left behind a little red wagon. It looks as if some enterprising imperialist army was building a fort of old tires, plastic milk crates and stuff that probably belonged in the basement if not the living room. Somebody left a shirt on the ground, and not recently. Somebody started digging a hole to China and forgot to put the shovel away. Somebody forgot to put the sled away, too. Mommy's got a hundred feet of small- and medium-sized clothes out on a line across the yard. It looks as if Daddy may have started to mow the lawn, off to one side of the house, but something called him away—a crying child, perhaps, or dinner, or lack of gasoline. Maybe he had to take someone to a Little League game or the emergency room. Maybe the grass was just too high and Daddy decided to let it grow till autumn, then burn it off, the way the Indians did. Maybe he jumped into his neighbor's Winnebego and shoved off, never to return. Hence the shaggy lawn.

Frankenstein hatches a good one. He's going over to the house and offer to mow their lawn. For five bucks. While he mows, Toots will get to play in the sandbox, swing on the swings, maybe even pedal around in the little red fire truck. He'll get five bucks and she'll get the suburban experience.

It's easy getting through the fence. The kids, or maybe a couple of bears, have pulled it up from the dirt, unraveled it like an old sweater, and worn a deep trail under the hole. Frankenstein ducks through, followed by Toots and Cleopatra. She heads straight for the swings. Her dog stays with her.

It turns out nobody's home. Frankenstein knocks on front door and back, even goes up on the deck, which extends from a sliding door upstairs. Nobody comes to the door. Now that he thinks about it, the whole neighborhood looks recently abandoned. He wonders if World War III is on the way and everybody but he and Toots is tucked away in their bomb shelters.

But they aren't. They're driving around in their station wagons, maximizing the suburban experience. They'll be back soon. The kids will see Toots dumping sand on her head, and they'll say, "Hey, who's that?" Mom will look askance at Frankenstein and consider dialing 911. Maybe she's already heard about him on TV. Maybe, now that he thinks about it, he ought to scram while he can.

But Toots won't go. She has already swung on two swings and galloped on a horselike contraption. All three of these are still swinging while she's over in the sandbox, filling a bucket and dumping sand on her legs. Frankenstein knows *exactly* what the cool, heavy, moist sand feels like on bare legs. It hasn't been all that long since he did the same thing, almost burying himself less than twenty feet from the shed where his father would suffocate himself. Indeed this nice little family has a shed of similar size a similar distance from the sandbox. Maybe that's where Dad is.

With that useless and unbidden thought, he can't pull Toots from her pleasure. Life is too short and too cruel to curtail the simple pleasures of childhood. Toots, no doubt, has had her share of the pain. If she feels the need to bury her little legs in the sand, let the sand flow.

The scene begs the background sound of a lawn mower and the sweet smell of cut grass. As long as he's going to get caught by this family, he might as well be doing something constructive. He's going to mow their lawn. When the folks get home, he'll be in a strong negotiating position. They'll never suspect he's the guy who broke out of the Wilmington jail. Escaping convicts don't mow lawns. It simply isn't done. It's in the convict's code of honor. When you're on the lam, you stay on the lam. If you need something, you steal it, if at all possible at gun point, ideally leaving a trail of blood. Everybody knows this. The perfect cover, then, is honest labor, loud and out in the open.

This is the boldest, dumbest, most exciting thing Frankenstein's done in a long time, besides busting out of jail. And kidnapping. He goes right on over to the lawn mower, figures right out how to start it, and yanks on the cord twice. The motor only sputters, but it feels *good* to yank on that cord, an effort simultaneously masculine and ordinary. In an intuitive move, he flicks the choke forward and lays one hand on the top of the motor for a moment of Zen. He inhales. He exhales. He gives the cord a medium-slow pull as if extracting three feet of dental floss from the machine. The motor pulls itself up by its own bootstraps, slowly at first but with determination. It sounds to Frankenstein like a case of impacted wet grass. He knows just what to do. He pushes down on the handle so the front wheels rear up, then lets it drop. The mower coughs hard and spits globs of grass as if clearing a weekend's phlegm from its throat.

He checks over his shoulder for Toots, performs a mechanical pirouette and sets off along the border of the lawn, the line where the neighbor's neat, short grass meets Frankenstein's shag. The cut grass shoots out in a visible cloud. Ugly lawn flows into the front of the mower; beautiful lawn issues out the back. He swings around at the end of the lawn and returns along the new frontier. He follows the line of his previous cut with the precision of an artist. Though he's just begun, it already feels like progress. He turns left at the side lawn, where Daddy left off. Within a few steps he stops to move a bicycle over to the cut section. He moves a green bucket, too, and then a decrepit, naked, paraplegic doll which may have been mown over once or twice before. It's just a few more steps to a basketball, but the trip will save him time later. All he has to do is kick it. Only when it rolls to a stop on the cut grass does he notice that he has set the bike, and the bucket and the doll, and now the basketball, in a precise line perfectly parallel to the line of his mow. It looks very organized, very neat. As he mows, *very* neatly now, he walks clear across the lawn to set toys in the row, and then a second row in front of the first, and then a third. They come to look like an audience of aliens from a dozen planets.

He picks up Toots at the sandbox. She rides his shoulders as he mows. When he comes to a toy, he lifts her down, holding her at the waist, hovering her over the target so she can pick it up and hold it as he carries her across the lawn to the ranks of their cohorts.

As he nears the final quarter, a grandma next door steps onto her second-story deck. She's holding a pie in two mittened hands. It's a beautiful sight, an older woman with a hot pie. Frankenstein smiles and waves. The woman smiles back, mostly at Toots, he's sure, but maybe at the whole sight of a lawn care guy with a little girl on his shoulders. The woman sets the pie on the corner of the deck railing. It steams. Terrifically hungry, Frankenstein can smell it, or at least imagine its smell, strawberry-rhubarb. This is the season for it. The smell slices through the background of mown grass. As he imagines the grassy, fibrous stuff of it, his jowls cringe. His gums ooze. He hasn't had a strawberry-rhubarb pie in a long, long time, and Toots has surely never had the pleasure.

And there by the grace of grandma sits one such pie, steaming, classic, perfect beyond the limitations of plain reality. It's more than mere cliché. It's a mythological manifestation, a morality play in which Frankenstein and Toots have been invited to perform. It's not something a person has the option of ignoring. Something divine has set this up, quite likely the same prankster divinity that has escorted him through the events of the last two days and put his empty stomach here, face to face with a pie from the Great Above.

Or the Great Below. Sometimes it's hard to judge these things. What better shape for the devil to take then the gentle aspect of a mother's mother?

And maybe Fat Lips is the Virgin Mary in drag.

Frankenstein mows to the end of the lawn, turns and mows back. He's going to steal that pie. He's supposed to. He's going to complete his lawn, tidy up a few spots that he missed, park the lawn mower, wipe it off so it's cleaner than it was when he found it, and then he's going to walk right over there and grab that pie. Nothing sneaky about it. He's not going to crawl on his belly, and he's not going to run away like a common thief. He's going to walk away, pie in one hand, Toots in the other, across grandma's lawn. He'll slide under the fence with as much dignity as possible and hasten down the railroad tracks like the good hobo he is. And if grandma comes and says, "And just where do you think you're going with the pie, young man?" he's going to blush and go "Aw shucks, ma'am" and tell her how good it looked and how he couldn't resist and how his little sister had never tasted rhubarb pie since her mother got sucked up by a tornado or something, he doesn't know exactly; he'll just play it by ear and see if the woman doesn't end up inviting them in for not only a slice of warm pie but some milk as well, maybe even a touch of hydrogen peroxide on his aching rat bite.

Frankenstein's lawn is mowed. It looks pretty good. The people will always wonder what happened. He likes that. He's going to disappear into the sunset, and they're going to say, "Who was that guy?" Grandma will recount the story a hundred times. The incident—the lawn and the pie—will remain in the neighborhood lore for decades. Every strawberry-rhubarb pie will remind them, and the story will be retold.

He does a pretty calm job of moseying on over to grandma's deck. He reaches way up to edge the pie onto the tips of his fingers. Yipes! It's hot. He lowers it to the ground faster than gravity itself could have done. He licks his fingers and blows on them. Cleopatra leans in for a sniff. Frankenstein shouts, "God *damn*," quietly. Toots says, "Hog-*wham*," not quietly at all. Frankenstein takes this as a sign of intelligence.

He's pretty intelligent himself, he thinks as he solves his problem so quickly, so efficiently. Under the deck there's a little piece of plywood barely a foot long. With the edge of his sandal he nudges the pie onto the board—a perfect little tray.

And off they go, as cool as three cukes just a tad late for lunch, across grandma's lawn, back to the fence. Feeling like a team leader on *Beat the Clock*, he feeds Toots and Cleopatra through, then the pie, them himself.

Just as he rises, he hears grandma come onto the deck, *pissed*. "Hey!" she shouts, as she must, her voice shrill, as sharp and accurate as a throwing knife. "Hey!"

He doesn't listen to the rest, doesn't even look back. He feels guilty about this, yes, but good, too. The woman has lost a pie but gained something to talk about for the rest of her life. Old women need this more than they need pie. She will talk about it with all the bitterness of rhubarb.

Either that or she's firing up the Dobermans and packing her grenade pouch. Frankenstein doesn't care. He has performed flawlessly, and now he must exit.

He feeds Toots pie by the finger as they hurry down the tracks as fast as her little legs will carry her. The pie draws her at an amazing speed, fueling her muscles as well as her desire. The residential stretch disappears behind them, and soon they round a bend to the south and come upon, glory be, a steel bridge, its girders silver-orange in the sun of late afternoon. It spans a stream much too small for such a structure. Somebody got carried away with this bridge. Frankenstein wishes it had been him.

They follow a path down to the stream. It's only a couple of feet deep. He can see the green rocks below the lazy eddies. With his hand he brings water to his mouth, then to Toots's. With his wet palm he wipes the rhubarb stickiness and day of dust from her face. Then they sit to eat. No more finger-helpings for her. She pushes handfuls into her tiny maw. He does the same. It is the best pie he has ever eaten, the best pie in the world. Someday, when he's rich, he will return to the woman that baked it and give her the Rolls Royce she deserves.

But first, a bath. What he's supposed to do, leave this poor girl dirty and in shorts that smell of pee? He knows what kind of trouble he'll get into if he gets caught taking her clothes off. That's what he thinks about as he does it. For the good act of bathing a child, the State of Illinois might well lock him up for the rest of his life. He thinks about this and how good it is to be innocent of any such lascivious intent. He's just a little ashamed of being conscious of the fact.

He picks his naked Toots up by the armpits and wades into the stream. She squeals as he lowers her toward the water, curls her legs up and sucks in her stomach. She laughs like crazy as he drapes her little bottom through the current and makes a noise like a motorboat. When he finally plunges her in, the cold traps her breath in her stomach. Up to her neck in water, she latches, arms and legs, onto the wet denim below his knee. As he pulls water up over her head, she sputters and gasps and finally lets go.

Frankenstein rubs her little shorts and shirt on a rock below the water. Rinsed out and wrung half dry, they at least look cleaner. He lays them on a bush to dry. Then, after looking around real hard twice, he quickly peels off his filthy pants and lowers himself into the water. It's cold but feels as good as the rhubarb pie tasted, as good as a hot bath in a regular tub, as good as a massage, as good as love itself. He sighs from the diaphragm.

While Toots flounders around, he rubs his face and body with handfuls of sandy gravel. He pulls up a nice flat rock covered with stringy algae and scrapes it across his flesh. It seems to remove at least the outer layer of his oily coating. He lies face down in the water, eyes open. The streambed is a beautiful green blur undulating with dull light. He blows bubbles at it and wishes he could stay under there forever. It is so much sweeter than the real Illinois. He's even tempted to try breathing underwater. Who knows, maybe the laws of nature have changed since he last checked. But no, he can't do it, can't quite even want to. He comes up for air.

Frankenstein puts his pants on before they're really dry, then builds a little fire to finish the job. He also just wants to look at fire. He feeds it crooked sticks of driftwood left behind by a flood. It's soothing to see and feel. He rolls a short thick log to place where he can lean back against it. He keeps thinking about what a good job he did on that lawn, imagines the people coming home and wondering *what the*....Toots, exhausted and full of illicit pie, dressed in clothes dried and warmed by the fire, settles back against him. The fire hypnotizes her as the sky turns orange, blue-green, dark blue, black. Little by little, against her own will, she melts into Frankenstein's leg and drifts into a snooze. Her weight against him is unbelievably light and flaccid. He doubts he could wake her even if he tried, but he also feels that if he budged her, she might come apart like an over-cooked chicken.

FRANKENSTEIN ON THE CUSP OF SOMETHING

He feeds the fire without moving his leg. It hypnotizes him, too. It's just a flameless, smokeless molehill of coals that throbs to his own heartbeat. With excruciating care, he maneuvers his jacket under his leg, puts his arm where his leg was, and eases down to curl around little Toots. Now he can hear her purr as she sleeps. It isn't the purr of cat but a gentle sigh with each exhalation. It's the sound of comfort and security, and he likes it very much. He makes the sound himself and likes that, too. He holds her tight, quite the way she held him as he horsied her through the cornfields, the way she'd have to hold on if he ever hopped a train. She's warm against his bare chest. Once she jerks as if jolted with electricity, but she doesn't wake up. Her purr recovers its rhythm. He kisses the top of her frizzy little head, takes one last squint at the embers, and sleeps.

- Chapter Fifteen -
No

Frankenstein and Toots wake up simultaneously, brought to life by the vicious huffing of Cleopatra attacking a flea in the center of her back. Toots wakes up faster than he. A quick snort injects air into her, and she peels herself off his clammy chest. She looks a little surprised, but not upset, to find herself sleeping on the bank of a little river. She rubs her knuckles in her eyes. He takes a lot longer to move. His joints and muscles have seized up in the night. It's hard to raise his chest enough to breathe. Mr. Sandman has dumped cement on his eyelids, and someone else has sprinkled him with the dust of river mud. His rat wound seems to have sealed itself during the night, but at his first full breath, it cracks down the middle. This, he thinks, is a preview of death. It's something to avoid.

Frankenstein pulls river water onto his arms, chest and face. The crust in his eyes comes out in glops. He presses a handful of water to Toots's face, holds it there while she scrunches into his palm. She giggles and chatters her teeth as he runs his wet hands around her neck and throat and back behind her ears. Then he shakes the dirt from his jacket, puts it on, and off they go, up to the tracks and across the steel bridge.

FRANKENSTEIN ON THE CUSP OF SOMETHING

The dawn is sweet, marred only by hunger, tacky skin and a long way to go. Frankenstein keeps his eyes peeled for more grandmothers with hot pies. He'd even settle for a freshly filled Dumpster. He'd steal pellets from a rabbit. Then he thinks of stealing the rabbit. He walks toward the liquid orange sun with that in his mind—somebody's bunny on a spit. He's never eaten rabbit, let alone bunny, but he can smell its golden-brown crust and the smoke of its fat dripping to the embers of a low fire. He could definitely eat a bunny like that. He would suck the marrow from its little bones.

But they pass no rabbit cages, no pies on sills, no apple trees, no place to spend the ten dollars he still has in his pocket. He thinks about the waitress in the Wilmington diner. He wishes she were here with him. He just feels like kissing her, like smelling her hair and feeling her head against his chest. She'd have food for them. She'd know what to do. He misses her.

They walk and walk and walk and walk, stopping now and then but mostly walking. Toots takes to sucking her thumb. Frankenstein rolls a pebble around in his mouth. When they come upon a black birch tree, it's as welcome as a turkey dinner. The twigs taste of toothpaste. Toots doesn't see the joy in it, but Frankenstein chews up the end of a thick twig and uses it to rub plaque from his teeth. He minces the flecks of bark and pokes them back toward his throat.

Frankenstein and Toots face two possibilities: death by starvation or salvation by food. The simplicity of the alternatives comforts Frankenstein and probably Toots, too. Food has always appeared for both of them. They assume it will arrive in time. Everyone assumes that. So a horrifying thought comes to Frankenstein: food will not come in time, and Toots will die under the assumption that a fed belly is an exceptional state. She'll die thinking that she's supposed to.

But no, something will happen. It has to. And it does. The train tracks pass behind a small shopping plaza. The main store is a supermarket. Three tractor trailers are backed up to the loading dock. The breath of refrigerated produce blows out of the supermarket, across the back parking lot, through the chain-link fence and into Frankenstein's face. They are saved. All the food in the world is just a hundred yards away.

They find the inevitable break in the fence and crawl through. Around front, the supermarket, an AmeriMart, has just opened. He's never heard of this kind of supermarket. He wonders if it sprang up during his days on the run. The electric door swings open to a wonderland of florescent light and chilled air. He and Toots are among the first shoppers through the door. Cleopatra knows enough not to walk through doors like that.

Toots gets to sit in little seat at the back of the shopping cart. Frankenstein's only got ten dollars, but boy is he going to get his money's worth. He's going to spend all day in this supermarket. He's going to invest his ten-spot on food that is both delicious and nutritious. He's going to check each and every unit price. He's going to massage the Oreos, fondle the grapes, mull the pistachios. The coffee grinding machine ropes him in, embraces him like a lover. He figures no one will miss one little coffee bean sneaked from the bin. He sucks on it as he heads for the candy, hoping to find an open bag. Alas, the shelf has been restocked in the night. Frankenstein walks on. Then he stops, puts the cart in reverse and backs up to a cellophane sack of snack-sized chocolate bars. Nobody's looking. Frankenstein devises a reasonable plan. He's going to open that bag, slip a couple of bars out, and walk away. Someday when he's rich, he's going to buy a bag just like this, pay for it, and then go put it back on the shelf.

He gets away with it. Toots chews hers up real fast and smiles a chocolaty smile. She's got chocolate all over her lips and chin. Frankenstein heads for the wipes department, checks behind him, opens a pack of moist towelettes and yanks out half a dozen. He wipes her off near the paper towels and gives his own armpits a quick, refreshing pass. He applies another towelette to his neck and face. Making absolutely certain no one at all is looking, he jams a wipie into his pants and gives his crotch a very quick bath. Oh yes, oh yes, it does feel very, very good.

He peruses the deodorants with great care, decides to go with the very best, that of a European designer known better for his clothes. He snaps the cap back on, returns the cartridge to the shelf. No one will ever miss what he has taken.

Frankenstein owes AmeriMart a bag of snack-sized chocolates and a pack of wipies. He might as well owe them some olives and a can of sardines, too. And a banana. And some pistachios. He grabs a little bottle of chocolate milk for Toots, tries to get her to drink quick hits as they dally among the pickles. Toots says, "Wow!" real loud.

The smell of the chocolate milk takes him back to elementary school. He says to Toots, "You like baloney?" He revs up his cart, shoots down the aisle, rounds the corner without looking, gallops to the deli section. He could go for a little baloney himself. With mustard. He heads for the condiments, back where he just was. He knows right where to go. He has to look interested in mustard until a stock boy gets done lining up a little army of ketchup bottles. By the time the coast clears, he's made his choice. He's going for the speckled brown one from Bordeaux. He twists the lid off the jar, rolls a quick cigar of baloney and dips it in. He feels himself quite the gourmand, munching thoughtfully, his baloney cigar between two fingers. Toots reaches for it, gives it a bite. She likes it, too. And the mustard's in such a nice little jar. Frankenstein vows to buy some someday. It will be his official mustard. He'll buy a lot. He'll make good for the jar he leaves open on the shelf.

Toots says, "Gimme!" at the potato chips, so he grabs her a bag. He swings around to the pet products. A container of flea powder won't fit in his pocket, so he just dumps the powder in. He hankers for cranberry sauce but first has to pick up a can opener and a plastic spoon. The cranberry sauce makes him think of creamed corn. Toots, as it turns out, likes creamed corn, too. They drink it straight from the can. Concerned about a balanced diet, Frankenstein heads for the produce, grabs a carrot and some scallions. Toots won't eat either, not until he dips them into a bottle of bleu cheese dressing.

Why didn't he think of this before, he wonders. He can graze the bounty of American agriculture from here to Baltimore. Toots doesn't have to go hungry. The morality of it doesn't jibe too well with the Scout Oath he took not so long ago, though there was a line in there about "help other people at all times." Surely that commandment would cover feeding one's young no matter what. He remembers something about honesty, but that was then; this is now. He's been beaten by the police, bitten by a rat, forced into hiding and all but obligated to take on a child. Society will have to owe him for a while. If the AmeriMart chain suffers a blip in profits, so be it. His Toots will be fed, and he, her provider, will sustain himself.

Frankenstein feels great. His stomach's full. Toots is satisfied. They had a good time. They're real pals now. Accomplices. He figures the nicest thing he can do for this supermarket is buy a couple of apples and get the hell out. He picks a Delicious and a Granny Smith, forks over his ten-spot at the express register, accepts his apples in a plastic bag way too big for them. He carries Toots through the electric doors into the welcome warmth of mid-morning.

He figures he should call his sister. He'll let her talk with Toots. A nice public phone stands at attention just twenty feet from the supermarket door. Toots on his left hip, Cleopatra attacking a spinal flea at his feet, he flips the phone off the hook and lets it swing as he dials for a collect call. He's got the receiver up to his ear just in time to say his name. His full-bellied merriment dips just a bit until suddenly his beloved Susie's on the line:

"Hey, Bub," she pipes, "where are ya?"

"Illinois, I believe. *Corn* country. And headed east." He pulls Toots in tight against his flank. She's warm, flaccid and almost asleep.

"You sound *good*," his sister says, almost as if surprised. He barely hesitates to wonder if he's only called her when things were bad. But those days, those cold, hungry, lonely times, are so far behind that they seem unreal. Toots is warm on his hip.

"Thing *are* good," he says. "Everything's hunky-dory. Hunkier and dorier than you can imagine." He's itching to tell her the news but doesn't quite know how. It's right at the back of his throat, just off stage, ready to dance out on cue. He grips the phone between his head and neck, extracts some flea powder from his pocket and sprinkles it along Cleopatra's back.

His sister says, "Have you called home recently?"

He senses seriousness in her voice, like maybe she's going to report a death. "No," he says. "Should I?"

"I don't think you'd better. She flipping out."

Frankenstein hesitates. He doesn't want to say anything bad about his mother, not even to his sister. He won't say he thinks his mother flipped out a long time ago, around about the time she had him wax and buff the floor of the garage. She still thinks he did something wrong in the process, but he still thinks that the brush on the rented waxer wasn't supposed to be used on concrete, that friction had caused it to catch on fire, ruining the garage, in her fastidious opinion, with a coat of toxic resin. She thought it was toxic, but Frankenstein could have lived with it. She spent $8,000 having the wallboard ripped out and a new layer of concrete laid down. Normal mothers don't do things like that, not until they flip out.

Frankenstein says, "Flipping out?"

"Within a twenty-four-hour period she found out she's got termites *and* lice."

"Lice! It is not possible. A louse could not live within fifty feet of her. It wouldn't even want to."

"Frankly I doubt the lice were real. But the termites were. Apparently they've been in her walls for a long time."

"And where there's termites, there's lice."

"Exactly." The second syllable comes through the phone like an arrow and hits a bull's-eye inside him. He knows what she means.

"So what's she doing?" he asks.

"She's down at the Motor Inn and she's *real* jumpy. She won't say it, but I can tell she thinks they might come looking for her."

"They?"

"The termites. She's talking about burning down the house. She wants me to find out if that's legal."

Frankenstein doesn't have to tell his sister to tell their mother not to burn the house down, nor does he have to tell her their mother needs a shrink. He says, "So you think I should call her?"

"I don't know. It might be weird."

"Might be like getting a phone call from a louse, huh?"

He meant it as a little joke, a little fun poked at himself, but it hurts to hear her say, in a tone a bit too close to serious, "It might." He wonders if his sister sees him that way, too.

He wants to tell her that he has turned a certain corner, that he's been clean since yesterday and has a pocketful of wipies. At this very moment he smells like the best of deodorants. Getting his pants washed might be a bit problematic at the moment, but that's temporary. As soon as he gets another pair, he's going to wash the ones he has on. Before he can figure out how to say all that, he pictures himself in white pants of crisp cotton. Maybe it's seersucker he's imagining. He doesn't know what seersucker is, but to him, it's the epitome of dapper, something worn only by a very clean person, the type who would never need to sit down outdoors or on public transportation, a person reasonably certain he will not spill food or contaminate his hands in such a way as to transfer a smudge to his pants. He will have clean, groomed fingernails. His hair will be shower-wet all day. He will not need Ramundo What's-his-face deodorant, but he will use it anyway. And matching cologne. And his daughter....

"Guess what I have?" he says.

She's too quick with "Impetigo?"—a joke, but it hurts.

"Funny," he says in two stressed syllables, then, "I've got a little girl."

"A little girl? What kind of a little girl?"

"The regular kind. I'd say she's about three."

"Come on, you can't just *have* a little girl."

"And yet I do. It's all pretty amazing."

"Well what did you, just find her or something?"

"Sort of. And her mother gave her to me. Sort of. It's all pretty complicated."

"I'd love to hear about it sometime."

"Well you can! That's the good news. We're on our way to Baltimore."

Silence on the telephone. Frankenstein presses it hard to his hot, hot ear.

She doesn't say anything until she finally says, "No."

His face pulses hard, twice. Saliva seeps from his lips and they turn numb.

His sister says, "No. Don't come here. I'm sorry, but that just won't work."

- Chapter Sixteen -
The Death of Frankenstein

Frankenstein sinks into a deep and desperate sorrow. Even sitting down, knees high, arms across them, forehead on arms, he feels faint. Toots leans against him. Her little arms reach halfway around him, and her little hands pat his head. Her little affection only makes him feel worse. The three fingers that hold the plastic bag with the apples are sweating. The sweat spreads to his palm and then to his chest. He really wants to put his head in the bag for a while, to be alone in there, to hear the inward rustle and breathe his own breath for a while. If he could, he'd live in there. He'd even die in there, but he can't. Toots's little hands are patting him lightly. He can't just leave her. His father did that to him. He won't do it to her. But still....

The flea powder has not helped Cleopatra. She's chewing most viciously at her back, snorting and huffing as she strains at an itch just out of reach. Frankenstein could reach it for her, but he figures why bother. Dogs have fleas. You can scratch a dog, but the itch never goes away. It's just the same for him. Happiness isn't his to be had. He's not going to Baltimore. He's not going anywhere, just as he's been doing forever. He's not going to have a little girl to take care of. He can't even take care of himself. He can't even asphyxiate himself in a plastic bag. But he keeps looking at it. His fingers keep sweating. He doesn't think he could move them. He can't even bring himself to try. Through a haze of tears, the fingers look distant and vague, a painting by a sad, drunk, failed impressionist who no longer needs his hands.

A tear finally gains enough weight to become a drop. It slips out of his eye and slides like a snail to the tip of his nose. And there it hangs, a cold, quivering itch. It tries hard to tempt him to shake it off or just blow it upward to knock it from its perch. He could see it if he focused his eyes, but he can make no such effort. In a way, he enjoys the irritation of it. When the inevitable trickle of snot arrives, he lets it. Her doesn't even sniff it back in. Why bother? Why not just let it run down to his chin to hang in a gooey pendulum? Why not? Who is he, Frankenstein, to tell snot what to do? Besides, nobody can see it here in the personal darkness below his crossed arms, behind his knees, above his deep lap. He can do anything he wants in here, anything but die. Toots's tiny hand sees to that. It feels like a mouse on his shoulder blade. He sighs, or tries to. He inhales it all right, but on the way out it breaks up into a guttural sob—just one, but it scares him in the way of a monster bursting out of a closet. He sucks it back in as fast as it came out, but it won't stay down. It returns, this time making a sound like a large goat. It hurts to breathe in again. His chest feels wounded around the sides and heavy in the middle. *Maybe this is a heart attack*, he thinks. *Maybe this is it*. He tells himself he doesn't care, but something inside him does. His sobbing continues. All he can do is suppress it. It sounds like a dog muttering in its sleep.

More tears join the drip at the end of his nose. His pendulum of mucus seems to have reached its maximum length. Below it is the stained, shaded concrete of the sidewalk. Frankenstein wonders about it without quite wondering anything. It's just there: concrete, a tarnished gray, minutely dimpled, sprinkled with sand. There isn't one damned thing about it. It's down there at the bottom of the cave formed of his legs and slumping torso. Light comes into the cave between his sandaled feet. Vague semi-shadows pass by—shoppers perhaps looking down at him, maybe with pity, maybe with disgust, maybe thinking the little girl is cute. One shadow doesn't pass by. It gets darker and becomes a black shoe. Frankenstein doesn't lift his head. He doesn't want anyone to see his tears and his dangling rope. The shoe, like all problems, will take care of itself. It will expire. He won't have to deal with it; it will deal with him. It will make the decisions, and he, bereft of all desire, will accept what it ladles him. A kick in the teeth would be all right. He wouldn't mind a bit.

The shoe, a medium-length, unshined, slightly scuffed thing that men wear when dressed neither up nor down, just stands there, much too close and much too patiently. It seems to know he's looking at it. It knows it can outwait him. It's just a shoe. It doesn't tap, twitch, scuff or shift.

Frankenstein's still hoping it will kick him in the teeth when Toots jerks and says, "*No.*" It's a *no* of fear and insistence. He has no choice but to look up. Before he sees the man's belt buckle, far above him, he knows who it is. It's Fat Lips. He's chewing gum slowly. Below his sunglasses he looks pensive. One hand rests on his little buddy, the nightstick. The other, hooked over his belt, holds handcuffs with just two fingers. He looks moderately concerned, perhaps with a bit of pity, the twisted kind one applies to a dying animal that one has just shot. Frankenstein likens it to the face of the man he imagines poked out the eyes of the accident victim in eastern Tennessee. It's the same look, the cold, philosophical appreciation of pain at its worst, helpless and slow.

Toots slides around him, leaning hard, squeezing between him and the wall. His hand oozes sweat with constipated intensity. Fat Lips's hand, the one with the cuffs, extends toward him, and one finger takes aim at a point between his eyes. It curls twice, slowly. It seems the size of a sausage.

Frankenstein can't move. Even his mouth is paralyzed, his lips throbbing as if recovering from Novocain. He just keeps sitting, holding tight to Toots with something that isn't arms. She's all but climbing into him. He wishes she could. If he had her warmth inside him, maybe he could move.

He doesn't have to move. Fat Lips spits his gum to one side and then, with a toothy sneer, explodes. Frankenstein feels like a rag doll as Fat Lips grabs his jacket at both shoulders, lifts him two feet off the sidewalk, presses him to the wall and kicks the wind out of his stomach. Toots squeals, "No!" in the long, angry, desperate screech of a small mammal.

Curled fetal, unable to inhale, Frankenstein wraps one hand around her little ankle. She wiggles behind him, screaming into his neck. He can only whimper, and all he can whimper is "No."

Fat Lips shifts to a lower stance, grabs Frankenstein's jacket at the neck and hurls him around flat to the pavement, cheekbone to the concrete. His fat black shoe slams into Frankenstein's ass so hard it brings blood to his throat. He's helpless as Fat Lips pulls his arms back and whacks the cuffs onto his wrists. He's still got the plastic bag and its apples in one hand. Fat Lips knocks Toots out of the way, leans down low and growls directly into Frankenstein's ear, "You're fucked now, asshole. You're fucked good." His breath hurts as much as teeth.

He drags Frankenstein by the scruff of his jacket like a sack of flour. The back door of the squad car is already open. With vicious strength he heaves Frankenstein's upper half onto the seat. With a shoving kick, he pushes him the rest of the way in. A few seconds later, Toots lands on top of him. When Cleopatra lands on them, her claws scrape deep into his exposed back as she struggles for balance. Then the door closes hard against his feet.

The car pulls away quickly. Frankenstein's sprawled across the seat, Toots atop him, her arms and legs around him as if he were a log in a river. Cleopatra's trying to burrow under him, and Toots is crying with a painful resignation that children shouldn't have. Maybe she's done this before, he thinks. Maybe she knows more than he. This wasn't supposed to happen to her. It wasn't part of his plan at all. But then again, nothing ever is. The fact drives through his chest like a spear of cold steel. He curls around as best he can, far enough to put his lips to her cheek. What can he say but, "It's all right"? It makes as much sense as saying *no* to a cop, but in a way, it might not be all that wrong. Everything's going to be the way it's supposed to. Toots is going to the Illinois Hole for Doomed Children, Cleopatra's going to the pound, and Frankenstein's going to die. He wonders if it's physically possible to get his plastic bag from his cuffed hands to his head. It might be possible. It definitely might if Toots helped. He wonders how he would explain such a thing to her and whether he would.

The fresh smell of a new cigarette swirls around. Fat Lips drives with a heavy foot but without benefit of siren except for once, apparently to whoop someone out of the way. The car tilts as he sways around. It takes ten minutes to reach the hard right turn onto the crunch of gravel. It's the police station. The car stops. Frankenstein's heart beats very hard, but the back door doesn't open, not until a few minutes later. He can't see what's happening until Toots's mother, arms cuffed behind her back, sails into the back seat like firewood. She lands on top of him and Toots and rolls to the floor. Cleopatra struggles to free herself from the weight of three entangled people. Toots's mother is groaning harder through clenched lips, crying silently from deep in the gut. He can almost hear her saying *no* low and hard. Her light brown dreadlocks shake stiffly.

Toots sticks with Frankenstein, but her mother's looking up at her. She's looking up at him, too. Their faces are only a foot apart, maybe less. All he can see, really, are her eyes. Thick with tears, maybe green, maybe brown, they look like tiny swamps. His own tears, draining to one side, leave an itchy trail to his temple. He tries to say something, but only an ugly gurgle comes out. He coughs up rat pus, swallows it back down and tries again. As if to an intimate lover, he whispers, "Now what?"

She can't talk. She clenches her lips harder and clenches her eyes enough to squeeze the tears out. Shuddering, she keeps them closed. She has a small bruise on one cheekbone, or maybe it's smeared eyeshadow. Her wet make-up is a primordial mess. Her nose looks like maybe it was broken, but it's too small to tell. It's kind of flat against her face. He imagines her face hitting a mailbox the way his did. He knows the punch-in-the-face pain.

Fat Lips patches out. The car rocks wildly as he maneuvers it into the street and takes off. Frankenstein wishes hard that he could just get up a little and look out to see if the friendly waitress has noticed. He wishes he could just say thank you for trying and tell her good-bye.

They go a pretty long way before their speed evens out and the car just goes straight. They're on an interstate. Frankenstein can tell. He can tell, even by the sun, that they're headed east. *Baltimore*, he thinks. Now we're going eighty miles an hour toward where we might as well not go. It's the first time in over a year that he dreads arriving somewhere. Right now, he suspects, cuffed, crying, choking, things are as good as they're going to get. He should be thankful for this limited misery. He should be thankful for having his beloved Toots atop him, clinging to him, warm, loving him. He should be thankful for being a foot away from a woman he loves.

Yes, he loves her. He knows this. He feels it wholly. They are both cuffed and helpless, fetal in the back of a cop car, doomed to something, and they share a sweet child. He doesn't know this woman's name, or even the name of the child, but they are all so close now, in so many ways, that they cannot help but be in love. It's stupid, maybe, but he cannot help but say to this woman, in what turns out to be a thin squeak, "I love you."

He can hardly believe he has said it. He wishes it didn't sound so weak and desperate. He wishes he didn't have to say it while he has snot across his face and breath that tastes of something dead. He wishes he could say it in moonlight, near an ocean, in clean clothing, perhaps with a flower in her hair. But as it is, he can't even touch her. She's a foot away, but he can't even touch her, and his words, I love you, sound perilously close to perverse.

But she opens her eyes, and for a second they're clear. For a second she sees him, and a second later she contracts with an abdominal spasm that jerks her back to a fetal curl, her arms behind her back, her mouth yanked open at a painful angle. She coughs hard, trying to bring something up, but her stomach is an empty knot. She manages a spit of bile. Frankenstein can taste it. This is love. He says it again, even more weakly; "I love you."

She spits. It's gummy stuff. It takes two spits, then a third. Then she breathes. She inhales a sob. She spits gain, pauses, then straightens herself. She forces her head to Frankenstein and presses her cheekbone to his. "I love you," he says, trembling hard. "I love you."

She says it, too, though it's only a high-pitched moan. He knows what she means. Then Toots presses her face into theirs and kisses them both. She knows how to do this; she knows how to kiss. It's the tiniest kiss from the tiniest of lips, but their warm voltage surges through him. It stuns him like an anti-adrenalin, shoots him with an instantaneous semi-numbness. Cleopatra's tail twitches. Frankenstein wants nothing in the world except for this moment to continue. He's happy.

He feels the end of it approach as the car slows and the turn signal clicks off several seconds, tick-tock, tick-tock, tick-tock, at a rate that would please Fat Lips more than he. His heart seems to match the cadence with a heavier and more dreadful throb. The car slows too much and too quickly for an exit ramp, and it doesn't veer to the right. With a sudden brake it heaves to the left and descends onto a thumpity unpaved road. Within seconds, it stops. Frankenstein feels obliged to maneuver himself up enough to see out the window, as if he might be able to do something about their situation. They're off the highway, in a grove in a kind of dell between the eastbound and westbound sides of the interstate, or so he guesses. He can't see very far.

He drops down as Fat Lips gets out of the car. He tries hard to think of something, a way out. If this were a movie, he'd kick Fat Lips and watch him fall unconscious to the ground. But when the back door opens, he can no more kick than fly. All he can decide is that whatever happens, he's not going to say *no*. He's going to take what he gets.

Fat Lips grabs Toots by an arm and tosses her to the ground as if cleaning out the back seat after a long, hard vacation. He grabs Frankenstein's belt, hauls him halfway out, then grabs his jacket collar and hurls him over backwards. Frankenstein lands on his cuffed hands, spraining or breaking a thumb under his own weight. No sooner has he recoiled from that than Toot's mother lands on top of him.

Fat Lips is quick. One foot shoves the woman away as he descends onto Frankenstein, straddling his belly and in one smooth movement pulling out his semi-automatic, tilting the hammer back with the palm of his left hand. Through crimped lips he says "Fucking asshole," then leans around, takes aim at Cleopatra just ten feet away and lets off a shot. The bullet smacks a big chunk of flesh off the back of her hip, throwing blood and fur into the air. The dog howls like an unearthly siren, blasting the air with bolts of pain. She lashes her teeth at the wound, but her hips stagger away from her, sinking away.

Fat Lips growls, "God *damn* it," and shoots again. Cleopatra's head, from the jaw up, explodes with blood and ash-white bone. She falls quickly and shudders in the leaves as her soul pulls out. Her tail wags in a circle, slowing with each pass until the just the tip of it twitches twice like a beckoning finger.

Before Toots can inhale a scream, Fat Lips crams the barrel of the gun into Frankenstein's mouth. He can taste the steel and the gunpowder and feel the heat of it. It stabs against the back of his throat. He gags with a horrifying, choking-vomiting sound. He wiggles involuntarily, keeps choking and gasping. He can't breathe through his nose. He has to breathe around the gun. He pictures the little bullet in there poised like a fist itching to punch through the back of his throat, through the upper tip of his spine and out the back of his neck. He pictures the bloody wad of mouth-flesh and bone twacking into the leaves behind him. He pictures the lights going out and the final, subaqueous silence. Fat Lips's thick, short thighs hold him firm, and his free hand pins Frankenstein's throat to the ground. Far, far away, Toots whines harshly, helplessly, a lot like the way she cried on the floor in the jail block, but much farther away. Her mother's crying, too, straining against a gut taut with fear. She sounds more distant than the trucks out on the interstate.

Fat Lips says, "This is it, asshole, I hope you've had a good time." His eyes gleam with wicked anger and glee. "Here we part. All I need is your name."

Frankenstein just coughs. He can't say anything with nine-millimeter steel against the back of his throat. But he doesn't want to die anonymously. He doesn't want to just disappear. He thinks of his mother and his sister. He doesn't want them to always wonder in the way he has wondered about his father. If he had ever decided to die, he would have left a note. He would have explained. Fat Lips isn't going to let him write a note, but if he at least knows his name, maybe an identified body will make its way home. He coughs again, emits an attempt at a syllable. The gun barrel pulls back an inch, but it tilts so that Fat Lips can gleam through the distant little notch of the rear sight.

"Fwangfif," he says, struggling to slide his name around the gun. *Francis.* Tears really gush from his eyes. "Fwangfif Holmef." The *l* and *s* blur beyond recognition. And with that he takes the only way out. He sinks into the ground, away, away, into a darkness that closes into a pinpoint and disappears.

- CHAPTER SEVENTEEN -
Something Ever After

By this point in her short, hard life, little Charlene knows how to walk. She knows better than to whine about it. She toddles along in pensive silence, heading in the same direction as before, away from the sun as it set, and now away from that horrible car and that horrible place in the woods with that horrible man. She toddles part way, sleeps the night in deep grass, toddles more. She toddles all the way to Indiana. She doesn't eat until they put her at a linoleum table in a diner. They give her a pencil so she can draw on the paper place mat until her scrambled eggs arrive—protein with a side of starch and a glass of vitamin C. She really likes the juice. Smart girl that she is, she glubs it down and says, "More." They bring her more. She glubs it down, half of it anyway. The waitress, pure Hoosier, thinks it just too-too cute. She brings a glass of chocolate milk, just to watch. Charlene glubs down a quarter of that, gives herself a light brown mustache.

Brenda attacks her eggs with equal gusto. She forks eggs with her right hand while her left pours ketchup. She adds salt. She adds pepper. She keeps her mouth full and moving. The food rolls around like something in a cement mixer and with almost as much noise. She tosses coffee into the churn. She talks and cries. She swears. She eats a spoonful of sugar, signals for more coffee. Though her hands are shaking, she handles things well. She pats Charlene's fuzzy head, adjusts her plate, erases her mustache with a paper napkin. She keeps collapsing into tears, sinking under momentary grief as if under a wave. But she always bobs up, shakes off the tears, sniffs, keeps chewing, even smiles a bit. The food is good.

The waitress loves Charlene. Even the cook comes out to look. He gawks as if at plane crash survivors, then comes back with a stack of tiny pancakes with whipped cream, cinnamon, crushed walnuts and on top nothing less than a maraschino cherry speared with a swizzle stick.

All this with money from Brenda's underpants. It's flat and warm as it hits the table. "Filthy fucking money," she says. "Let's get rid of it. There milkshakes in this place?"

There's milkshakes, all right. "Chocolate," she says. "Large if you got a choice."

No choice. It's as large as all milkshakes are, in a frigid steel container with a glass on the side. Two straws. She uses them both to suck the sweet thick brew straight from the steel. Where does it go? She's not much bigger than a milkshake herself. She washes it down with more coffee. "How about grits?" she says in the tone of a challenge. "A large grits."

Large grits come right up. She melts four pads of butter in a crater. She adds a tablespoon of maple syrup precisely in the center. It sits there like a pupil in a jaundiced eye. "My mother taught me that," she says.

She speaks in the soft twang of a central-state girl whose mother can do tricks with grits. She looks like somebody who could milk a cow if she had to, though she probably hasn't seen one since she probably got thrown out of 4-H about ten years ago. That would make her twenty-three or twenty-four, though her face carries the hard smarts of somebody thirty-two.

She drops her fork into a half-finished side order of home fries on which she has ordered extra paprika. "Done," she states. "Done."

Little Charlene looks like she can't decide whether to fall asleep or throw up. She lowers her head to her mother's lap. Her mother, looking down at first, then straight across the table, says, "Francis."

The name sounds sweet from her chapped and oily lips. It slides right out on a carpet of buttery grits. He wouldn't mind hearing it again. With all the openness of an invitation, he says, "Yes."

"We need a plan. And some cigarettes."

Francis fingers a warm flat five from the mess of bills, gets change at the cash register, goes out to the cigarette machine in the sunny little foyer. Brenda has struck him as someone who has moved beyond Marlboros. He could ask, but he's sure she'll love anything with nicotine in it. He feeds in a mess of quarters and pulls the Raleigh knob. He also plunks two quarters into a newspaper machine. He likes the way it trusts him not to take them all.

"Raleighs," she says as he slides them onto the table with the pack of matches that came with them. "All right." She raps them on the table, opens them with fluid panache. As she lights a match, he notices the book of matches suggests that he become a tractor-trailer driver. She shoots blue smoke straight up and says, "We could back to Illinois, kill that son of a bitch."

"Let's let him go. We have more important things to do."

She smiles over the cigarette between her knuckles. It's a nice smile, almost motherly in its assessment and approval. "Yeah?" she says, curiously almost seductively.

"Yeah." He snaps open the newspaper, moves the first section to the bench, opens the classifieds with a certain expertise.

"Employment," he says. "Administrative/Managerial. Nope. Automotive. Nope. Banking. Forget it. Carpentry/Construction. Maybe. Computer/Data Processing. No way. Cosmetology. You know anything about cosmetology?"

"I suppose I could fake it. What else they got?"

"Education. Electrical. Engineering. Financial/Accounting. *Jeez.*" College hasn't done him a whole lot of good. He remembers why he hit the road after graduation. It was because he was a useless human being. He still is.

"Dog groomer, must have experience. HVAC. Don't even know what it is. Inspector. Janatorial supervisor. Hotel/Motel. Maintenance-slash-handy man, trailer park. Manufacturing. Medical...."

"Hey, wait," Brenda says. "Go back. Go back to the trailer park."

"Maintenance-slash-handyman, trailer park. Must know plumbing, lawn care, bookkeeping. Three years experience. Live-in. References. 982-4311."

He loves her smile. It says so much. He's going to kiss it as soon as soon as he can get close enough. He's pretty sure she'll let him.

"Plumbing?" he says with an emphasis on the question mark.

"We'll figure it out before they figure out we can't."

He wants to kiss her—*we'll*. He wants to eat it. Of course they can figure out plumbing. If Brenda's there, he can do it. *They* can do it. Looking up at her from under his eyebrows, he says, "Lawn care."

"Perfect. Who in the state of Indiana knows plumbing *and* lawn care *and* needs a job?"

"Just us, I guess. And I guess bookkeeping narrows it down even more."

"My father was a bookkeeper. The prick."

"And I suppose he taught you all he knows."

"If he could keep books," she says, "a drunk monkey could keep books."

"References?"

"*You* got a father?"

"Well...no." He realizes he'll get to tell her about it. He'll do it while they're in bed, smoking. She'll hold him. He'll whisper the details against her little breast.

"*Somebody?*" she suggests.

"Well, yes, there is somebody." He can call her collect. He'll be glad to. He nods.

"Then it's done. We're maintenance-slash-handy men." Her smile's so big it squeezes her eyes shut. He could swear he sees a happy sheen of tears on her teeth.

Brenda says, "You need a shirt. You can't apply for a job looking like that. And I need some long pants or a skirt or something. We have to walk in there like we're a nice couple. You're with me in this, right?"

Oh, yes. Oh, yes, he certainly is.

With one hand she separates the money. They've got a couple of tens, a five, some ones. He extracts nine dollars and change from his jeans. He says, "If they've got a Goodwill store here, we're rich."

They've got one. The waitress points the way. They settle up, leave her a moderate tip. That's the end of a ten and some ones. Francis carries a sleeping Charlene against one shoulder. She fits against him as if in a mold. Brenda puts her arm under the bottom of his jacket and around his bare waist and leans against him as they walk down the sidewalk. Her fingers squeeze him just short of his rat bite, but he doesn't tell her. His arm shelters her little shoulders. It feels very good. He could walk down this sidewalk forever.

Brenda's arm tightens a bit. She says, "That poor dog."

Frankenstein stops and puts his other arm around her, around her and Charlene, pulls them both against him, both their heads to his chest. His throat's so constricted he can barely speak. He says, "That could have been us."

Brenda's fingers dig into the small of his back. "Can we get another one?"

"God, yes. First thing."

"From the *pound*."

"Damn straight."

But first some clothes. The Goodwill store's got pretty good stuff—good enough for Francis and Brenda, and cheap. She finds a sunny yellow skirt that reaches just below her knees. It goes well with her striped shirt. She goes through the racks as only a woman can, even a drug addict, examines a pair of navy blue pants that might have been the bottom half of a suit. "Three dollars," she says. "Not bad." She finds a nice white shirt with white stripes, Pierre Cardin, no less. "Two bucks," she says. "This is great." She heads for the ties. There's darned little to choose from, but Brenda knows which one's least bad, a polyester job so busy with paisley that you can barely see the word "Virgo" swirled down the middle in psychedelic bamboo.

She peeks through the curtain of the little changing room as he sheds his sweat-laden jeans and pulls on his new pants. He's going to need a belt with a lot of holes in it. By the time she fetches one, he's got the shirt and tie on. The belt cinches it all together. In the mirror he thinks he looks a little wrinkled at the waist. The sudden containment draws cold perspiration from his ribs. He turns around, faces his palms toward her and says, "How do I look?"

She tugs his shirt a little here, a little there, tucks it in a bit more. She smooths some wrinkles from his chest. "You look good," she says, her fingers still on him, her eyes probing his face. "You really do."

- THE END -